THE RUBY KNOT

The Dirty Boat Guys of Coronado Series

JANE JOSEPHS

SOUL MATE PUBLISHING

New York

THE RUBY KNOT

Copyright©2018

JANE JOSEPHS

Cover Design by Rae Monet, Inc.

Published in the United States of America by
Soul Mate Publishing
P.O. Box 24
Macedon, New York, 14502

ISBN: 978-1-68291-746-6

ebook ISBN: 978-1-68291-717-6

www.SoulMatePublishing.com

To my children,

Laura Irion and Michael Josephs.

You delight my heart always.

Acknowledgments

When I decided to write *The Ruby Knot*, I had only a few plot points and a simple story in my head. But early in the writing, my daughter Laura continually encouraged me, asked pointed questions, gave thoughtful, challenging insights, and prompted me more than a few times to write and re-write. My deepest appreciation, honey! Who you are is a constant inspiration to me.

To my son, Michael, thanks - more than I can ever express - for joining the Navy and making me the proudest mom, ever! Without your willingness to serve our country, and share with me a few insights into life as a Special Warfare Combatant Craft Crewman, I wouldn't know the first thing about this amazing group of special forces who call themselves "Dirty Boat Guys." My hat's off to all of you! I love you, my dear Mikey!

The friends I've made in the Poway Critique Group of the San Diego Christian Writers Guild have my unending thanks for your encouragement, support and honest criticisms. Some of my characters had to undergo major surgery because of you – and I'm so grateful!

Big hugs and kisses to my awesome beta readers who also keep me lifted up in prayer. I would be nothing without your love, your faithfulness, and your encouragement! Of this amazing, wonderful group, Kirsten Kelleher provided invaluable editing and thought-provoking comments for *The Ruby Knot*. All my love, sweet girl!

For taking a chance on me and inviting me into the Soul Mate Publishing family, thank you, Lori Polito and Debby Gilbert. I hope this is just the beginning of a sweet ride!

To the husband of my crazy youth, Steve, who has stuck with me all these years, enduring my technology challenges, and letting me occasionally win at Scrabble, all my love, always, no matter.

And last, but first in my heart always, all praise and thanks to my Lord and Savior Jesus Christ for loving me with an everlasting love. To Him be the glory forever and ever!

Chapter 1

Katie Ryan smiled at the picture of her first trimester ultrasound sitting among the baby supplies on her dresser. "Not long now, little one," she said, smoothing her hand over her protruding stomach where a mild cramping sensation had begun. "Just a couple of hours of quick, easy labor, okay?"

Her shoulders slumping, Katie turned away and scanned the bedroom suite she rented from her friend at church, Julie Skidmore, in the north inland suburbs of San Diego. So much had happened since she moved from South Carolina a year and a half ago with her best friend, Ashley Davis. But nothing had been as life-changing as those two days in Las Vegas nine months ago.

The phone rang in the family room next to her bedroom and Katie tensed, listening for news she had known for days was coming. News she didn't want to hear.

She clenched her teeth when Julie's calm "hello" gave way to an excited yell. Her delight could only mean one thing: her husband Brad, a Navy SEAL, was home from his deployment in the Middle East. Katie reached for the ultrasound picture and held it against her pounding heart. If Brad was home, there was a good chance the boat guys were, too.

"I don't care, I don't care, I don't care," she whispered.

Forcing herself to take slow, steady breaths, Katie put the picture back on the dresser, pulled clean clothes out of a drawer and went into the bathroom. Noah would be here in less than an hour to pick up the *Life Together* project she had designed for Pastor Dale's next sermon series, and she hadn't yet showered. *Should I tell him?* "No, not yet. Not now," Katie murmured under her breath and turned on the shower.

Ten minutes later, Katie opened her door to find Julie about to knock.

She grabbed her friend in a fierce hug. "I heard. Brad's home, right?"

"Yes! He's got to put his gear away, but he's home! He'll be ready in an hour or so for me to pick him up at the base."

"Oh, Julie, I'm so happy for you! I know you and Megan have missed him so much!"

Julie stepped back but didn't let go of Katie, her expression somber. "The boat guys are home too, Katie. I asked Brad, discreetly of course, and he said he saw their boats coming on the truck to the base. That means . . ." She glanced at Katie's stomach. "That means your CJ is home. It's decision time for you."

Katie swallowed but the knot in her throat wouldn't budge. She tugged the belt of her robe tight over her middle and turned away. "He's not *my* CJ, and I couldn't care less that he's home. What the Navy boat guys do is no concern of mine."

Julie slid her hand down Katie's arm. "It is when the boat guy is the baby's father, don't you think?"

A spasm seized Katie's belly, rippling the surface of her skin from left to right. She turned to Julie, both hands clutching her stomach. "Whoa, that was crazy!"

"Are you having contractions?" She patted Katie's arm. "It's okay. Take it easy."

"No, no, I don't think so." Katie blew out a calming breath.

Julie smiled. "You're sure? First babies usually take their time."

"I know, I know. Look, Julie," she said as the sensation in her belly eased, "we've had this conversation about the baby's father before. And I've told you I want to forget I ever heard of Special Warfare Combatant-Craft Crewmen. Especially one crewman, whose name I never want to hear again!"

She turned to her desk. The *Life Together* design project filled the computer screen. The logo blurred as tears welled in her eyes.

"He used me, then left while I was asleep. I'm not about to go begging for more." Katie shut her eyes against the pain in her heart.

"Do you want Brad to see what he can find out?"

Katie's eyes flew open and she turned. "No. No! Keep Brad out of this. Please. What more do I need to know than what his name stands for? First name *Conniving*. Second name *Jerk*. How's that sound for the father's name?"

"Not so good. And not anything I've ever heard about the SWCC guys. Sure, they're alpha males. All the special forces guys are. But Brad says they're as highly trained as the SEALs and just as disciplined."

Katie swallowed her anger. She already knew all she wanted to know about the Navy's elite SWCC community near San Diego, in Coronado, California. *Swick.* They called themselves Dirty Boat Guys. On Time. On Target. Never Quit. Well, one of them had quit on her. No name other than CJ, no contact number, just a romp in the sack and no trace of the guy in the morning. She had to stop thinking about what had happened that weekend in Las Vegas. And start thinking of the baby and what his coming into the world was going to mean for her life.

Katie picked up a blue newborn sleeper off the laundry pile she had tossed on her bed that morning. She had to stay busy or go crazy. "I can't believe I'm about to have a baby. Just look at how tiny these clothes are. They're like doll clothes."

"And you have no idea how many of them a baby can go through in a day," Julie said. "I have a couple of minutes. Let me help you fold these." She picked up a sleeper. "When I had Megan, we did laundry every other day."

"You mean Brad did laundry?" Relieved that the topic of the baby's father had been dropped, Katie turned to the pile, picked up a sock and rooted through the laundry until she found the match. But her stomach wouldn't settle. *Was CJ home?*

"He did, actually," Julie said, adding the sleeper to the stack on the shelf. "Especially after my mom went home." She picked up a T-shirt. "It was nice of the Myers' to loan you the changing table, wasn't it? The Pack 'n Play, too. It fits nicely in your room. For now."

"Most of the people at the church have been so nice. It's overwhelming." Katie picked up a tiny pair of blue jeans to fold. "I thought—" Katie stopped, her hands clutching the jeans. "Well, you know I thought, being pregnant and all, with no husband, well, that most people at the church would want me fired. Or wouldn't want anything to do with me."

Julie shook her head. "I know you went through a rough patch with some people who can be like that, but they're the exception. Most people love you, Katie, just like I do." She picked up a handmade quilt. "And those women who came to your shower are the most nonjudgmental women I've ever known. Seriously. They've been wonderful role models for me in my Stephen Ministry group. God can use this baby, if you'll let him."

"I know that's what you believe, and I want to believe it too, really, I do. But it's just so hard." She shook her head. "I never should have gone to Vegas with Ashley in the first place. She got me to move out here with her to San Diego. Now I'm pregnant, thanks to her."

Julie shook her head. "I agree Ashley hasn't been the best influence in your life. But she loves you. And Katie, she didn't force you to go to Vegas, or to go into that bar. I think you managed that and more all on your own. You and this CJ fellow."

Katie felt her eyes fill with tears at Julie's rebuke. She turned away and put the baby jeans in the changing table. Why couldn't Julie understand how lonely she had been feeling the day Ashley suggested the trip? How depressed she'd been since she found out her old boyfriend was married? Why was she always on the losing end in relationships? Only Noah had been a constant, gentle reminder of God's love.

"I'll do that, Julie." Katie took the quilt Julie had folded. "You don't have to fold my laundry along with everything else you and Brad have done for me."

Julie sighed. "Katie. You have to stop beating yourself up. You made a mistake. But you're doing the right thing by having this baby. Let's take it one day at a time, okay? See what the Lord has in mind. I'm going to pick up some milk before I get Megan at preschool. Then we'll be off to get Brad. Do you need anything?"

"No, I'm good. Noah's coming over in a bit. I'd better get dressed and see about some lunch."

"If you're still craving Froot Loops, there's a little milk left, at least enough for one bowl. I'll get a fresh supply of cereal when I get the milk."

"You're the best, Jules, really. I'll play with Megan this afternoon so you and Brad can take a nap."

Julie laughed on her way to the door. "Now, that's a deal I am not going to pass up!"

Thirty minutes later, Katie was awakened by the doorbell and pushed herself up from the sofa. When it rang again, she called, "Noah, is that you? I must have drifted off for a minute."

At the front of the house, Katie smiled at Noah, her heart giving a funny flutter at the sight of him. His bald head and black chin beard never failed to amuse her. All he needed was an eye patch to be pegged for a pirate. "Hey you," she said, and pushed open the screen door. "How are things at the church?"

"Hey yourself." Noah cupped her cheeks, his eyes making a thorough inspection of her face. He smiled and kissed her, a delicate touch of his lips that left her wanting more. "I heard Brad's home. Is he here yet?"

"Nope, but soon. Julie and Megan are probably on the base by now. How did you know?"

"Julie stopped in the church office after she picked up Megan. I came in the room when she was talking to the staff about you. She seemed to think you might be in labor." His eyes darted to her stomach and back to her face. "Are you?"

"I've had some cramp-like stuff. Nothing that's too bad. Or even regular, so I don't know if it's labor or not. I sat down on the sofa to wait for you and just drifted off!"

"Understandable. We're all with you, Katie, and praying for you."

"Thanks. I'm counting on it. Do you want something to drink?" She turned and walked with him past the formal living room to the family room and kitchen in the back of the house next to her bedroom suite. "Water, lemonade? Or we have some Dr. Pepper. Julie stocked up the minute she heard Brad would be home any day."

"Sure, Dr. Pepper sounds good." He sat at the table and clasped his hands.

Katie fixed the drinks and brought them to the table. Heat flooded her face at Noah's intense gaze. "What? You're staring at me, Noah. Has something happened?" *Had he changed his mind about wanting to have a relationship with her, given her condition?*

"No, no, nothing's happened. It's just you. You've got this glow about you, Katie." He winked at her and smiled. "I hope that means you were looking forward to seeing me today."

"Of course I was, silly," Katie said, feeling her cheeks heat. Noah's smile did crazy things to her stomach. "Even if I did just see you most of yesterday at church." She laughed, remembering how good it felt to be with Noah, to see that gleam in his eyes that told her he thought she was special. "I think it's those tacos we ate last night that are giving me trouble today."

Noah laughed with her. "Yeah, I guess I did see you most of the day, didn't I? Too much?"

Katie sipped her drink. "Not for me, it wasn't." Another cramp caused her to wince. "Ooh," she moaned. "I think that one actually was a contraction."

Noah's face paled and he jumped to his feet. "What should I do? Do you need to get to the hospital? Should I call Julie?"

Katie laughed at his panic. The contraction had built sharply, but was already easing. "No, no, I'm fine now. It was just a little cramp, that's all. I could have another week. Nothing to worry about."

"Are you sure?" He sat back down. "I could take you to the hospital. After that, I'm not sure. Is anyone helping you, like, during the labor part? I faint at the sight of blood or I would be there for you."

"Julie's helping me. Don't worry." Katie's fears went into overdrive. What if something went wrong? What if the baby had the cord wrapped around his neck like had happened to Julie's daughter?

"Katie, are you all right?" Noah reached for her hand.

"We're home! Katie? Noah?" Julie called. Megan skipped into the room first. Brad and Julie followed.

Noah stood, his face flaming with color. "She's having contractions, I think." He pointed at Katie. "I was just trying to help her, you know, just keep her calm."

"Are the contractions coming regularly?" Julie asked.

"Mm . . . no, still the same. I'm okay now." Relief coursed through her. Julie had been an ER nurse before having Megan. She would know what to do if there was any problem.

"Noah, I'd like you to meet my husband, Brad." Julie put her arm around Brad and leaned in to him. "You started your internship at the church right after he deployed. Brad, this is Noah Davidson. He's here to pick up a flash drive of a new sermon series that Katie's designed for Pastor Dale."

The two men shook hands and began talking about the church. Katie couldn't help comparing them. Brad was six-two and solid as a rock, his arm and leg muscles bulging in a T-shirt and worn jeans. The climate in the Middle East had favored his olive skin and deepened his tan. Noah, on the other hand, was average height, somewhat pale, slim, and had the look of a scholar with his wire-framed glasses. Katie smiled. Noah was charming and sweet. It didn't matter that he preferred reading to physical exercise. Training kept the special forces guys in top shape. Their lives depended on it. Thoughts of CJ in the hotel spa in Las Vegas flashed through her mind, and she stood quickly, almost knocking over her chair.

"Easy there," Julie said. "Brad's folks will be here any minute to welcome him home. Did you talk about the new design with Noah yet?"

"He just got here a few minutes ago. I'll get it now." Katie gave Brad a quick hug. "Welcome home, Brad. I'm so glad you're back safe and sound." She hurried to her bedroom to get the flash drive.

"Yoohoo! Brad, we're here. Yoohoo!"

From her bedroom, Katie heard the reunion. She grabbed the flash drive off her desk and turned. "Ooooohhh." Water gushed from between her legs. "Oooohhh . . ." She looked down as a pain hit unlike any other she had experienced so far.

"Excuse me," she said from the doorway. All eyes turned and conversation stopped. "I think it's time to go to the hospital. My water broke."

Julie hurried to Katie. "No problem. Let's get you into some dry jeans. You still have plenty of time. Did you pack your bag?"

Noah took her hand. "I know you've got everything worked out with Julie, but call me as soon as the baby's here, okay? Or as soon as you feel up to it. I'll be right over to see you." He kissed her on the cheek. "I'll be praying for you."

Katie could only nod as another contraction took her breath away.

~ ~ ~

Connor "CJ" Jansen pulled his truck into the hospital parking lot and found an empty space after circling twice. His adrenaline pumped hard and fast. He wanted to blast a hole in something, anything. Instead, he adjusted his cap, making sure his hometown SD logo was front and center, and started walking to the front entrance of the hospital. The July heat sucked the air out of his lungs. He swiped his hand around the back of his neck where perspiration had gathered. A wave of anxiety hit him and he stopped short of the door. He turned and lifted the cap off his head, running his fingers through his thick, dark hair. *I'm a father? I have a son?*

CJ stared at the parking lot. Why had Katie left him in the dark? She had known she was pregnant for three months before he deployed. He hadn't called her. But it didn't mean she couldn't call him. He hadn't left his number, but it wouldn't have been impossible for her to find. Anger clawed at his gut. He could get back in his truck and drive away. Katie would never know he called six hospitals before finding her. He could wash his hands of the whole mess.

He sat down hard on a bench, angry at where his thoughts were taking him. Where was his honor? Did he have no shame? What kind of man walked away from his responsibilities? From his own flesh and blood?

He scanned the rows of windows on the side of the hospital. Somewhere up there on the third floor, in room 312, Katie was with her baby. His baby. The baby they had made together in one amazing, unforgettable Saturday night in Las Vegas.

He could still see her that first night. Friday. The night he and Dustin arrived in Vegas, thirsty and ready to blow off some steam. Katie had been sitting at the bar with her friend, Ashley. Her long brown hair had the kind of curls that refused to be tamed. She had flipped a handful of them over her shoulder and looked straight at him before getting off the stool and disappearing down the hall to the restroom. It had only taken a few minutes of talking with her when she returned to know she was one of a kind.

"Fool!" he bit out as he stood to pace.

He couldn't and wouldn't walk out on his son. But how could he walk back in? Would Katie expect him to marry her? He shied away from the thought. Not that she wasn't gorgeous. She was. Long legs, the toned body of an athlete, and dark-chocolate brown eyes that sparkled when she laughed. But there was no way he was ready to settle down at his age. He had celebrated his twenty-fifth birthday in Bahrain a month ago. Katie was a couple years younger. They barely knew each other. One weekend didn't count for much.

Except it did. He was a father.

As he paced, a plan came together in his mind. He would go in and see Katie. He would simply explain he wasn't ready to settle down, but he would support her financially. Set up an account for the baby's future as well as provide for monthly support. Maybe they could go on a few dates. Take it slow and see if the chemistry was as hot as he remembered. That was reasonable, wasn't it?

A guy coming across the parking lot caught his attention. He held a balloon bouquet tied around a vase of roses. One of the balloons was shaped like a baby bottle. The man wore the silly grin of a new dad. CJ's stomach churned at the turn his life was about to take. From the looks of him, the guy couldn't wait to get to the new arrival in his life. His gifts said it all. An idea came to CJ, and he followed the guy to the door.

Chapter 2

A Subway sandwich shop was on the left of the hospital's front door. The aroma of sizzling bacon made CJ's mouth water and his stomach growl. He ignored it and walked into the gift shop. An assortment of flower arrangements filled a refrigerated cabinet. He picked up a porcelain baby shoe filled with a potted plant and put it down. *Is this really happening?* Jet lag hit him and he yawned. The shoe had a blue bow at least. He turned to find the clerk. Instead, he spotted a small display cabinet of jewelry.

He scanned the contents of the cabinet, seeing a bracelet he liked. CJ smiled. Not just any bracelet, but one with a knot in the center, set with a small red stone. *Knots, basic boat guy stuff.* Would Katie wear it? Or throw it at him? Maybe she would see it as a keepsake for their son, something he could give to his own wife one day? CJ drew a long breath. He was getting way ahead of himself. He hadn't seen Katie for nine months, and had no idea what her reaction would be at seeing him now. Would she slap his face, shout at him, demand he get out his checkbook? Or would she see a gift like this bracelet as an apology? A new beginning for them? CJ lifted his hat and re-settled it. What did he want from seeing Katie today? At the very least they needed to talk. Figure out the next step. Why had she left him in the dark about the pregnancy?

He stared at the bracelet. *Why am I making this so hard? It's just a gift.* He turned to the clerk. "I have a question about this silver bracelet with the red stone. Is that a ruby?"

"Yes, that's a genuine ruby, the birthstone for July, and it's set in white gold. That's a love knot that holds the ruby. We always feature the current month's birthstone for new dads like you. It's one of our most popular gifts, and moms love it, of course! I can gift wrap it for you, if you'd like."

CJ sucked in his breath. *Love knots.* How did she know he was a new dad? He had only picked up the baby shoe. And smiled at the knot bracelet. She probably had years of experience, judging from her silver-gray hair. "Okay. Yeah." She took the bracelet out of the case. "Wait. Do you have a card I can put in with it?"

"Here you go." She handed him a blank business-size card and a pen.

For several minutes, he stared at the card. What should he say? He needed to get this right. Finally writing a brief sentence, he signed his name and handed it back to the clerk. "Do you have any other baby shoes with flowers instead of a house plant?" A common house plant wasn't the message he wanted to give. Not when the other dad brought roses. "How about balloons? Do you have any of those?"

"We do, but we're all out of helium right now. I'm sorry. It was a busy weekend. We're supposed to get a new tank tomorrow. And the houseplant in the baby shoe is all we have right now, too."

He couldn't go in with only the bracelet. After no communication with Katie for so long, it screamed of intimacy. Already second guessing his decision to buy it, he said, "Okay, I'll take the plant. And that teddy bear in the sailor suit over there."

"Are you in the Navy?" the clerk asked as she took the bear off the shelf.

"Yeah," CJ said, his heart rate accelerating. What was he thinking? Katie could very well spit in his face. He'd left her in Vegas. He hadn't made any effort to get her number, before or since. The last thing she might want staring at her was a bear that reminded her of a dirty boat guy.

"How would you like to pay for these?"

"Debit," he said and pulled out his wallet. He looked at the gifts on the counter. Every one of them screamed *Remember*. His stomach growled. Maybe he could get a sub and put off the confrontation a little longer. Gathering his purchases, he went out of the store and stopped in the lobby. He eyed the sub shop. His workout routines burned a lot of calories, so he ate often. A sub would be perfect. But his mind refused to give in to his body. No one had ever called him a coward, and he was not about to be one now. He squared his shoulders and headed for the elevators.

At the third floor, the elevator doors opened and CJ took a deep breath. He followed the signs to Room 312, his heart nearly beating out of his chest. Just inside the room, he stopped and stared in disbelief. "What the . . . ?"

Katie sat propped up in bed holding the baby and kissing a man.

CJ cleared his throat.

~ ~ ~

Katie gasped and jerked away from Noah, her heart racing. "CJ," she whispered, hugging the baby in a protective gesture.

"How are you, Katie? It's been a while. I hear we have a son."

CJ's calm voice and solid presence filled the room. "Yes," she whispered, pressing against the mattress as he advanced into the room.

He tossed the teddy bear in the empty bassinet and held out his hand to Noah.

"I'm CJ Jansen," he said. "And you are . . . ?"

Noah cleared his throat and shook CJ's hand. "Noah Davidson, I'm a good friend of Katie's, obviously. I'm an intern at Cornerstone Church, in my last semester of seminary."

Katie beamed at Noah, her heart melting at his defense of her. He hadn't backed down from CJ's towering presence. She, on the other hand, wanted to die of shame. Who had told CJ about the baby? Her heart pounded and her eyes filled with tears. She dashed them away. All the months of feeling so alone during her pregnancy came rushing back. This was the guy who had treated her like a princess in Vegas—until he got what he wanted and ran out on her.

CJ put the baby shoe with the plant and the gift-wrapped box on the table at the foot of the bed. He touched a red rose and turned to Noah.

"I take it these are from you?"

"Yes, Katie and I are very close." Noah put his arm around her.

CJ pierced her soul with his next words.

"I see you wasted no time finding someone else. Are you sure this baby isn't his?"

Katie cowered beneath his hostility before a flash of anger filled her. "I, we, of course this baby isn't his! Noah's a pastor!" How could CJ think such a thing? He had no idea what she'd been through at her church, the scorn and the gossip, the blatant attacks on her character and the near loss of her job until Pastor Dale had stepped in and allowed her to work from home. Her voice hitched. "You didn't even bother to leave me your phone number before you ran out on me in Vegas! If it hadn't been for my friends, and Noah, and Life Choice Pregnancy Center, I would have been alone. Totally alone." She turned her face away, her sobs filling the room.

Both men started for Katie at once. But CJ pulled up short when Noah shot him a look that said back off. Noah had won, this round at least. But it rankled. He hadn't gone to Vegas looking for a relationship, but he'd found one.

And lost it, judging by the scene playing out before him. CJ concentrated on taking slow, steady breaths, fatigue clouding his usual clear thinking. He studied Noah. *What would a girl like Katie see in such a puny punk? A pastor, of all professions.* CJ took a step back. Time to rethink his options.

The sound of Katie's sobs tore through his defenses. CJ clenched his teeth, wanting to punch the guy whose hands were all over Katie. Instead, he talked himself down, detaching to get a grip on the situation. He trained so he could handle pressure, compartmentalized to keep his emotions in check and get the job done. He knew what to do in heavy seas battling wind-waves. He knew how to extract a team of SEALs under heavy enemy fire, and take over a ship undetected. But unlike the resources he had as a SWCC, or his teammates, who always had his back, there was no high-powered combatant craft or 50-cal machine gun here that would get him out of this trouble. He didn't even have a rubber raft.

CJ considered his next move with the same attention to detail as he gave a SWCC mission. He could stay and be the unwelcome third wheel. Or come back another time. Maybe do a little reconnaissance in the meantime; ask aunt Aubrey for advice, since she was a pediatrician and one of his family's closest friends. He jerked at the sound of a commotion at the door, his senses on full alert. A little blond girl came running in the room, followed by a woman and a man who CJ recognized immediately.

"Skid." CJ tensed, surprised to see a guy he knew from his deployment.

"CJ." Brad nodded. He looked at Katie, then back at CJ. "So, you're the one."

The two men shook hands.

"Congratulations?"

CJ looked away, embarrassment swamping him. He rubbed the back of his neck. "I guess you could say that. A shock for sure, coming on the heels of getting home yesterday. I heard the news this morning at about eight."

Brad nodded at the baby. "I think he got here about three. The only reason I know that is because my wife helped with the delivery." Brad gestured to the tall blonde who had come in with him.

"So, how do you and your wife know Katie?" CJ asked, his mind racing for the connection between one of the SEALs he'd worked with in the Middle East and the woman he had left in bed in Vegas.

"Julie and I go to the same church as Katie. I was on the Council when we hired her to design publicity for the church. I knew from Julie that she got pregnant with some guy on a weekend in Vegas. Didn't know the guy was you, though. Until just now." He shook his head. "Katie came to live at our place a few months ago. Money problems, I guess. Julie knew more than me about the situation. She's her Stephen Minister, you know, a person who comes alongside someone who's having a tough time, and they keep things confidential."

Brad moved to pick up the little girl who was now clinging to Julie. Megan. CJ remembered Brad telling him his daughter's name one day when they were working out. He'd seen her picture, too, although Brad didn't go overboard with bragging like some guys.

CJ studied the people surrounding Katie. Noah had draped his arm around Katie's shoulder in a possessive gesture that made him see red. Brad had one arm wrapped around his wife and held Megan with the other. Julie lifted the baby out of Katie's arms and cradled him in hers. Megan threatened to fall out of Brad's arms in her excitement to see the baby.

"Can I hold him? Please, Daddy?" Brad looked at his wife for the answer.

"Sure, if that's okay with Katie," Julie said.

At Katie's nod, Brad put Megan in the rocking chair the hospital provided. Julie knelt and put the baby in the child's outstretched arms.

Jealousy and hurt swamped CJ at the sight of them gathered around his son. He glanced at Katie. She ignored him. The day could have been a new beginning for them and their baby. A day to talk about the whys and the what now. Instead, everyone, it seemed, was welcome to hold the baby but him. He didn't even know his own son's name.

Chapter 3

Katie jerked awake, disoriented. Outside in the hallway of the hospital a cart rolled by making enough noise to wake the entire floor. She turned on her side and hugged a pillow. Yesterday had been exhausting, physically and emotionally. After appearing suddenly and silently in her doorway, CJ had slipped out of the room without anyone seeing him while Megan held Timmy.

Just like Vegas.

This time, though, he had left gifts, his name, and his phone number. Did he really think she would call him? Wasn't it enough that she had agonized over whether to put his name on Timmy's birth certificate? She wanted to be done with him. To put the time with him in Las Vegas behind her. She shook the gift-wrapped box, curious when it rattled. *Jewelry?* Did CJ think, after all this time, he could win her with jewelry; that she would pick up with him where they left off? Katie tossed the box on the tray table and flopped back on the pillows. *Think again, Mister SWCC Dirty Boat Guy.*

She rolled over and pressed the call button, her attempt to purge CJ from her life giving her no peace. Guilt ate at her. She should have told him she was pregnant. *How had he found out about the baby?*

Katie chewed on a thumbnail. Hadn't one of the nurses told her she could have juice and crackers any time she wanted? The digital clock on the wall showed the time. 4:36 a.m. Three hours or more until breakfast. Her stomach rumbled. She'd hardly touched last night's supper. Noah had scarfed down her dessert and left with barely a kiss on her cheek. The untimely appearance—and disappearance—of CJ was to blame, she was sure. Why couldn't she get him out of her thoughts?

Fifteen minutes later, when no one had answered her call, Katie untangled her legs from the sheet and put on her robe. If juice and crackers weren't going to come to her, she would go to them. The non-skid pads on her hospital socks made a slight scraping noise as she walked down the hall. The nursing station was deserted except for one woman in dusty pink scrubs. She looked up when Katie stopped at the desk.

"Can I help you?" She went back to typing on her keyboard.

"May I have some juice and crackers, please?" Katie asked. "I didn't eat much supper."

"Well, you should have," the woman snapped before standing up and disappearing around a corner.

"Bad night for you, I guess," Katie mumbled under her breath.

"This is all we have; take it or leave it," the woman said and set a cup of cranberry juice and a package of saltines on the counter. Without another glance at Katie, she sat and resumed typing.

"Thanks, this will be fine. I'm so sorry I troubled you." Katie took the snack and turned away. She shot an arrow prayer for the woman, just as Noah had taught her, opened the juice box and drank the entire cup. Needing some exercise, she walked down the hallway to a small reception room. A cap with a SD logo on the front had been left on a chair. She picked up the hat and turned it in her hand. Was it CJ's? Is this where he'd gone after sneaking out of her room? She closed her eyes, seeing him again, his lean six-foot frame, his commanding presence and firm jawline, that lethal charm and ready smile. Without meaning to, she lifted the hat to her nose and inhaled the scent of him. The memory of their time together rushed over her in waves. Tears filled her eyes and she dashed them away. She glanced at the clock and forced herself to return the hat to the chair. After five already. Timmy would want to nurse soon. She tossed the juice box in the trash and opened the crackers, eating them as she walked back down the hall. Denying the feelings.

"There you are," a nurse said, looking up from her computer in the hallway.

"I was hungry," Katie said, holding up the empty cracker packaging.

"Timmy will be, too." She got up from her work. "Here, I'll take that." She took the empty wrapper and walked away.

Katie stopped at the door to her room, the sound of "Anchors Aweigh" startling her. She raced into the room.

CJ sat on the bed, his back to her, holding Timmy.

"Are you crazy? What are you doing?" Katie fumed, circling the bed. "Give him to me." She reached for Timmy.

"Easy, Katie, easy." He held up his arm to display a wristband that identified him as Timmy's father. "I'm here legally, but here you go." He stood and held the baby out to her.

Katie reached for Timmy, her hands shaking.

"Careful now," CJ said, completing the transfer. "Sit down, Katie. We didn't get a chance to talk yesterday."

"Wha . . . How . . . ?" Katie couldn't get a coherent question out. She was shaking like a leaf, tears filling her eyes. Somehow CJ had managed to get a wristband. Clutching the baby against her chest, she perched on the edge of the bed.

CJ huffed out a sigh and sat next to her, his hip touching hers. "Why are you crying? I just wanted a few minutes with him. Honest, Katie, that's all. Just a few minutes to meet my son. In person. If you'd been here when I arrived, I would have explained that."

"I can't believe this." The panic was easing, replaced with anger and disbelief. "I'm going to file a complaint."

"For what? I'm his father. It says so on the birth certificate you filled out. Thank you for that, at least."

A knock on the door startled them both. A petite Asian woman in a lab coat with a stethoscope around her neck came in to the room and stood at the foot of the bed. She looked at CJ. "So, this is your Katie. And your son."

Suspicious, Katie felt her heart lurch. Who was this woman, and what had CJ said to give her the idea they were together?

"I'm Doctor Chang, Katie." She came around the bed and held out her hand. "I'm a longtime friend of CJ and his family and a pediatrician on staff here." She nodded at Conner. "Call me old-fashioned, but I believe Dad needs to bond with his baby as much as Mom does. CJ explained that you two are not together at this time. That makes me very sad." She glanced at Timmy. "He's ready to nurse, so let's give Katie some time to do that, CJ. Then the two of you can talk." She patted Katie's shoulder.

CJ left the room with Dr. Chang. As if in a trance, Katie unbuttoned her robe to nurse the baby, raised the mattress and scooted down into the bed. She closed her eyes, reciting scripture Noah had taught her. Within minutes she dozed off cradling Timmy against her breast.

In the hallway, CJ put his arm around Dr. Chang's shoulder. "Thanks for steering me in the right direction so I could see my son, aunt Aubrey."

"You know how much I care about you, don't you? I'm glad to help."

As they passed the nurses' station, a doctor looked up from a chart he was studying.

"Morning, Aubrey, CJ. Good to have you home."

CJ nodded. "Thanks. Morning, Dr. Ben."

"Don't forget, cards at seven at Mary's tomorrow," Aubrey said to the doctor as they continued walking.

"Wouldn't miss it," Ben said and headed in the opposite direction.

"Praise the Lord for his mercy and faithfulness," Dr. Chang said under her breath. At the entrance to the nurses' station, she turned. "Keep me posted, CJ. The way I see it, you need to make every effort to work things out with Katie."

CJ nodded. "I know."

She pulled gently on his ear. "And CJ, talk to your parents, you hear?"

"Soon. I will. Thanks again, aunt Aubrey. Love you." CJ stooped to hug the petite doctor.

"Love you, too. Always, no matter." She turned and walked to her desk.

CJ sighed and returned to Katie's room. *Always, no matter.* A phrase his family used often to express their unconditional love. He sighed. The caffeine energy drink he had gulped an hour ago had deserted him, but he didn't know if he would get another chance to talk to Katie alone again. They had some things they had to get clear.

Propped up in bed with her eyes closed, Katie cradled the baby against her exposed breast. He looked away. Remorse filled him. If things were as they should be, being with her as she nursed the baby would be the most natural place in the world for him to be.

"Ah, Katie, I'm sorry. Really." His chin dropped and he leaned against the bed at her feet.

Katie opened her eyes with a start and hastily covered herself. A blush rushed to her cheeks. "What in the world were you thinking? Coming here in the middle of the night?"

"It's not the middle of the night. It's already after five. Not that I know exactly what time zone I'm in right now." His velvet brown eyes were luminous. "I wanted to see you, that's all. And hold my son."

"You could have asked."

"You could have offered."

His criticism stung. Tears pooled in her eyes. "I need a tissue."

"Promise not to go away, and I'll get you one."

"And just where would I go?" When he didn't move to get up, she sniffed loudly. "You want me to use my sleeve?"

"I've used worse," CJ said, going around the bed to the box of tissues on the rolling table.

He moved with cat-like grace, his presence filling the room. Katie's breath caught in a half sob. Memories rushed at her.

"Here you go." He sat down on the bed, this time alongside her hip.

Katie tore off a couple of tissues and wiped her nose. "Thanks," she said, refusing to meet his gaze. She placed the tissues within easy reach and pushed her hair behind her ear. How long since she brushed it? Or her teeth? Why did he have to see her looking like such a wreck? Katie kept her head down, looking at Timmy. He had fallen asleep again.

The silence between them lengthened. Katie began to feel drowsy. CJ's presence calmed her. But his next words made her instantly defensive.

"Were you ever going to tell me?" CJ asked. "About our son, I mean."

Katie clenched her teeth, ashamed, but not about to admit it. "No."

CJ stared at her, searching her face. "You think I deserve that?"

She remained silent.

"Come on, Katie. You think that would have been fair to our son? To never know his dad?"

Katie looked away. If things worked out with Noah, Timmy's dad would be a pastor. Why should it make her feel so guilty? CJ had run out on her, not the other way around. His next question intruded on her thoughts.

"How did you choose his name?"

"Oh. His name. Well, it's from the Bible. My favorite books. And I like the sound of the two names together with mine."

CJ shook his head and chuckled. "That may be, but do you realize you named the baby after my father and me? Dad's name is Timothy, and my middle name is James."

Katie crushed the tissue she was holding in her hand. "Noah and I chose Timmy's name."

"So, you call him Timmy. I like it." He looked away, his jaw clenching before he pierced her with eyes that smoldered. "How serious are you and this Noah dude?"

Katie looked away, unable to meet his eyes. "Very. He's been there for me since he came to Cornerstone last January."

"The month I deployed." He leaned in enough that she couldn't escape his gaze. "So, you've known him six months, and you think you love him?"

Do I love him? Katie looked away again. "We're getting there." She stuck out her chin. "Not that it's any of your business."

He didn't hesitate. "Actually, it is my business."

A sharp edge of panic pierced her heart. She stared at him. "What do you mean? It's been nine months since I last saw you, and you wouldn't be here now if someone hadn't told you about me. That's the kind of guy you are!" All the anger and pain of his rejection was back, so powerful she had trouble breathing.

"You have no idea what the last nine months have been like for me! And fortunately, someone did tell me. But not the person who should have. You've got a lot of nerve, Katie, judging me! I'm here now. And nobody said I had to be. I could have ignored this whole thing. Pretended I never knew about it."

"Who told you? Tell me. Who?"

CJ stood and paced to the window. He opened the blinds; sunshine poured in the room. "Timmy's one day old."

Katie ignored his attempt to distract her. "Who? I want an answer."

Turning, CJ strode to the foot of the bed. "Does it really matter? I don't want to hurt you, Katie. Or Timmy. But if you're serious about a relationship with Noah, maybe even thinking about marrying him, then we need to talk about custody. I'm Timmy's father, whether I'm ready for it or not, and I'm not ditching my responsibilities toward my son."

Katie glared at him, a shiver giving her away. "You want custody?" Judging from the doctors he knew and his military status, he could probably get plenty of people to side with him. Who did she have? Insecurity swamped her. What if Noah didn't love her? He said he did, but wasn't she, after all, damaged goods?

"No, I'll never agree to that." She closed her eyes, shame washing over her. She had given away her virginity to this guy. And paid for it with a baby. Her baby now.

She glared at CJ with loathing. A day's growth of beard had heightened rather than diminished his good looks. But to her, he might as well be the devil himself. Stubborn determination was written all over his face.

"Who told you?" she ground out between clenched teeth.

He rubbed a hand around the back of his neck several times and sighed. "It doesn't matter, but it was Dustin. He and Ashley got back together right before we deployed." He shot her a challenging look. "I thought you and Ashley were best friends. At least you were in Vegas. You must have known they were back together. You could have reached me, if you wanted to."

Katie glared at him, so angry she could hardly speak. "Let's just say Dustin is a sore subject between us. Ashley knows better than to talk to me about him."

"Why? What did he ever do to you?"

"Dustin's your friend. Ask him!"

In the hallway, a baby cried.

"You need to go, CJ. What more is there to say? I'll fight you with everything I've got to keep Timmy with me. I'm his mother. No judge in their right mind will ignore that."

"Don't be too sure about that, Katie. It's a different day out there. I have better resources than you do." CJ moved to her side. With his hand on the mattress behind her, he leaned in, his voice hard. "I hope it doesn't come to that, Katie. And that's the honest truth. But I'm going to see Timmy for starters. After that, we'll see. I'll be at your place on Saturday, nine sharp. I'll get your address from Brad."

Timmy woke with a start and began to wail. CJ left the room without looking back.

Chapter 4

Midmorning sunshine filtered through the blinds in Katie's hospital room. CJ hadn't returned, but his words wouldn't get out of her head. What did he intend to do? Besides make her life miserable? She glanced at the present he'd brought with him yesterday. Gift-wrapped in blue-and-white striped paper, a hospital logo sticker held the white grosgrain ribbon in place. It sat on the side of the table where she'd shoved it to make way for her food trays. Not that she had much appetite. *An impulse buy?* Katie got out of bed and stopped at the rolling table, reluctant to touch CJ's gift. *Should I open it? Throw it in the trash?* Determined to ignore it until she got home, she turned and picked up Timmy from his bassinette. Laying him on her bed, she stripped off his T-shirt and wet diaper. "You are a hungry boy, aren't you, doll baby?" She crawled in bed and plopped against the pillows to nurse him. A while later, a knock on the door startled her. At least the curtain provided some privacy. "Yes?" she called.

"It's Dr. Chang, Katie, may I come in?"

"Oh, hi, yes, come in," Katie said.

Dr. Chang came around the curtain and stood beside the bed. Wary of the doctor and her connection to CJ, she concentrated on Timmy.

"You're nursing. That's good." She patted Timmy's arm. "I see you've freed him from his diaper for a while. I hope he doesn't pee on you." She smiled and gave Timmy's big toe a wiggle. "After all these years of working with babies,

I still love tickling their toes. Their feet are often genetically similar to their mom or dad's, as you're probably aware."

"I guess I hadn't thought about it." Katie wiggled her own toes, comparing hers to Timmy's. "I don't think Timmy's toes look like mine, do you?"

Dr. Chang considered Katie's toes. "You're right. You're second toe is a little longer than your big toe. You should ask to see CJ's."

Katie nodded, stifling a laugh. She pictured the conversation. *By the way, CJ, can I see your toes?* Would he shrug in that easy way of his, give her a quizzical look, and sit down to take off his shoes? Or tell her to take a hike?

Timmy's cry brought her back to reality.

She lifted the naked baby to her shoulder and soothed her hand over his bare back. Dr. Chang acted as if nothing out of the ordinary had occurred that morning. Except it had. CJ had been here, and Katie suspected this was the woman who had helped him.

"Would you mind handing me a diaper? They're in the cabinet under his bassinet." Sitting cross-legged in the bed, Katie could feel her cheeks turning pink. "I think he's getting cold. I guess I shouldn't have undressed him." She laid Timmy on the sheet with his feet in her lap.

Dr. Chang found a fresh diaper and some powder. "It's good to get to know your baby, Katie, while you're still in the hospital, in case you need help or have questions. You might want to ask to bathe him, too, before you leave."

Katie diapered Timmy. "I hadn't thought of that, but I'll ask. That's going to be nerve-wracking on my own at home. I guess I need a T-shirt, too." She started to get out of bed.

"I'll get it." Dr. Chang walked back to the bassinet and brought out a T-shirt. With an efficiency foreign to Katie, she pulled the shirt over Timmy's head. "He looks just like CJ, doesn't he?" She slipped one of Timmy's arms, then the other, in the T-shirt and picked him up.

Did he look like CJ? Katie hadn't thought about it. But now that the doctor was holding him, she could see how much he looked like his father. Katie sighed. Would CJ really insist on custody? The question wouldn't go away. Or the nagging worry.

Her gaze on the baby, Dr. Chang rocked him and said, "I went to med school with this little guy's grandpa, CJ's dad. We went separate ways for some time, courtesy of the Navy, but we both ended up at Balboa, and then in private practice. Did you know Tim's an orthopedic surgeon at this hospital?" Katie shook her head. "CJ's mother, Mary, is my best friend. We're playing cards with some friends tonight, so CJ had better have broken the news about this little guy." She gazed at Katie with compassionate brown eyes. "Whatever's going on between the two of you, don't take it out on Timmy, please. The innocent suffer for the guilty. I've seen it too many times." She placed Timmy in Katie's arms. "I had better see to business. God bless you, dear one. And grant you His peace." She turned to go.

"Thank you, Dr. Chang. I . . . I'll think about what you said."

"Good. I will be praying for you and CJ. Oh, and by the way, if you haven't found a pediatrician for Timmy yet, let me know. I took care of both CJ and his sister while they were very little." She shrugged. "I'm not taking new patients right now, but I'll make an exception for Timmy."

"Thank you." Katie barely got the words out before the doctor was gone.

~ ~ ~

The room was quiet, the baby asleep. Katie hugged a pillow to her face to stifle her sobs. *The innocent suffer for the guilty.* Shame and fear washed over her. How could she protect Timmy from the stigma of being born out of wedlock? It was too late. She could never turn back time. What did CJ mean about wanting custody? He couldn't be serious about taking him away from her, could he? Turning on her side, Katie cried until she finally cried herself to sleep.

The rustling of pages woke her, and she opened her eyes. Noah sat balancing a notebook and his Bible on his lap. "Hey you," she said without lifting her head from the pillow. Sometime during her crying spree, she must have lowered the hospital bed. Now, she stretched under the covers and explored the contour of her tummy. Considerably shrunk from the mound it was, but plenty more to lose. The thought made her want to get out of bed and get going. Instead, she stretched again.

"You're awake." He closed his Bible and notebook and set them on the floor. At her bedside, he smoothed his hand over her hair. "Hey, beautiful." He leaned down and kissed her on the lips. "How are you feeling? Did you get any sleep at all last night?"

"I look terrible and you know it!" She took his hand. "A little sleep. Not enough. That's the number one complaint about a new baby, Julie says. Not enough sleep." *Should I tell him about CJ's visit?* Katie rejected the impulse.

"Well, we'll have to work on that. Can't have your creative abilities stifled by lack of sleep. Pastor Dale loved the art work you did for the *Life Together* series, by the way. I don't think I even got a chance to tell you that, did I?"

Katie found the switch and raised the bed. "It's been crazy around here. I've barely had time to shower. But he called. Yesterday early evening, I think. Time is running all together for me. I can't wait to get home!"

"Me too. Hospitals aren't my favorite place." He laughed. "But I guess I'll get used to them as a pastor. Do you know when they're letting you go? Julie seemed to think she would be coming for you right after lunch when I talked to her earlier. It's about one o'clock now. I've got to get back to the office in a few minutes or I would be taking you home.

Pastor Dale put me in charge of selecting the daily Bible readings, making up the small group questions, and listing at least three resources that go along with his message this Sunday. All he gave me to go on was the memory verse he had chosen."

"Which verse did he choose?"

"One from one of your favorite books." He quoted, "'Consider it pure joy, my brothers and sisters, whenever you face trials of many kinds, because you know that the testing of your faith produces perseverance.'"

"Okay, I've got it. James, chapter 1, verses 2 and 3, right?"

"Right! Atta girl!"

Katie smiled. It was one of Noah's favorite expressions, and he used it often. Katie pulled on his sleeve. "I could use a kiss to go with that encouragement."

His beard tickled her chin. For a pastor's son, he certainly knew how to kiss. *Almost as well as CJ.* Why was she thinking of him? She pulled away and palmed his cheeks, focusing all her attention on him. "Mmmnn . . . that's exactly what I needed."

"Me too. Listen, once you get home and get settled, let me take you and Timmy out to Del Mar. We'll sit in the car and, you know, get reacquainted. Watch the sunset. We can walk on the beach. Whatever you feel like." His wink said he had something besides watching the sunset in mind. "Maybe Saturday?"

She took his hand. "That would be perfect. I love the idea of walking on the beach with you. But it might be too soon for Timmy to be out, I don't know. I'll ask Julie. Anyway, we can sit in the car, at least." Being with him would surely chase away any trouble CJ might dish out in the morning. "You have to go, don't you? I see you drifting."

"You got me. I'm sorry. It's a big assignment, that's all, and I don't want to let Pastor Dale down. He got some emails from a couple of small group leaders about the last set of questions I did. Get this, they didn't like having to look up so many different scripture passages for each question."

"You're kidding? I loved those questions, especially going over them together. But I guess it did help to be with you and have access to your knowledge of scripture. Keep challenging me, okay? I love it."

Noah leaned down and kissed her again. "I love you, sweet Katie. I've never met anyone who inspires and encourages me like you do."

Katie's heart fluttered and her breath caught. "Oh, Noah, I love you, too."

This time when he leaned down to kiss her, she wrapped both arms around him and pressed up against him. He responded, deepening the kiss.

"Well, isn't this cozy." Brad Skidmore stood inside the doorway.

Noah pulled away quickly and backed up.

Katie blushed. "Brad. I-I wasn't expecting you. Where's Julie? I haven't been given the okay to leave yet. As far as I know."

Noah grabbed his books off the floor. "I'd best be on my way." Once behind Brad, he blew Katie a kiss and winked. "See you later, Brad."

"See you, Noah." Brad turned back to Katie. "Julie got a call and thought I should check since Noah's got other stuff he has to do. She said the hospital usually sends new moms home after twenty-four hours. Megan's with her at my folks' house baking sugar cookies, so here I am."

As if on cue, a nurse entered the room. "Oh, you're here to get her. Good. Dr. Chang said she called your wife." Turning to Katie, she said, "The doctors are signing your release forms. Yours and the baby's. I'll have some instructions for you. We'll go over those in a bit, and then you can take them home as a reminder." She walked back out the door.

"Dr. Chang called?" Katie looked at Brad.

"I guess. Julie didn't say who, just that you were probably going to be discharged. Looks like you'll be awhile though. I'll get some coffee. Be back in fifteen."

"Oh, okay." The days of being on her own with Timmy were about to begin.

~ ~ ~

In the hospital cafeteria, CJ rubbed a hand around the back of his neck to ease the tension. Considering the circumstances, and his colossal mistake in sleeping with Katie in Las Vegas, the conversation with his Dad had gone surprisingly well. He hadn't hidden his disappointment. But he hadn't heaped burning coals on CJ's head either. CJ looked out the window, his eyes moist. He felt small, and there was nothing about the feeling he liked. *Humility comes before honor.* Hadn't his parents preached that message from as far back as he could remember? A few of his dad's choice words had done the job of humbling him, all right. As had his advice: do whatever it takes to reconcile with Katie. Period.

CJ wiped his eyes then picked up his coffee cup and took a drink, grimacing at the taste. It had gone cold.

"Hey man, am I interrupting?" Brad extended his hand.

CJ shook his hand. "No, no, sit down. Just finished talking to my dad about how I . . . ah . . . well, what a mess I got myself into. I could think of a few other words for it, of course, but my dad doesn't like swearing. I try to rein it in when I'm around him."

"Yeah, I have to watch myself, too. Especially around Megan. I just came from Katie's room. She and the baby are being discharged. So, your dad didn't take it too well, huh? What about your mom? Are your folks together?"

"If you mean are they still married, yeah, twenty-five-plus years. I'm talking to Mom next. I would have told them together, but Dad's surgery schedule goes till eight tonight, and Mom's playing cards with a bunch of friends at seven, so she invited me for an early dinner. The way she eats, I'm pretty sure I'll have to pick up a burger or two on the way."

"It's none of my business, but what are your plans? I mean, do you want to be part of this baby's life? In any kind of real way?"

The words stung, but CJ couldn't read anything but kindness and concern in Brad's expression. It made him want to find a hole and crawl in. He sighed and looked out the window. What was done, was done. Nothing he could do now but go forward and try to set things right. But it wouldn't hurt to have Brad on his side with Katie. "Yeah, I do. Can't see it any other way, seeing as Timmy's here. It's still sinking in that I'm a dad, but I want to be part of his life." He shook his head. "I haven't had a chance to talk to Katie about it, but as soon as she gets a social security number for Timmy, I'll set up an account for him. Give her monthly support, too. I told her this morning that I want to see Timmy on Saturday. I hope it's okay if I come over."

"Sure. Any time. We're going to the zoo on Saturday, so you can have the place." Brad took a sip of coffee, then nailed CJ with his next words. "What's your plan with Katie, CJ? Obviously, there was a certain amount of attraction in Vegas. What happened?"

CJ looked away. Admitting his faults to Brad was every bit as hard as telling them to his dad. But he looked back, meeting Brad's gaze. The guy was married. He knew what it was like to be with a woman who made you feel out of control, crazy high. "Yeah, Vegas was hot. Katie was, well, she was . . . I don't know . . . It was . . ." He laughed. "She's amazing."

Brad shook his head. "That good, huh? Pretty sure that's a sign you're in deep."

Blowing out a long breath, CJ flopped back in his chair and crossed his arms. "Yeah. You could say that."

"So, why'd you ditch her?"

CJ tensed. He sat forward again, on the defense. "That's harsh, man. I didn't exactly ditch her."

"I'm pretty sure she sees it that way."

CJ's stomach clenched at Brad's cold stare. There was a reason the guy was a SEAL: he didn't back down. Didn't give any slack. A trickle of sweat ran down CJ's back.

"Time just got away from me that weekend, that's all. Then it was Sunday and I had to get back for a big anniversary party for my parents." Without thinking, CJ took another sip of his cold coffee and barely kept himself from spitting it out. "This coffee sucks!" He pushed it to the side. "You've been deployed, what? Three times? You know how the work-up before deployment goes. Long days, weekends, meetings, briefings, drills, and then the waiting. It's a constant ride, tense. And then, there's the paperwork. Who to notify in case of death, blah, blah, blah. I didn't think I could handle getting involved in a relationship along with the prep, especially like the one I wanted to have with Katie after Vegas. I guess somewhere in my head I thought I was doing her a favor. I never dreamed she'd get pregnant. Stupid of me. Just plain stupid." CJ lifted his hand to remove his hat, and discovered it wasn't on his head. He smoothed his hair instead, trying to remember where he'd left it. "I planned to look her up when I got back. Honest. My teammate Dustin is dating Katie's friend, Ashley. I always thought I could find Katie through her."

"Instead, you found out you're a dad."

"Yeah, Dustin woke me yesterday with the news. I couldn't believe it. Thought he was playing a bad joke. I'm still in shock, sort of. What I hadn't figured on was Noah. You've seen how she looks at him." He looked away, angry. "I think I've missed my chance."

"Could be, if the kiss I interrupted when I got here is any indication. Maybe you should shave your head. Grow a beard."

CJ rose halfway out of his chair, his temper flashing. "You think this is funny?"

"Actually, I don't think it's funny at all. Look, CJ, sit down. I'm on your side. We spent a lot of time sweating in the gym overseas. Not to mention the missions we did together. So, I know you don't back down. 'Never Quit,' remember? So, here's how I see it. I figure if anyone can give Noah some competition, it's you. But it won't be easy. Katie's had nine months on her own without a word from you. And Noah's well liked at the church, or so Julie says. He's almost got his degree to be an ordained pastor, he's from a family of pastors, and from what Julie tells me, Katie's on fire for Christ."

The news crashed over CJ. "A Bible-thumper like my dad, huh? Great. Just great."

"Wouldn't hurt to brush up on it. Just saying." Brad stood. "Time to get Katie and get this show on the road. Let me know if I can help. I'll be praying for you."

"Appreciate it." CJ slumped in his chair. *How could he possibly get God on his side?*

Chapter 5

The teddy bear stared at her from the bassinette. It's sailor suit mocked her. Katie picked it up and squeezed the bear's tummy, seeing CJ's face again as he tossed it in Timmy's bassinette without looking, his gaze intent on her. *Only a day and a half ago?* So much had happened. Clutching the bear to her chest, she breathed a prayer for strength. For courage to ignore CJ's charisma and keep to her plan. She turned away, and pulled her bag out of the closet. Brad said he would be back in fifteen minutes to get her, and she wanted to be ready. In the bottom of her bag she found clean underwear, a nursing bra, and a T-shirt. Stripping off her robe, she stuffed it into the bag with the teddy bear and turned to get her jeans off the closet hanger.

Five minutes later, showered and dressed, she tackled the job of packing her toiletries and the baby's supplies. Noah's roses sat beside CJ's houseplant. Had he chosen it for the baby shoe or because he knew, long after the roses turned to dust, she would still be nurturing the plant? Still thinking of him every time it needed water?

The gift-wrapped present drew her. Intrigued her. Made her want to cry. It had to be jewelry. What else could be in a box so small? She shook the box. It rattled, a muffled scraping. A guy's go-to kind of gift. *What did it mean?*

A sound at the door startled her. Katie sighed and stuffed the box on top of everything else in her bag. "Thanks for coming to get me, Brad. I'm so sorry to take you away from your family. You just got home and haven't had more than a few minutes to be with Julie and Megan! I can't believe how bad my timing is."

He shook his head. "A baby comes in God's timing, Katie. All we can do is go with the clock. And sometimes we can't see the blessing of it till later." He picked up her bag. "I'll take the balloons, the roses, and your bag if you can get the plant and Timmy. "Is there anything in the bathroom I need to grab?"

"No, I checked twice. This is all."

"I'll get the car and be at the curb."

As Brad left the room, a hospital volunteer arrived with a wheelchair. Katie lifted Timmy out of the bassinet and snuggled him in her arms. "That's a good boy, sweetheart. No crying, you hear?" She picked up the plant and sat down in the wheelchair. On the way down the hall, she called goodbye to Dr. Chang.

Dr. Chang waved. "God bless you, Katie. Enjoy your new baby."

At the curb, Brad got out of Katie's car. "Julie gave me your car keys, so I brought your car. Good thing you got the car seat installed. They can be difficult, and it's been a while since I installed one. You'll have to give me a refresher so I'm ready for our next baby." He lifted Timmy out of Katie's arms and strapped him in.

So, Brad and Julie were planning to have another baby. Katie smiled. Maybe Megan would have a brother or sister in nine months. A deployment baby. "Thanks so much, Brad, for helping me out."

Katie got in the front seat and fastened her seat belt. More than anything she wished Noah would be waiting for her and Timmy at home. Or better still, that he would be the one driving them home. But she pushed the thought aside, knowing he had work to do for the coming weekend at Cornerstone, and thanked the Lord for her loving friends. She chewed on her thumbnail, anxious. Brad deserved to have a day with his family. But it meant she would be alone for the first time with Timmy. She stared out the car window and silently prayed.

Brad pulled into the driveway then backed out to park the car on the street. "Let's get you and Timmy settled. I think it's been decided that we're having dinner with my parents. Julie texted me there's a container of leftover chili in the fridge, if you want it. We should be back around seven or eight. Is Noah or CJ coming over?"

"No, no, not tonight. Noah's got a big project at church, and I need to regroup. Maybe catch a nap."

In the house, Brad put her bag on the bed and set the roses on her desk. The balloons floated to the ceiling.

"Thanks for coming to get me, Brad. You guys are the best friends ever. Have fun with your family, and I'll see you later."

~ ~ ~

The next two days passed in a blur. Worn out from getting up in the night with Timmy, Katie tried to nap every time the baby did, and still get her work done. The Men's Steak Dinner at the church needed publicity, and Noah, since he was in charge, wanted a fresh logo for the event. She had just finished sketching out her last idea when he knocked at the door.

After a quick kiss, he sat down beside her on the sofa and put his arm around her. "You're worn out, aren't you? I'm sorry to add to your work, but I guess you can tell this dinner is important to me." He smiled. "It's going to be a real treat for the men of Cornerstone, too, with Dad coming to speak. Let's see what you've come up with, okay?" He opened her sketchbook.

Cradling Timmy, Katie munched popcorn and enjoyed Noah's methodical scrutiny of her sketches. "Am I going to get to meet him?"

Noah's head jerked up. "You mean Dad? Sure, sure, one of these days. I want you to meet both my parents. When Timmy's older, don't you think? One of the ladies at the church told me newborns shouldn't be exposed to a lot of people."

"Yeah, I've heard that too, but I'm not too worried about it. What do you think of the sketches? Like anything?"

Noah rubbed his head and stroked his beard. He scooted closer to her, turning pages again. "Okay, I think this third sketch works. Maybe use the cowboy from the last drawing with it. I like the western theme."

"Okay, I can do that. It means another sketch for you to approve, though. And I'll need a few more days to get the final drawing done. You okay with that?"

"Sure. I'm planning on being over here a few times a week anyway. If that's okay?"

"Perfect. I love seeing you. And studying together." She took a deep breath. "Did I mention that CJ is insisting on seeing Timmy?"

Noah's head jerked up. "No. No, you didn't. When? How often?"

"Saturday morning. To start. But I'm not letting him stay long."

Noah stroked his beard. "Well, he *is* Timmy's father. He should take some responsibility for him."

Katie fumed. "I don't want to see him."

Noah closed the sketchbook and took her hand. "I wish you didn't have to see him. But you have to be realistic, Katie. Give the guy a chance to be with Timmy. He didn't strike me as the type to let himself be pushed around, so you might as well let him visit—on your terms, not his."

She grimaced. "Yeah, I guess you're right. I'll get him in and out of here as fast as I can. I'm looking forward to going to the beach with you."

He turned to kiss her. "And I'm counting on having you all to myself."

"Then put Timmy on your prayer list, that he doesn't cry the whole time. He's been a little grouchy since we got home."

Noah touched the baby's head as he stood. "Peace, Timmy. Gotta go, honey." His kiss consoled her. "I'll see you tomorrow about six. No, let me check to see when the sun sets and I'll text you the time."

Katie grabbed another handful of popcorn, too tired to get up. "Okay. See you." Within minutes, she closed the bag and snuggled down for a nap. Noah's project could wait. Maybe she could ask CJ to watch Timmy while she worked.

~ ~ ~

"Katie," Julie whispered on Saturday morning. "We're heading out to the zoo now. It's eight-thirty."

Katie groaned but didn't move. Timmy had cried four times in the night. She had dragged herself out of bed each time, nursed him, changed him, and went back to sleep. Except for the one time when her mind wouldn't shut off.

"I don't think I can do it," she moaned when Julie shook her shoulder. She didn't want to see CJ. But even in her sleep-deprived state, she knew he wouldn't back off. His body language had made that very clear. The custody threat had done the rest. With another moan she rolled over on her back, her eyes still closed. "Okay. I'm awake."

Still whispering, Julie said, "We're off then. There's turkey from the deli in the fridge. We'll see you about six if you haven't left with Noah for the beach by then."

Noah. Katie smiled. One hour with CJ. That's all he was getting, and he'd be gone. She would wash her hair this afternoon and braid it in a French braid, Noah's favorite. With a contented sigh, she rolled over toward the wall and fell back asleep.

Timmy's cries woke her. Her eyes popped open. What time was it? She rolled over and gasped. CJ sat in the glider chair holding Timmy.

"Hey, sleepyhead."

Pushing her hair out of her face, she sat up and pulled the sheet to her chin. "How did you get in here?" First the hospital room and now her bedroom. She would have to get a lock for her door.

"I pulled up as Brad and Julie were leaving. Brad said to come on in and make myself at home. So I did. I brought you a mocha from Starbucks, but I'm afraid it's cold now. I put it in the fridge."

Timmy continued to cry. CJ didn't look a bit flustered by it, which infuriated Katie. Was the guy made of stone? "You need to leave. Timmy's hungry."

CJ got up, but instead of leaving, he handed Timmy to her in the bed and sat back down. "You've got the goods. Have at it."

"You need to leave. Now." Katie glared at him. He set the chair in motion, sitting back with one bare foot resting on the opposite knee. "Now," she said again.

"Feed the baby, Katie, I won't look. Have a bottle ready next time and it won't be an issue."

Katie fumed. Noah would never presume to be in her bedroom. Turning toward the wall, she pulled the sheet around herself. Timmy's rooting reflex made her smile. He tried to nurse through her nightgown, his cries accompanied by one of his legs striking the air. "You're as pushy as your father, aren't you?" she whispered, fumbling with her nightgown. "Well, you can wait a second."

Fifteen minutes later, Katie lifted Timmy onto her shoulder to burp him. "See that man over there, Timmy," she said to the wall. "Well, he's got a lot of nerve sneaking in here." She was about to say more when a burp cloth was placed over her shoulder from behind.

"I'll change his diaper when you're done, if you like."

She could feel CJ's presence directly behind her. Solid. Unyielding. He lifted her hair and she tensed. "What do you want, CJ?"

He sat down beside her. "This, Katie, this is what I want. To be with you and Timmy for a few hours. For now." He ran his fingers lightly up and down her back.

"Don't touch me, CJ." She turned and thrust the baby at him. "Timmy's diaper's full. He needs it changed."

Without a word, CJ took Timmy and walked to the changing table.

Throwing off the sheet, Katie got out of bed, raced for the bathroom and locked the door. She turned on the shower and stripped off her nightgown. The smell, although not terrible, caused a blush to race to her cheek. CJ had been sitting close enough to get a good whiff. "Good," she ground out under her breath. "I hope that'll keep him far away from me."

After twisting her hair and securing it with a clip, she took off her underwear and stepped in the shower. How long did she dare stay? Closing her eyes, Katie stood with her back to the warm spray and tried to think of something beside the man in her bedroom. She imagined herself back in the swimming pool at the apartment complex where she and Ashley had lived when they first came to San Diego. They had raced each other in the pool every night, just like they used to do on the swim team in high school. Katie pulled back from the spray, grabbed the soap and lathered her body. She and Ashley had been inseparable friends for as long as she could remember. *Until Vegas.* Another reason to be mad at CJ.

Katie turned off the shower, grabbed a towel, and groaned. She hadn't brought a change of clean clothes and wouldn't last long without underwear to keep a pad in place. Her face flaming, she put her ear against the door. Where was CJ? She pulled the towel snuggly around herself and opened the door a crack. The room was empty. She tiptoed out of the bathroom, closed her bedroom door, and got dressed. Her heart pounded as if she had just finished a marathon. She glanced at the clock. It wasn't even ten.

With a sigh, Katie headed back into the bathroom and released the clip from her hair. She grabbed her hairbrush, leaned over, and began brushing her thick hair from the roots to the tips. When she stood and threw her head back, the curls cascaded over her shoulders. She opened a drawer in the vanity and withdrew a thin pink headband to match her T-shirt. "Nothing's going to help these eyes," she said to the girl in the mirror. Puffy from lack of sleep, she nevertheless pulled a tube of concealer from a drawer and did the best she could to cover up the damage. She had nearly finished when she caught the reflection of CJ standing behind her with Timmy. She whirled and stabbed the air with the concealer wand. "You can't be in here."

CJ glanced left and right. "It appears that I can."

He laughed, and his face took on such an expression of relaxed happiness that Katie's breath caught in her throat.

"You look beautiful, Katie. Whatever that stick is that you're waving around, it worked magic on your eyes. You don't look quite as tired as when I arrived."

She backed him out of the bathroom. "And now it's time for you to leave. You've had plenty of time with Timmy." She closed the concealer and dropped it on her desk.

"Not so fast. My folks want to meet Timmy. They're bringing lunch."

"What? You can't just invite them here. This isn't even my house, as you well know! Julie and Brad will be home any minute. Megan's toys and books are right out there in that cabinet and Brad will probably want to watch TV."

"Nice try, Katie. I talked to Brad. He said to make myself at home; they won't be home before six."

Her pulse pounding, she pushed past CJ and headed toward the family room before turning back abruptly. "You never said a word about your parents coming with you. I-I'm not ready for company." She marched up to him and pushed on his shoulder. "I've been a mother exactly four days. I'm exhausted. All I do is feed Timmy all day and all night, too. I can't have company. I'm not ready . . . You don't know . . ." Her sobs filled the room.

Shifting Timmy to his shoulder, CJ went to Katie. He wanted to touch her, but held back, not wanting to be rejected again. "Katie, come on. You're tired. I get it. I know a little something about sleep deprivation." He tried to distract her, give her time to collect herself. "On the Tour—that's the SWCC version of the SEALs hell week—we stay up almost around the clock for three days. It's insane. But we do it. We have to or we're out." He stepped closer. "You'll get through this, Katie, I promise. You've got what it takes." He waited, hoping he didn't have to call his mom and renege on his invitation. When Katie wiped her eyes, he said, "Look, Timmy's quiet now. Why don't you go back to bed for an hour? I need bonding time with my son, right?"

Katie sniffed and turned to him. "Okay. But don't ever surprise me like this again."

"I promise." He nodded and left the room, pulling the door shut behind him.

Chapter 6

Throwing off the sheet, Katie sat up and stretched. She glanced at the clock and yawned. *Almost noon.* Had CJ's parents arrived? She got out of bed and tiptoed to the door. A low murmur of voices reached her. She turned and went into the bathroom. If she couldn't get out of this, she would at least look presentable. She finger-combed her hair, brushed her teeth, applied a light coating of mascara to her eyelashes, and stroked her lips with gloss.

Seated in the family room, facing the TV entertainment center, CJ and his parents turned in one accord when she opened her door. Katie glanced from one face to the other. CJ stood to his feet, followed by his dad. Timmy started to fuss in CJ's dad's arms. Katie released a shaky breath. "Hi," she said and lifted her hand in greeting.

"You're up." CJ crossed to Katie. With his hand on her back, he drew her forward. "Katie, I'd like you to meet my parents, Mary and Tim Jansen."

Mary came around the back of the sofa, holding out both hands. "You're even more beautiful than CJ told us." She let her hands rest on Katie's shoulders. "I'm so glad to meet you, and I apologize for coming so soon after you had Timmy. I-I didn't think I could wait a minute longer to get to know my grandson. Come, sit with us." She turned. "Are you hungry? I brought chicken salad and croissants."

"That's so nice of you. Maybe a glass of milk, to start. Thanks for letting me get a little extra sleep."

"You need all you can get with a newborn, don't you?" Mary rounded the counter to the kitchen. She found a glass, opened the refrigerator and poured the milk. "Here you go." She handed the glass to Katie. "I also brought a vegetable tray and some cheese and crackers. And some artichoke dip I made for my card party last Wednesday. It's even better a few days later, you know. Does that sound good?"

"Thank you, yes, ma'am."

"What charming Southern manners. But please, just call me Mary."

"Okay, Mary." Katie said and smiled.

CJ pulled out a chair for her at the table. "Best to give in and eat, Katie. Mom loves to see people well-fed and happy." He took the vegetable tray and dip Mary offered and put it on the table. The cheese and crackers landed next.

Katie downed half of the milk in a few gulps, grabbed a piece of cheese, ate it, and took another. Timmy had quieted. She glanced at Mary. CJ's mom might like to see people enjoying their food, but she personally didn't look like she overate. White capris and a blue-and-white striped top showed off her fashionably trim figure. Her sable-brown hair was knotted in a thick bun low on her neck. Small diamond stud earrings caught the light as she moved around the kitchen.

CJ took a seat beside Katie, grabbed a stalk of celery and filled it with a generous load of dip. The crunch of his first bite filled the room. He loaded the end of another stalk and offered it to Katie. "You like artichokes?"

"I guess. Haven't really had them that I know of. But I'll try it." She took a small bite and chewed. "This is delicious," she said, finishing the portion with the dip. "But I either need more dip or less celery. The ratio's off."

CJ held out the bowl to her. "Go ahead. No one in this room will fine you for double-dipping."

"CJ's dad joined them with Timmy, who was now starting to fuss. "I didn't get a chance to say hello yet, Katie. Please call me Tim." He held out his hand. "CJ was right.

He told us you like to live on the edge. Not everyone would have tried something they'd never tasted, but Mary's dip makes artichokes one of my favorite vegetables." His smile was every bit as lethal as his son's.

Katie looked at CJ. "You told him that I like to live on the edge?"

"The edge of the fountain, remember?"

Katie blushed, the memory returning in a rush. Their first kiss. After he saved her from falling in the fountain. "Oh, that." She stood and took Timmy from Tim. "Actually, I'm rather boring. If I'm going to enjoy my lunch I think I'd better feed this guy first. But I'll be back for more of that dip, so save me some, okay?" She went into her room and closed the door.

While Timmy nursed, Katie leaned her head back and closed her eyes. She had stuffed the memory of how charming CJ could be deep into her mind. She didn't want to let it out again, or get taken in by his good looks. How could he be so much at home in his own skin? Did he ever feel insecure? Probably not, with parents like Mary and Tim. They hadn't let him come alone, and they hadn't come empty-handed. Not only had they brought lunch, but on the coffee table in front of the sofa she had glimpsed a pile of presents. The sound of their voices in the kitchen was relaxed and happy. Several times she wished she knew what was so funny when their laughter filtered through the door. Was this show of family togetherness just part of some bigger plan to get custody of Timmy? The thought caused her stomach to clench.

Fifteen minutes later, she opened her bedroom door to find CJ, Mary and Tim in the same seats where she had left them. The men stood as she entered.

"I hope we didn't make too much noise out here," Mary said. She got up and brought chicken salad sandwiches on croissants, fresh fruit, and homemade chocolate chip cookies to the table.

CJ crossed to Katie. "I'll take Timmy while you finish the artichoke dip. See, we did leave you some, although I had to remind Dad to go easy." He nuzzled Timmy's neck and cheek before draping him over his shoulder.

"Don't believe him, Katie. It was the other way around," Tim said. He resumed his seat and met her gaze across the table. "So, CJ says you're a graphic designer. What made you choose the field?"

Katie finished chewing a carrot stick. "I had a teacher who got me interested in computer work. She was my art teacher, and even though she was older, she liked learning new things. She told me about some programs she found on the Internet. So, that was the start. I always knew I wanted to go to college and have a career, and graphic arts seemed the best fit."

"What college did you attend?"

"I can tell you that." CJ winked at Katie. "Charleston Southern University. See, I was listening in Vegas."

Katie laughed. "Listening and giving me a hard time for going to a school you'd never even heard of. Remember that?"

"Yeah, I remember you called me a few choice names, none of them flattering."

"But deserved. You West Coast snobs . . ." Katie felt herself blushing. With a few words, CJ had transported her back to the first night they had been together in Vegas.

Mary brought her back to the present when she set the milk and some glasses in the center of the table. "Tim, why don't you offer a prayer, please." She sat and held out her hands to her husband and Katie.

Katie swallowed and glanced at CJ. She took Mary's hand. CJ's hand was palm up, waiting for hers to fill it. Katie stared at it, seeing the hard callouses, remembering the rough texture on her skin. Tim was waiting to pray. She closed her eyes and put out her hand. CJ's closed around it. The feel brought a wave of memories so intense she nearly cried out.

"Heavenly Father, we're so thankful that you've brought CJ safely home, and you've brought Katie and Timmy into our lives. Bless them, Lord, with your favor. Guide them in your ways. Nourish us now with this food, and help us serve you wholeheartedly. Amen."

Mary released her hand and reached for the plate of sandwiches. Katie pulled, but CJ didn't let go. Instead, he tightened his grip and stroked his thumb over the back of her hand. When she looked at him, he smiled in a way that made her almost faint. It said they had history. Only two nights and a day together, but history all the same. Did he think she could forget nine months with no word from him? Not likely.

"CJ, stop playing and let Katie eat." Mary held the plate of sandwiches out for Katie to choose one.

He released her hand and waited until she had a sandwich to take his. Still holding Timmy, he filled his plate with a hefty portion of cantaloupe, honeydew, strawberries, grapes and blueberries.

As the meal progressed, conversation flowed easily. Katie looked from Mary to Tim to CJ, jealousy welling up inside her. Mealtime with her own family had been nothing like this. Of course, her dad had reason for his bitterness and his bad temper, didn't he? And her mom, though she always worked hard to keep peace, didn't always get her way. Just thinking of her made Katie sad. Peggy Ryan had wanted to be with Katie and meet Timmy, but she was her husband's sole caregiver and couldn't get away. Katie reached for a second cookie.

The meal finished, Tim stood and began stacking the used plates. "I'll wash these. Why don't you and Katie get started on those gifts, CJ? You too, Mary. I'll have these done in a minute and join you. I can see everything from here."

"Let me hold Timmy awhile," Mary said. "Come here, my darling grandbaby." She took Timmy, nuzzled his tummy, and sat on the love seat across from Katie and CJ.

"Where do you want to start?" CJ asked. "Small, medium, or large?" He held a box to his ear and shook it. "If it's not a rattle, I just broke it."

"Now you have to open it. I'm not taking the blame for any damage you've done."

CJ ripped off the wrapping and opened the box. Inside was a rattle in the shape of a giraffe. "Just what I always wanted." He shook it a few times, laid it on the sofa, and reached for the biggest box. "Here, you open this one."

Not wanting to disappoint Mary, Katie kept it to herself that she already had a giraffe rattle. She worked on opening the big box without tearing the wrapping paper.

"Just rip it," CJ said. "Live dangerously."

"No, I might need this paper for something else." But as she peeled open the tape to expose the contents, she clapped her hands and laughed. "This is perfect! I totally needed this since Timmy shares my room." She finished unwrapping a large diaper trash can with built in odor control.

Shaking his head, CJ handed her another gift. Between them, it took twenty minutes to finish unwrapping toys, clothes, bibs, disposable diapers, a baby swing, and play mat. In the smallest box she found a gift card for a jogging stroller and gave a shout of joy. But the gift that took Katie's breath away was a cashier's check in her name, to be saved for Timmy or used as needed, and a promise in writing from Tim and Mary to faithfully stand by her no matter where her life's path took her.

With tears pouring down her cheeks, Katie could no longer see the writing on the check and note. "You don't even know me, and you would do this for Timmy and me? I don't know what to say. I'm overwhelmed. Thank you. Thank you." CJ pulled her against him, and she didn't protest. Instead, she wrapped her arms around him, turned her face into his chest and cried.

Embarrassment and confusion swamped her. Why were they doing this?

Mary offered her a tissue and sat down beside her. Her hand gently stroked Katie's back. "We didn't mean to make you cry, Katie. We just want you to know we love you and want the best for you. Tim and I are going to head home now, but I hope we can come back. And we'd love to have you and Timmy come visit us in our home. We only live about fifteen minutes from here. Whatever is best for you. No strings attached. Tim wants to pray a blessing over Timmy before we leave. Is that okay with you?"

Wiping her nose, Katie stood. "Sure, that would be beautiful."

Cradling Timmy, Tim made the sign of the cross on Timmy's forehead and said, "In the name of the Father, and the Son, and the Holy Spirit, I bless this child, and I ask for your protection, direction, and favor to rest on him, this precious child of yours and ours, Lord, that he would grow strong in the knowledge of you and your ways, and love you all the days of his life. Amen."

Tim handed Timmy to Katie and kissed her forehead. "You're in our prayers, sweetheart. Don't hesitate to call if we can help you in any way, okay?" Mary moved to his side and slid her arm around his waist.

Katie blinked back tears. "Thank you so much. I don't know what else to say. You have been so kind and so generous. Thank you." She hugged Mary as best she could with Timmy between them. "Bye, and God bless you."

CJ helped his parents take dishes to their car. Not knowing what else to do, Katie went to her room, nursed Timmy, and put him down in his crib. She washed her face and brushed her hair, exhausted and overwhelmed.

She made her bed and tidied the bathroom. No sound

came from the family room. *Had CJ left, too?* Why were his parents being so nice to her? It had been subtle, but the more Katie thought about it, the more she was sure that Mary at least was trying to make up for her son's behavior. She and Tim were wonderful, but CJ was nothing like Noah. He had never even said he was sorry. Now he was hiding behind his parents and their money.

A soft knock on her door startled her. "Katie, are you okay?"

Katie opened the door. "Shh . . ." she whispered. "You're still here. I thought you left with your parents."

"No, I wanted a minute to talk to you. Is Timmy asleep?"

Katie glanced at the crib. "Almost," she whispered and stepped out of the room, closing the door quietly behind her. "I'm really tired, CJ, and I have something else tonight. Will this take long?"

CJ looked away, a muscle flexing in his jaw. "No, no." He stepped to her and ran his hands up her arms. When she stiffened, he dropped them and rubbed one hand around the back of his neck. "So, that scene of you crying and hugging me on the sofa was for show, huh?"

"What do you mean? I was blown away. Why would anyone give someone like me that kind of money? What are they trying to buy?" A thought came unbidden. "Is this your way of trying to get custody of Timmy?"

CJ stared at her, his eyes flashing. "Is that what you really think? That my parents are trying to buy you? They plan to come in here and take Timmy away from you? Come on. You read the note they wrote. They care about you. You're the mother of their grandson. Their first and only grandson. No matter what you think of me, they're the real deal. They care about people. Don't hurt them, Katie. Please. You may not think much of me, and that's okay, but don't take it out on them." He pierced her with a hostile stare, turned on his heel, and walked out of the house.

Katie worked her lower lip with her teeth, regretting her behavior. Whatever he wanted to say, it was too late now.

~ ~ ~

CJ got as far as the park near Katie's house before he had to pull over. Anger and hurt ate at him, threatening to make him do something foolish. Like run his truck into a tree. Leaning against the headrest, CJ closed his eyes. Where was the easygoing, fun-loving woman he'd met in Las Vegas? Today she'd been fickle. One minute crying and hugging him, the next pushing him away. He could still walk away. Forget about Saturday visits. Let his parents deal with her. Except he was the one who had made the mess. He and Katie. Why couldn't she see he was trying to make things right? At least for Timmy's sake. His son. Already he loved him with an intensity that scared him. He wanted to ask her about the present. The ruby knot. Had she opened it? Read his note? CJ shook his head, discouraged. His parents had wanted to meet Timmy. He hadn't put up a fight. Maybe that was the problem. He wasn't fighting. He hadn't even picked up a weapon. If this was the Tour, he'd be cut from being a SWCC already. *Never quit.* The slogan he lived by. The one he'd die by, if it came to that. But not today. Not if he still had a chance with Katie. Determined to keep trying, he started his truck and pulled away from the curb. He needed a strategy. His mother had used food and gifts. But instead of winning Katie, it had made her suspicious, and hadn't done anything to help his cause. With a final glance at the street where Katie lived, he headed for the base. Maybe a couple hours of working out at the schoolhouse would help him figure out what he really wanted. And how to make it happen.

~ ~ ~

Multiple layers of pink and orange streaked the sky as the sun slid over the edge of the gray-brown waters of the Pacific Ocean. The beach was filled with tourists and locals alike, their pop-ups and umbrellas dotting the sand. Seated in the front seat of her car with Noah at the wheel and Timmy sleeping in the back, Katie soaked in the sight of a family who had brought a kite. The dad was helping a boy of about five or six get it off the ground and into the air while the mother dug in the sand with her little girl.

"How did this morning go?" Noah asked.

"It stretched into the afternoon." Katie sighed and turned away from the tranquil setting on the beach to face Noah. "CJ brought his parents and they brought lunch. And presents. Lots of presents."

"You're kidding. What kind of presents?"

"Some little things like bibs and a rattle, and some big things like a swing and a gift card for a jogging stroller, which I really want. And then there was the check. A cashier's check. For a lot." She blew out a long, steady breath. "It doesn't seem right to take it, even if Timmy is their grandson."

"Sort of like they're trying to buy you, you mean?"

"Yeah, I guess that's it. CJ hasn't offered to help support Timmy. It's really his responsibility, not his parents'."

"Have you asked him to help?"

"I shouldn't have to."

"Yeah, you're right. From the looks of him, he's all muscle and no brains."

Katie laughed. "That's not very nice. And I wouldn't say that exactly. CJ graduated magna cum laude from college."

"That doesn't mean anything. Especially if he went to a community college."

"Hey, watch it. I went to community college for a year before I transferred to CSU. It saved a lot of money. But CJ went to Berkeley. Joined the Navy right after he graduated."

Noah was clearly not happy with Katie's defense of CJ. "And just what else do you know about the guy? Beside that he took advantage of you?"

He was jealous. But the words stung all the same. Mostly because they weren't exactly true. She had been a willing participant, caught up in the moment and enamored with CJ's charm that weekend in Las Vegas. If only she hadn't gotten pregnant. The thought brought her up short. She was crazy in love with Timmy. He was her life now. She wouldn't go back for a minute, even if she had to spend many Saturdays with CJ and his parents.

Noah broke into her thoughts. "I want us to be together, Katie. I love you and Timmy. The sooner you can break it off with CJ, the better." He took her face in his hands and leaned toward her. Inches away, he smiled. "I want you all to myself. Is that so wrong of me?" His lips met hers in a gentle, possessive kiss, followed by another. "All for myself."

The ocean breeze drifted in the car windows and fanned Katie's face. She felt hot all over, surprised by the intensity of Noah's words and kisses. But not unhappy. Surely this was the man God intended for her. His divine plan for her life. As Noah's wife, she could serve alongside him in the ministry with the rest of his family. Wouldn't her gift of communicating through images and designs always be needed in the church? His next words sent a thrill down her spine.

"I think you should meet my parents, too. How about next Saturday? I'll work out the details."

Chapter 7

With her six-week post-delivery appointment three hour away, Katie grabbed her phone and headed for the kitchen. Certain she had dodged the postpartum depression bullet, she still had a few questions for the doctor. Guilt over having a baby out of wedlock ate at her, especially since Noah's parents couldn't agree on a time to meet her.

There were good reasons for the delay, Noah had assured her. His father pastored a mega-church and served as chairman of the board of his denomination. He was busy the next few weekends with speaking engagements and a staff retreat at the church's summer camp. They very much wanted to meet her and Timmy, Noah said.

Katie sighed. She wanted to meet them, but was nervous about it, too. Pastor Davidson was a well-known author and speaker. Noah had told her about his three books, theological tomes that were on the shelves of seminary libraries throughout the country. Katie had googled one title, and given up reading after the first page. Her own meager knowledge of Christianity and how to interpret the Bible paled in comparison.

Refusing to give the Davidsons any more thought, Katie opened her Facebook page and scrolled through the messages from friends. Ashley's post stopped her. *#Celebrate Recovery works! #NoMoreGambling #TwoMonthsClean.*

Katie hit "Like" and sent a message to congratulate her. She missed her friend. Nothing had been the same for them since Ashley took up gambling in Vegas with CJ's friend, Dustin.

She closed her phone and went to the refrigerator. Time for lunch. Time to think about re-connecting, seeking reconciliation with Ashley. She had already forgiven her. Why not get together again?

She opened the refrigerator and pulled out fresh spinach and romaine lettuce to make a salad. Leftover grilled chicken from last night's supper looked good, so she chopped it and threw it in the bowl along with a few sliced almonds and some dried cranberries. In the middle of her silent table prayer her phone rang.

"Hey, Pastor Dale, what's up?"

"Hi, Katie. How are you and Timmy doing?"

"He's six weeks old already. Can you believe it?" Katie mixed her salad as she talked, popping a few dried cranberries into her mouth to squelch the hunger pains.

"They do grow fast. Say, listen, can you come by the office next week? We've got a few more projects we'd like to talk about with you."

"Sure, sure, no problem. I'll see if Julie can watch Timmy for me."

"Does Tuesday at nine work for you?"

"That's fine. I'm going for my six-week checkup today, so I'm hoping the doctor okays me to start jogging again. If he does, I'll jog down to the church."

"Well, don't rush it. Just take your time. Maybe start with a few walks. You and Noah can get some exercise together." He laughed. "Get his nose out of a book once in a while."

Katie laughed, too. "I'll try, but I think he'd rather get mine in a book than get his out of one."

Pastor Dale sighed. "It's something to think about, Katie, those differences in your personalities and interests. I know you two are getting pretty serious, so you might want to talk about it. Doing the things you like best—but having to do them alone because the other person isn't interested or willing—well, that's the kind of thing that can cause tension in a relationship."

"Hmmm. You're right. I-I've seen that in my brother's family, and . . ." Katie hesitated. She didn't like to talk about her family, especially with her brother's marriage trouble. "And I'll talk to Noah. I know we're very different, but there's so much about him that really helps me be a better person."

"I can see that. He's learning a lot from you, too. Just think about it, okay? And I'll see you Sunday."

Katie hung up the phone and got up from the table to get a glass of milk. The conversation with Pastor Dale rattled her. Was he trying to tell her that she wouldn't make a good partner for Noah? Just because he liked to read and she didn't? Except for a short daily walk, her days were spent taking care of Timmy. The doctor's appointment would be her first outing and she was more than ready for it. How long had it been since she really exercised?

Finishing her salad and milk, Katie cleaned the kitchen and went outside in the backyard. Brad had bought a shed that he planned to put up on Saturday. Several boxes sat leaning against the fence in the corner. The temperature on the outdoor thermometer read ninety-two. *A swimming pool would be perfect right now.* With her artist's eye, she laid out a plan in the yard for a pool, a spa, and a backyard kitchen. All she needed was a deed to the house in her name and plenty of cash. Katie laughed at her daydream and went back in the house.

~ ~ ~

The bedroom had never felt so small, or so hot. Standing in front of the fan, Katie bounced up and down with Timmy. To no avail. His cries bounced off the walls. He had been bathed and fed. His diaper had been changed. She had massaged him with lotion. But nothing made him happy. Not wanting to wake the family, Katie remembered Julie telling her that Brad would drive Megan around in the car to put her to sleep. Grabbing her phone, her car keys and her wallet, she headed for the door.

It took twenty-five minutes, but Timmy had finally fallen asleep. Katie was almost to Pomerado Road, where she could turn and circle back to the house, when her car died. Stopped at a red light, the engine only revved when she pressed on the gas.

Her heart began to pound. A horn honked behind her. She put down her car window and waved the car to go around. Where were the hazard lights? When she finally found the switch, she pressed her fist to her mouth to keep from waking Timmy with her panic. She was on a busy road. It didn't matter if it was late, traffic was plentiful. Her mind raced. Oh, why hadn't she signed up for AAA road emergency service? Who could she call? Julie was home alone with Megan while Brad was out on a training exercise. Noah, the pastors, and the staff of Cornerstone Church were at their annual retreat and unavailable. Did she dare call CJ? She immediately rejected the idea. He was probably at the base or at home, at least thirty minutes away. The police were her only option.

A knock on her window stopped her from dialing. She let out a startled cry. A couple of young men stood a few feet from her car, motioning her to put down her window. Her nerves jumping, she cracked it a few inches.

"We can push your car for you. There's a parking lot just a little way ahead." The taller of the two pointed up the road.

"Oh, okay," Katie said. "Thank you so much." Timmy started to fuss.

The car began to roll, and the Smart 'n' Final grocery store appeared on her right. She turned the car in to the lot, pulled in a slot near the back, and pressed the brake pedal. The guys gave a wave and hurried back to their own car.

Now that she was out of traffic, Katie heart rate slowed. She tried to pray, but couldn't think what to say. She needed a way to get home with Timmy. And what was she going to do about the car? She had no idea what had gone wrong. Timmy started crying. It broke her heart to hear her baby so unhappy. She found CJ's number in her contact list and dialed. He answered on the first ring.

"Katie, what's wrong?"

She heaved a sigh of relief. "It-It's my car. It broke down. Some guys pushed me into a parking lot, but Timmy's crying again, and I don't have Triple-A or Uber or anyone else I can call. I'm stuck and I don't know what's wrong with the car. And I just called you because everybody else is away, and Julie can't leave Megan."

"Slow down, okay? Where are you?"

She told him.

"I'll be there in five minutes. Stay put. I'll send for a tow truck."

Grateful that he hadn't demanded to know what she was doing out at ten-thirty at night with Timmy in the car, she got out and unstrapped the baby from his car seat. His unhappy cries filled the night air as she walked and danced and bounced around her car, mopping at her dripping nose and tear-streaked face as best she could while trying to soothe Timmy. Nothing seemed to help her poor baby. She wanted to collapse on the pavement and sob. But instead, she kept bouncing. When CJ's truck sped across the parking lot and jerked to a stop beside her car, she burst into tears.

Without a word, CJ took Timmy from her and draped him over his shoulder. With his other arm, he scooped her to him and held her. She wet his shirt with her tears. "Shhh . . . it's okay. I'll take care of you."

Part of her knew she should protest him holding her so close, but he felt so strong and safe that she ignored it and pressed against him, her arms circling his waist. It took her several moments to realize he had a partially wet beach towel wrapped around his waist and his T-shirt had damp patches that weren't her tears.

"You're wet. Were you in the ocean? How did you get here so fast?"

"No, at my parents' house. Using their spa. My place doesn't have one, so I come home sometimes to use Mom and Dad's. It helps my aching muscles after a tough day on the ocean."

Held against CJ's shoulder, Timmy had quieted. Katie looked up and met CJ's gaze, but she didn't pull away. She couldn't, the attraction was so strong, so powerful. Just like in Vegas. It had led them down the wrong path that weekend. The path to Timmy. Forcing herself to look away, she stepped back and turned to her car. She was shaking, her voice uneven from such intimate contact with his body. "Did you say you called a tow truck?"

"Yeah, there it is." He nodded toward a tow truck pulling into the lot. He passed Timmy to her. "I'll take care of it, Katie. Why don't you and Timmy sit in my truck? This shouldn't take long. I'll have your car towed to the place my dad and I use. They do a good job and they're reasonable."

With CJ taking charge, she could think again. "I need Timmy's car seat. The base is attached to the back seat in my car, so I don't know how we'll strap it in your truck. But I'll figure out something."

"I've got the same base. Brad told me what kind to buy since he picked you up at the hospital."

Katie was dumbfounded. "You've got the base?"

The tow truck driver was coming toward them.

"Yeah, just get in the truck, okay? It's no big deal."

She climbed in the passenger seat and nuzzled Timmy's neck. "Your daddy is a take-charge kind of guy, little man. You know that? And he makes me feel things I shouldn't feel. Cause he's so . . . so . . . oh, I don't want to go there. I

can't go there." Katie forced herself to pay attention to wha
was happening with her car. She needed to block all thought
of what it would be like to be with CJ again. He wasn't the
right man for her. *Was he?*

Ten minutes later, as her car was being towed away
CJ opened the back door of the truck and settled Timmy'
car seat in the base. He closed the door and came around to
Katie's door. "Have you fed him recently?"

"Yes, while you were dealing with the tow truck driver
He should be ready to go to sleep. I just hope he stays asleep
when I take him out."

He took Timmy and strapped him in. Once in the driver's
seat, rather than starting the truck, he turned to Katie. "I have
a favor to ask."

"A-A favor? Like, what kind of favor?"

"I have something I'd like you to see. At my parents'
house. It won't take long. They're close to here."

Katie hesitated. "Won't they be asleep? I wouldn't want
to bother them."

"They won't be home until later. I think they're down
town at a jazz club tonight. Thursday is their date night."

"Well . . ." Did she dare be in the same house alone with
him? For how long? But he had rescued her. The least she
could do was let him show her whatever it was he wanted
her to see at his parent's. "Okay, but I should get Timmy
home right after that."

"Whatever you want," he said and started the truck.

From the main road, they made a few turns into a
neighborhood of large homes and climbed a hill next to a
water tower. Near the top, CJ turned up a long driveway.
A sprawling ranch-style home came into view, illuminated
by two porch lights and a lamp post. He parked outside a
four-car garage and came around to open her door. Once she
was out of the truck, he opened the back door and lifted out
Timmy in his car seat. He was sound asleep.

"Let's go in the front. If I open the garage door, it's going to make a racket. As is, the dog might wake him anyway." He guided her around to the ornate double doors at the front of the house. Katie could hear barking. CJ set Timmy down a few feet away from the door. "Let me get Dexter to settle down, then I'll get Timmy."

CJ opened the door and rubbed the dog's ears. He spoke a few commands and Dexter quieted immediately. Katie tucked her wallet, house key, and phone in the carrier, picked up Timmy and followed CJ.

The home was incredible, with large rooms, high ceilings, and a view out the back wall of windows that took Katie's breath away. Beyond an outdoor seating area, Katie could see a large infinity pool and spa.

"So, this is why you're wearing the beach towel?"

CJ pulled it off to reveal his board shorts and tossed the towel over his shoulder. "Let me take Timmy and show you around. The view's the reason my dad bought the house." He took the carrier from Katie. Once outside, he tossed the towel on a chaise and put Timmy in his car seat on an outdoor sofa.

"Will your dog bother Timmy?"

"No. He's already back in his bed. He's an old dog and needs his rest."

"I was just day dreaming about a pool. I used to swim every day back home." She walked to the edge of the pool and looked out at the lights in the distance.

"Your folks had a pool?"

Katie laughed and shook her head. "Not my folks. We lived, well, we didn't have a pool. No." After seeing his home, how could she admit that she'd spent the last seven years of her life in a mobile home park on the edge of town? She had left that life, and didn't ever want to go back.

"So, where did you swim?"

"We have the Atlantic Ocean, you know? The beach towns around Charleston are some of the best on the East

Coast. My favorite is Folly Beach because of the pier. But I usually swam at the city pool or the high school. That's how I met Ashley. We were on swim team together."

"How about college? Were you on the swim team there, too?"

"No, I had too much else going on by then. I worked my way through school." Katie knelt and ran her hand back and forth through the water. She looked up when CJ stood over her. He had taken off his T-shirt. His eyes said it all. "Don't you dare," she said.

"You'll wake up Timmy if you scream."

She stood quickly. "Now why would I scream?"

In one lightning fast move he picked her up and jumped in the water with her. He let her go as they plunged down to the bottom of the pool.

She pushed back to the surface, brushing hair out of her eyes. "You are in so much trouble!" She splashed water at him and swam for the wall with CJ in pursuit.

Truthfully, the water felt wonderful, and she really didn't care about her clothes. She'd been wearing flip-flops, so even those had floated to the surface. The night air was warm on her skin. The stars filled the sky. Off in the distance a coyote howled. When she reached the wall without CJ catching her, she challenged him. "Twenty laps, choose your stroke. See if you can catch me." But she had already left him behind.

Each time she turned, she felt better, happier. As if a weight had been lifted. It didn't matter if she beat CJ or not, she was so happy to be swimming again.

When she had worn herself out, she turned to find CJ. He was sitting on the edge of the pool, watching her. "You barely beat me, and you know it!"

"Had enough?" He eased back in the pool and glided to her. "You're amazing for a woman who had a baby six weeks ago, you know that? I only beat you by a couple of laps."

Katie blushed, warmed by his compliment. "It was more than a couple, but who's counting? I like to swim, that's all. And I know you were hardly trying. But you shouldn't have thrown me in. How am I going to get home now without getting your truck all wet?

"I thought you might like to stay. Let's get dried off, and we'll talk about it."

"Are you crazy? No way."

"Come on." He headed for the steps.

With no choice, Katie followed, trying her best to keep her eyes on the house, or the stars, or the outdoor furniture. Anywhere but where she wanted to look.

Tossing her a towel from an outdoor cabinet, CJ grabbed one for himself and rubbed it over his chest and legs. Katie did her best to stem the flow of water from her white jean shorts. After wringing out the hem of her T-shirt, she wiped her legs and feet. She wasn't about to leave wet footprints and water droplets all over Mary's hardwood floors if she could help it. But when CJ picked up Timmy and headed for the sliding doors into the family room and kitchen, she had no choice but to follow.

Down a hallway, he opened a door, flipped the light switch in a bedroom, and stood back. "There's a bathroom in here you can use. Mom's got a robe hanging on the bathroom door, and there's some stuff on the bed she bought for my sister. She shops year-round for birthdays and Christmas, so just help yourself to whatever you like. You and my sister, Lynn, are about the same size."

"What about Timmy?" She glanced in the carrier. "It looks like he's still asleep."

"He's doing fine." He smiled at the sleeping baby. "I'll take him in my bathroom with me, so I'll hear him if he wakes up."

"Oh, okay, thanks." She went into the room and locked the door. But when she turned around, she gasped. Along with a beautiful four-poster queen-sized bed, there was a full-size crib along the wall near the door. It was already made up with a blue gingham sheet, tailored bed skirt, and bumper pads with a sailboat theme. A mobile of fish and sailboats hung over the crib and several stuffed animals filled the corners. A fully stocked changing table sat near the crib with a diaper trash can identical to the one Mary and Tim had given her six weeks ago.

Shaking her head, Katie went in to the bathroom and turned on the shower. Could she possibly tell Noah about any of this?

Chapter 8

Katie's awareness of her surroundings came slowly. The guest room at the Jansen's house was dim; the sun already up. She stretched, enjoying the feel of the velvet soft sheets against her legs, until she remembered CJ's mom had talked her into texting Julie that she was spending the night. She moaned softly into the pillow. CJ had moved Timmy to the crib and left the room with a soft-spoken good night. What could she do but stay, since he hadn't offered to take her home? The more troubling question was: What would Noah think of her giving in and staying?

Throwing back the light comforter, Katie got out of bed and walked to the crib. Timmy was sleeping as if he didn't have a care in the world. *And why not?* He had nursed twice in the night, and thanks to Mary, he had dry diapers and a clean sleeper to wear. Katie's clothing was a different story. She had totally forgotten that she was going to ask CJ if she could use the dryer. Her shorts, T-shirt, and underclothing were still wadded up on the bathroom counter. She headed for the bathroom to assess the damage. Where was the laundry room?

Donning the robe she had worn last night over her borrowed boxer shorts and tank top, Katie opened the door a crack and peeked out. The aroma of frying bacon and fresh coffee made her mouth water. She tiptoed out of the room, grateful to see the laundry room close by. But she didn't feel right using it without asking. She turned down the hall toward the kitchen, passing a family photo gallery on the way. The dog met her when she was almost to the kitchen.

"Oh, you're not such an old dog," she said, bending t
pet his thick black coat. He followed her as she made he
way to the kitchen.

CJ's dad, Tim, was at the stove when she rounded th
corner. He turned as she came in the kitchen.

"Good morning," he said, coming around the islan
counter to give her a light hug and a kiss on her hair. "Di
you sleep well?"

"Yes, the bed is heavenly. And that coffee smells divine."

Tim crossed back to the counter by the stove and poure
her a cup. "CJ said your car broke down. That can be scar
late at night. Here, sit down." He pulled out a stool at th
island. "Do you take cream or sugar?"

"No thanks, just black." She lifted the cup to smell the
aroma. "Would it be all right if I throw my wet clothes in the
dryer? I went swimming last night. Rather unexpectedly."
She smiled. "But the water was wonderful."

"CJ threw you in, huh?" He shook his head. "I could
offer to take him to the woodshed, but we don't have one.
And as you can see, he's stronger than me. I'm pretty sure I'd
lose." He picked up his own coffee. "You're welcome to use
the dryer. Did you see the laundry room by your bedroom?"

"Yes, thank you. I'll be right back." Leaving her coffee,
she smiled at Tim and got up.

"I'm counting on it. I don't have clinic until eleven, so
as soon as CJ gets done with his swim, I'm making Belgium
waffles. Hope you like them."

"Yum. I love waffles. That's so nice of you."

Mary, in her own white terrycloth bathrobe, intercepted
her in the hallway and hugged her. "Good morning! Did you
sleep okay? I heard Timmy once, but it seemed like he only
cried a minute before it was quiet again."

"He was up twice, but I'm used to it by now. I'm just
going to throw my wet clothes in the dryer. If that's okay?"

"Oh, sure, sure. But why don't you wash them first. It only takes twenty minutes for a light load. Here, I'll show you."

In no time, Katie's clothes were in the washing machine and Timmy was awake demanding his breakfast. "I guess my coffee will have to wait," she said as she went into the bedroom. "I'll be with you in a few minutes." She lifted Timmy out of the crib and sat in the big armchair near the window. She loosened the belt of her robe.

Mary followed her in the bedroom and pulled the comforter over the bed as she talked. "Take your time. Tim's making waffles, did he tell you? CJ's favorite. Do you want scrambled eggs? CJ will, so we can always throw in a couple more eggs."

Katie laughed. "That sounds delicious, but maybe just one egg. I've still got a few pounds to lose."

"You look wonderful just the way you are." At the door, she turned. "I'm so glad you stayed, Katie." She pulled the door shut.

Twenty minutes later, Katie was changing Timmy when there was a knock at the door. Her robe hung open and untied but she couldn't take her hands away from Timmy to retie it. "Just a minute," she called, and picked up Timmy even though his sleeper was only half on. She opened the door expecting to see Mary, but it was CJ. She blushed, aware that she looked like she had just tumbled out of bed. CJ, on the other hand, looked as if he had just finished a photoshoot for some hot new ad campaign for Rogue Fitness. His hair was spiked and a day's growth of facial hair made his strong jawline even more pronounced.

"Can I help you with Timmy?" He glanced at her attire. "Mom's still in her robe, so you're welcome to come to breakfast in yours." He took Timmy from her. "I'll finish getting him dressed. Looks like you've changed his diaper. Are you hungry?"

Katie could hear the washing machine. Unless she wanted to borrow more of the clothes Mary had bought for Lynn, the robe would have to do. Swallowing her pride, she said, "Sure, if it's okay, I'll come like this." She tied her robe. "I'm definitely hungry."

CJ stepped back to let her pass.

At the table, Tim put a steaming cup of coffee in front of her. "I hope you don't mind, I drank the one you left. I figured you wouldn't want it cold."

"Thanks. You're right, cold coffee is not my thing, unless it's an iced latte from Starbucks in the middle of a hot afternoon."

Within minutes, the table was loaded with waffles, bacon, scrambled eggs, smoothies, and an assortment of pastries, fresh fruit, and juice. Mary said the blessing, dishes were passed, and plates were loaded. Once again Katie was in awe of how easily the family talked and laughed as they enjoyed the meal. Seated next to her, CJ kept his attention on Timmy and his food, but several times when their eyes met, Katie was the one who had to look away. Other than hugging her in the parking lot and throwing her in the pool, he hadn't touched her. *Did he want to?*

"Katie, my family is coming for the Labor Day weekend this year, and we would love to have you join us if you can," Mary said. "They're all excited to meet Timmy. My niece and her husband and two children are coming this time, too. Their youngest little boy is eighteen months. That's part of the reason I went looking for the crib and changing table."

With three pairs of eyes staring at her, Katie felt her cheeks grow hot. "I-I'm not sure. I might have another commitment that weekend." Noah was still trying to schedule a time for Katie to meet his family. "Can I let you know?"

Mary looked crestfallen. "Sure, I understand. You're busy with work and other things. Just let me know."

Tim rubbed his wife's shoulders. "We haven't had everyone in Mary's family together for quite some time, so if you can manage even an hour or two, that would be wonderful."

Katie nodded, distressed at hurting Mary. "Sure, I'll try. It sounds like a fun time." She didn't know what else to say. Already she was feeling herself pulled into the family by Mary and Tim. But CJ's silence made her edgy. Did he care whether or not his relatives met Timmy? Was he embarrassed to admit he had fathered a son before he had a wife? She couldn't tell from his guarded expression.

"I think the washing machine is finished," Tim said. "I'll get these dishes cleared."

Mary jumped up. "I'll get those clothes in the dryer for you. Why don't you have a swim while they dry? Lynn left several bathing suits here at the house. I'm sure one would fit you fine."

In minutes, Mary had produced two of her daughter's bikinis for Katie to select from. Not wanting to cause any more distress, Katie thanked her, took the suits, and closed the door to the bedroom. She held up the coral bikini bottom and groaned. Her tummy would have no place to hide in the skimpy bottom. The other suit wouldn't hide much more, but it would do. She stripped off her robe and pajamas.

Suited up, she grabbed a towel from the stash under the bathroom counter and wrapped it around herself. Making as little noise as possible, she made her way out to the pool, relieved when she saw no one in the kitchen or family room. Even the dog seemed to have disappeared.

Without some way to tie back her hair, Katie floated on her back and let the water ease her troubled mind. She wanted to please Mary, but she also needed to meet Noah's family. Finally deciding she would have to wait and see if anything would work out with the Davidsons, she launched out doing the backstroke. Within minutes, her troubles were forgotten.

Finished with her laps, Katie floated on her back, enjoying the warm August sunshine. A wolf whistle pierced the air. She stood up to see CJ standing at the side of the pool.

"Where's Timmy?" she asked, sinking up to her chin.

"Mom's with him. She's playing with him and talking baby talk, trying to get Timmy to smile at her." He squatted beside the pool. "You coming out of there any time soon?"

"I don't know. What time is it, anyway?"

"It's close to ten."

Stunned at how late it was, and how easily she had let herself relax while CJ, Tim and Mary took care of her, Katie made her way through the water to the stairs. She didn't want CJ gawking at her post-pregnancy body, but it didn't seem as if she had any choice. He had stood up, but he hadn't gone back in to the house.

He met her with her towel, not bothering to hide his interest in her body. "You look great, Katie."

She felt her cheeks heat then grabbed the towel from CJ and wrapped it around herself. Head down, she said, "Getting there. Swimming felt great. But I should get going." Her legs were dripping but she didn't want to take the towel off to dry them. She smoothed her hair back with her hands, and finally looked at CJ.

"Dad's mechanic called. Your car won't be ready until about three. I'd like to take you and Timmy to the zoo for the day, then I'll take you to get it."

"The zoo?"

"Yeah, you know, that place where they put wild, exotic animals on display for the public."

Katie bit on her lip to keep from choking. "I know what a zoo is. I just, well, I just never thought about going there.

I mean, with you." She wasn't about to tell him that she'd never been to the San Diego Zoo, and very much wanted to go. Sometime.

"Oh, I get it. You'd rather go with the guy who built the ark, huh? The one who brought the animals in two by two."

He was mocking her. She lifted her chin. "Noah and have talked about it, yeah. And don't make fun of him. Or that story. You probably don't even know it."

"Oh, I know it. And it's amazing alright. How a vengeful God is sorry he ever made people so he drowns them all. Some story."

"He doesn't drown Noah and his family, because Noah is a righteous man."

"Righteous, huh? So, it's okay that later he gets rip-roaring drunk and his son finds him naked? The same son, by the way, who becomes the father of the nation of Canaan, one of Israel's fiercest enemies. So much for Noah's parenting skills."

Katie tried hard to remember the part of the story about the son, but couldn't. Where was *her* Noah when she needed him? CJ seemed angry. How could she possibly win the argument when she didn't know the facts? Or what had set him off? Defeated, she started for the house.

"Wait, Katie. I'm sorry. I've got the day off. It's been a rough three weeks of training. I'd just like to do something fun. With you and Timmy."

Katie stopped. Her need for self-preservation fought with her need to show support for someone who put his life on the line for her country. Didn't her church pray for people in the military every week? Including CJ, whether he was named or not? The least she could do was show some interest. "What kind of training?"

"It's just Navy stuff."

"What kind?"

CJ rubbed his hand around the back of his neck. "It's called MIO. Stands for Maritime Interdiction Operations."

"What in the world does that mean?"

CJ laughed. "Navy stuff, okay?"

Katie waited.

"Okay. It's when we disrupt or destroy the enemy so they can't get their men or supplies to the places that will do us harm. In our case, we stop and board ships transporting stuff we don't want to get through to the bad guys."

"It's dangerous, isn't it?"

"It can be. Which is why I'd like to go to the zoo."

For the first time since he had rescued her the night before, Katie looked fully at CJ without looking away. She could see the truth of his words in his eyes: the last few weeks had been hard on his body. His mind, too? He had just returned from deployment six weeks ago, but already he was back in training for the next time. He had been in the spa when she called; he had come for her anyway. She had challenged him to swim laps; he hadn't said a word about being tired. He had watched Timmy without a hint of protest. Against her better judgement, the least she could do was give him some company at the zoo, wasn't it? But part of her knew it might be a costly mistake.

~ ~ ~

CJ watched her go and breathed a sigh of relief. Maybe if he could have some time with her, alone without his parents or her work responsibilities or any interference from Noah, they could start over. Go slow, and figure out if they could have a future. He sat in one of the deck chairs and stared out at the vista beyond. He always thought he had plenty of time before finding a wife. A weekend in Vegas—and being a father—put a whole new spin on the matter. But did his attraction for Katie add up to love? Frustrated, he got up to go inside.

His mother came through the back gate holding Timmy before he reached the door.

"Your father's off on his bike to the clinic. He said the repairs on Katie's car are about four hundred dollars. Do you think she has that kind of money? Or do you?"

"I doubt if she does. She only works part-time. I have an emergency fund I can use to help her. If she'll let me. She's agreed to go with me to the zoo today."

"The zoo? Oh, CJ, I'm so thrilled. Your dad and I have been praying for you and Katie. We would love to see Timmy living with both his mother and father."

"Don't start, Mom. It's just a trip to the zoo."

"But you're attracted to her, I know you are."

"We made a baby, didn't we? Sure, I'm attracted to her. She's gorgeous. But she's also got a boyfriend. And religion."

Mary patted his arm. "So, you've got some challenges, don't you?" She handed Timmy to him. "Whether you and Katie get together or not, you still have the responsibility to raise up this child in the way he should go, just like Katie does. And if that's not the way of Christ, just what way will it be? There's a lot of trouble out there in the world, CJ. Who will Timmy's anchor be, if not Jesus?"

Raking his teeth over his bottom lip, he opened the door to the kitchen. "We'll have to see, won't we?"

Chapter 9

At the zoo, CJ found a parking spot in the flamingo section of the parking lot. He came around the hood of the truck to open Katie's door.

"The zoo has strollers to rent, so we don't need his car seat," he said.

"Even for a baby as little as Timmy?"

"Well, we'll see, and if not, I'll come back and get it." CJ unstrapped Timmy and they walked together to the entrance.

While CJ bought their tickets, Katie sat on some flat rocks and applied sunscreen from a tote bag Mary had packed with diapers and supplies for Timmy.

"Your mom thought of everything. There's even a couple of protein bars in here."

"Speaking of protein bars, I'm hungry," CJ said. "Are you?"

Katie laughed. "After all you put away at breakfast, you're hungry again?" As she said it, her phone rang. She pulled it out of her back pocket. It was Noah. She blushed, guilt-ridden to be out with CJ when she hadn't even left Noah a text message. "Excuse me," she said to CJ and walked a few feet away. "Hey, Noah," she said. "How's the retreat going?"

"Great, just great. Lots of good ideas for the coming year. Of course, I'll be with Dad by then, but it's fun to hear what will be happening at Cornerstone."

Katie bit on her lower lip. Had she not had Timmy, she would be on the staff retreat, fielding ideas with the others. As is, Noah only had a few more months at Cornerstone before going back home to join his father's ministry. Did she have a chance of going with him?

A rowdy bunch of teenagers went by, laughing and bumping into each other.

"Hey, it sounds like you're not at home. Where are you?"

Katie swallowed. "Well, actually, I'm at the zoo. Just decided to get out since the doctor said I could start exercising again." Her fist came to her mouth; was she lying by not saying anything about CJ? Committing the sin of omission? "I'm just about to go in, so can I call you later?"

"It's best if I call you. The next session starts in a minute, but talk to me until then, okay? So, why'd you choose the zoo? Wouldn't the park be just as good and not nearly as pricey? Not as many germs either. Timmy's with you, right?"

"Well, yes, of course he's with me, but I'll keep him away from people. I just needed to do something different, go someplace new." Guilt at choosing to spend the day with CJ ate at her. Would Noah lose his temper if he knew?

"So, you got the jogging stroller, huh?"

"No, not yet. I'm renting a stroller here at the zoo. I have an umbrella stroller, but he's too little for that right now." Katie rubbed her forehead. How could she justify being at the zoo with a six-week-old baby? She turned and nearly bumped into CJ. He was holding up his ticket and pointing to the turnstiles. "So, we're off to see the elephants and tigers and bears, oh my!" She tried to get her breathing under control. "I'll take some selfies and send them to you."

"Sounds perfect. Well, have a great time and don't overdo things, okay? The retreat ends at two and I have someplace special in mind to take you and Timmy tonight."

"Tonight?

"I know it's last minute, but I've got a surprise for you."

"What kind of surprise?"

"Can't say, just trust me."

Katie laughed. "I do. A surprise sounds wonderful. I can't wait."

"Okay, I'll pick you up at six. I love you, Katie."

She lowered her voice, not wanting CJ to hear. "Love you, too."

Letting out a long, slow breath, she turned to find CJ waving to her from the entrance turnstiles. Tucking her phone in to her back pocket, she hurried over. "Okay, ready, let's go."

"Just a minute," CJ said, shifting Timmy to face her. "Since I bought the tickets, I want us to get a few ground rules straight before we go in."

Katie bristled. "What kind of ground rules? If you'd rather not take me in there now, fine. You can just take me back home."

CJ sighed. "There are only three. That I remember. Ground rule number one: The fun. We're here to have fun, not to fight."

The baby was wide awake, his little hands clutching the air. He looked so adorable, everything but how much she loved her baby went out of Katie's head. "Oh, you precious baby!" She stroked his cheeks and touched his nose, enthralled with his coos and rapt attention on her.

CJ's laugh interrupted her. "Ground rule number two: the gear. The one who has the baby doesn't have to haul the gear." He nodded toward the tote bag. "Your turn. Let's get the stroller and find some food. You're also going to need a hat. Timmy, too."

"Fine, but I have a feeling this little guy is going to go from happy to hangry in a minute so he'll need the food first. And I have it, you don't. Ha ha!" Katie led the way through the turnstile. On the other side, a photographer waited to take their picture. He ushered them to an area with a lion statue and snapped away.

"Here's your number," he said and handed a ticket to CJ. "Just check back at that photo booth over there right before you leave and your pictures will be ready. Have a great day!" He moved off to photograph the next family.

CJ pocketed the ticket and turned. "Let's get the stroller while Timmy's still doing okay."

She followed him to the rental place. He had been right about the zoo's strollers. CJ propped several blankets around Timmy and put the tote behind the seat. Turning to Katie, he asked, "Are you okay with a hamburger or do you want something else?"

"A burger sounds good." Katie couldn't get the conversation with Noah out of her head. What was she doing here with CJ?

A little way down the main street, they stopped at Front Street Café. CJ parked the stroller near an outdoor table shaded by an umbrella.

"What would you like on your burger? And what to drink?"

"Everything but onions and tomatoes. And I'll have a water.

"You want fries? How about milk?"

"I'll have both water and milk. No fries."

"Your turn." He transferred the baby to her arms.

"If I'm not here when you get back, it's because I need the restroom."

CJ checked the map he had picked up at the entrance. "There's one on the other side of the Skyfari East." He looked up and pointed to a cable with a gondola hanging from it. "You see those buckets up in the sky over there? There's a family restroom right beyond them. Do you want to take the stroller or leave it with me?"

"I'll take it and see if Timmy needs a change."

Twenty minutes later, she spotted CJ with his hands full of food, making his way to a table. With Timmy draped over her shoulder, she wheeled the stroller ahead of her. CJ left the food and hurried to her.

"I'll get this," he said. "Come and eat."

When they were seated with the food divided, he said, "If you want to say a prayer over this, it's okay with me."

"That's okay." Katie said, "I'm not so good at praying out loud." She looked away. Noah had been encouraging her, but it was so much safer to pray in her head. She closed her eyes but couldn't think of anything to say, even silently.

"Hmmm. Interesting." He took a big bite of his burger, chewed and swallowed. "You don't talk to God out loud, huh? But you're a Christian, Brad told me. I guess I didn't know that when we were together."

Katie looked away, her face turning a bright pink. Shame filled her once again. "What we did in Las Vegas was a mistake. I never should have . . ." She faltered, embarrassed.

CJ waited. "What? Never should have started talking to me that first night? We had fun, didn't we, Katie? Maybe drank a little too much, but still, I thought we had a good time." When she didn't respond, he went on. "So, what are you saying? We never should have had sex?" He took a giant bite of his burger and chewed as if what they had done was no big deal.

"Yes, that was wrong." Her appetite had vanished.

"You didn't think so at the time."

Her stomach clenched. He looked so smug, so confident in himself. And so sure that he knew what she had been feeling that night. "I-I was, well, you . . ." What could she say that wouldn't feed his ego? The truth was, he had been the most fun date she'd ever had. Not to mention that his looks, and the way he treated her—with respect and consideration—were a killer combination. But she couldn't admit to any of that now. She searched for some excuse for her actions. "I was, well, I was trying to get over somebody. You came along at the right time. That's all."

His intense gaze narrowed. "So, you're saying you used me. That I was your rebound guy." He stared intently at her. When he finally looked away, he grabbed his water and chugged it. Wiping his mouth with the back of his hand, he leaned back in his chair. "I'm not buying it."

"Well, it's true!" She had to get control of herself. Get control of the conversation and get him to back off. She was drowning in his furrowed brow and mocking smile. "I had just learned my old boyfriend got married. You were a good diversion, that's all."

If her remark hurt him, she couldn't tell. He didn't move for several moments. Then his expression grew thoughtful. "What happened? Why'd he break up with you?" He finished his burger, wiped his mouth, and crossed his arms on the table, waiting.

Under the intensity of his gaze, she felt perspiration running down her back. She didn't want to talk about it, any of it. "Shouldn't we get going? I'd like to see the elephants."

He didn't budge. The silence stretched until she caved. "Oh, all right, if you must know, I don't know what went wrong. He went to college a year ahead of me, and found someone else, I guess. Someone better than me. I discovered some notes she wrote to him when I went to see him for Homecoming. We hung on for a while, but then it was over.

"The first guy you ever loved?"

"Yeah. I wanted to marry him, I was so in love."

"When did you stop loving him? Or have you?" He finished his water and crushed the bottle. His voice turned hard. "Or was it his face you were seeing when you were in bed with me?"

"What? No! Listen, I don't want to talk about this!" She stood and wadded up the paper with the food she hadn't touched.

CJ stood, too. He grabbed his trash and hers and strode to the trash can without saying a word. When he returned, he picked up her unopened milk and water, slammed them in the tote, and pushed the stroller out of the restaurant. In a few long strides, he was on the main street of the zoo. When he turned, Katie caught a glimpse of his clenched jaw. Then he was gone, heading down the street the way they had come.

Her stomach in knots, she hurried after him, hugging Timmy to her chest. She had wounded CJ's pride. But he had planted the bomb that did the damage, not her. Did he really think she could be so intimate with him in Vegas if she still loved her old boyfriend? Katie would have laughed if she wasn't so distressed about the way the conversation had gone.

At a large shop near the café, he stopped. "I'll get Timmy settled while you get a hat or some sunglasses or something." He pulled his wallet out of his pocket and pushed two twenty-dollar bills toward her. He reached for Timmy. When she hesitated to take the money, he took her hand, forced it in her palm and closed her fingers around it. "Get a hat in there." He took Timmy and turned away.

Near tears, Katie went in the gift shop. It was bad enough that he was mad. She should be the one who was angry. He had accused her of being manipulative and deceptive. What had he said, that she had used him? Well, he had used her, too. And left her to face the music alone.

She wandered around the store, not really seeing anything until she was standing in front of a display of stuffed animals. She picked up a large lion and stroked the soft fur.

"What about this one?"

Startled, she turned to find CJ holding out a lavender hat with a zoo logo. She took it from him and tried it on without meeting his eyes. "It's fine." She turned away and went to the checkout stand. Still holding the stuffed lion, she dropped the hat on the counter.

"Are you buying the lion, too?" the sales clerk asked.

Katie looked down at the lion tucked in her arm. "Uh, how much is it?" For some reason she couldn't explain, it was more important to her to have the lion than the hat.

CJ appeared at her side. "Whatever it costs, we'll take it. And these two hats." He added a blue-and-white floppy hat for Timmy to the lavender one she had laid down.

Katie scooped up the stuffed animal. Without thinking, she pocketed the forty dollars and left the store. Once outside, she stopped and buried her face in the animal's soft fur to stem the flow of her tears. When CJ stopped beside her, she shifted the lion and looked away.

"It's a hike to the elephants. Here's your hat."

He started walking, leaving her to follow or not.

She caught up to him but didn't speak. Neither did he. The temperature had climbed into the nineties and perspiration dripped down her back. The lion's fur pressed against her skin. Hot. Itchy. But she kept walking, grateful that CJ controlled the stroller when they came to a steep decline.

Walking had helped her get control of her emotions, but nevertheless, she was grateful when the elephants came in sight. CJ pushed the stroller into a short tunnel and out the other side. A little further on, he stopped and sat on a bench in the shade of the Elephant Care Center. He pulled out Katie's water and offered it to her. When she took it, he lifted the edge of the blanket he had draped over the front of the stroller to keep out the sun. The baby reflexively jerked and settled back to sleep. Since they were in shade, CJ propped the blanket on the awning of the stroller so the air could circulate. A slight breeze caught the edge.

Katie sat down next to CJ and handed the water to him. "Here, you can have the rest." Words she wanted to speak lodged in her throat. Her phone rang. *Noah.* She stood and walked beyond the center to an enclosure holding several llamas. Beyond the llamas, an elephant pulled hay from a tube with his trunk. "Hey you," she said, without any enthusiasm.

"What's up?" Noah's upbeat voice soothed her. "You sound beat."

Katie closed her eyes. She wanted to be with him. Feel his arms around her and hear his words of comfort. Ask him to help her sort out her crazy emotions. Instead, she did her best to perk up. "It's hot, that's all. I'm at the elephant exhibit watching an elephant have lunch. Very entertaining." She glanced behind her. CJ pushed Timmy on down the curved walkway.

"How's Timmy doing?"

"Great. He's been sleeping almost the whole time. I-I bought him a beautiful stuffed lion. It's as big as he is but I couldn't resist. The zoo is huge and the elephants are a hike from the entrance. I'm going to get a workout just getting back." Her stomach rumbled with hunger pains. In her pocket, CJ's forty dollars burned against her skin. A dad and mom with their toddler crowded against the fence beside her.

"Who was that?" Noah asked.

Katie bit on her lip. "What? Oh, just someone nearby. Listen, I'm going to get moving. It's too hot to stand still, and there's still a lot to see. I'm going to send you a picture of me in front of the elephant, so look for it, okay?"

"Okay, I'll be waiting."

"Okay, love you."

"Right back at you. Bye."

"Bye." Katie felt sick to her stomach. How could she so easily deceive Noah like this? Where had CJ gone with Timmy? The whole day was a disaster. She had come to please CJ, to help him have fun and relax. And it had been anything but fun. She was a mess. Emotionally, physically, and mentally. And she had not been honest with Noah. With a moan, she moved away from the family to get a better shot of the elephant, held her phone in the air and took a picture of herself. She texted the picture to Noah, and started walking the way she had seen CJ go.

Within minutes, she came to the jaguar exhibit. A crowd had gathered to watch something happening behind the glass. She moved closer, looking for CJ. No rented strollers in the crowd. Next was the lion exhibit, also crowded. Her breath ragged, she trotted to one exhibit after another. People milled about and crowded together, but no CJ. Had he stopped in a store? Gone to the restroom? Timmy would need to nurse soon, and she hadn't eaten since breakfast. Lightheaded, she pulled out her phone to call him. His phone went to voice mail. She had to find them. She half-ran, half-walked, finally stopping when she arrived at the Skyfari West station. She pulled the map out of her back pocket. There was only one road, wasn't there? Where could they be? Tired and worried, she clenched her teeth to keep from screaming. At an empty bench, she sat down hard, hugged her knees to her chest, and cried into the lion's neck.

A few minutes passed while she tried to pull herself together and think what to do next. When she looked up, relief flooded her. CJ was pushing the stroller toward her. She quickly tried to wipe her tears away.

"Hey, hey, what's wrong?" CJ sat down beside her. "Katie, what's happened?"

She sniffed loudly and hit him in the shoulder several times.

"Hey!" He caught her hand in his. "What did I do? I thought you wanted to talk to your boyfriend." Turning aside, he said under his breath, "You're out with me, and you think that doesn't bother me?"

She turned tear-filled eyes on him. "Where were you? I-I couldn't find you." She jerked her hand away and swiped at the tears on her face. Pulling away the blanket covering Timmy, she unstrapped him and lifted him out of the stroller.

She buried her face in his neck, heedless of the lion falling. Beside her, she could feel CJ's solid presence. Calmer this time, she asked, "Where were you?"

"We were at the lion exhibit. You must have gone right past us. Then I went back to find you and you were gone." Timmy was starting to fuss. "Why didn't you call me?"

"I did. It went to voice mail."

CJ pulled out his phone. "Oops. I had it turned off. Sorry."

"You're kidding! No one our age turns off their phone, CJ!"

"Well, I did. I'm sorry."

She stood. "I'm going to feed Timmy and then we have to go." Without giving him a chance to speak, she went to find a restroom.

When she returned, CJ held up the slip the photographer had given him when they arrived. "Rule number three: don't forget your pictures."

Chapter 10

Stuffing the picture from the zoo into her desk drawer, Katie sighed. The day had not been a total loss, once CJ agreed to head back to the entrance. Along the way, she had returned his forty dollars, apologized for jumping to conclusions, and concentrated on the animals and birds at the zoo. The stuffed lion sat in the corner on her bed, a reminder to keep on guard against CJ's charm.

Katie stripped off her clothes and went into the bathroom to shower. Thankfully, her car had been ready earlier than CJ's dad had been told, and she and Timmy had both taken a nap when they got home. But now she was in a race against time to get ready for the evening with Noah. Did she even have any clean underwear? Where were they going? Should she wear her sundress? If they were going to be in air-conditioning or at the beach, she might need a sweater or her denim jacket.

Doing her best to block out the day at the zoo, she turned off the water and grabbed a towel. Through the door, she heard Timmy's cry. "Coming, baby, Momma's coming." Dropping the towel, she dashed into her bedroom, naked, and picked up Timmy. The phone rang. She laughed when she saw it was Noah calling to FaceTime. She could only imagine his shock if she answered.

Her sanity returning, she put down the phone. A few seconds later, Noah called again. She let it ring until it went to voice mail. Still wet, she nursed Timmy while she listened to Noah's message. Did she have time to fix her hair in his favorite style—a French braid—since she would be meeting his parents tonight? Katie gasped. She wanted to meet them but she wasn't ready. What if they asked her where she'd been all day? More to the point, what if they didn't like her?

Katie chewed on her thumbnail, debating what to wear while Timmy finished nursing. Her black sleeveless dress was her best outfit, but would it fit? She had been able to wear it up until her fourth month of pregnancy. But that was then. What about now? It was too hot to wear control-top panty hose, not that she even had any.

Obsessing over her looks and her lack of professional grooming, she alternately laughed and moaned as she burped and changed Timmy's diaper. Even he needed his nails clipped and a bath. Instead, she smeared lotion all over him and dressed him in his cutest newborn overalls and T-shirt. When she added the booties that looked like tennis shoes, she thought he looked adorable.

Until he spit up on himself and her.

"Oh, man, it's a good thing I didn't have my dress on, young man. Now I need another shower, but that's not happening, now is it?" She stripped Timmy as quickly as she could and grabbed another outfit for him. This one was a three-month size but it would have to do. She cleaned him with a wipe and started again to dress him. Her phone rang. This time the screen identified CJ. He wasn't calling on FaceTime, but still Katie groaned. He had already seen her naked. She had to get a grip. Why was he calling? They had already been together way too much today.

With Timmy dressed again and in his crib, she finished drying herself and reached in to her drawer for her underclothes. CJ's gift brushed her hand where it lay unopened near the back of the drawer. Katie groaned. The lion mocked her from the bed. A constant reminder of the day. Slamming the drawer, she turned away and began working on her hair. It was too clean to cooperate. And she needed a trim. Timmy began to cry when she was halfway finished. She couldn't do anything but let him cry if she was going to be ready on time. But it was heartbreaking, and she huffed out a shaky sigh. "In a minute, doll."

She finished the braid haphazardly and turned to get Timmy. This time when she picked him up he felt hot. Was he running a fever? Panic filled her, and she barely stopped herself from going out in her underwear to get Julie. Laying Timmy down again, she hastily put on her robe before going out to the family room.

Brad looked up when she skidded to a stop. "Hi, Katie. You going out with CJ?"

"No, no, Noah's parents are in town and want to meet me. But is Julie here? I think Timmy's got a fever."

"I heard him crying. Julie's not here."

Katie spotted a Dr. Pepper can and a bowl of popcorn on the coffee table. "Do you know when she'll be back?" It was almost six, and Noah would be early, a habit she usually admired.

"Megan's with my folks tonight, and Julie's out with her girlfriends. Remember? It's their once-a-year, celebrate-everyone's-birthday-at-once, night. She'll be late. They get a limo for the occasion."

"Oh, that's right. I totally forgot." She rubbed her forehead.

Brad muted the TV. Timmy's cries filled the room. "There's something bothering the little guy, for sure. Do you have some children's Tylenol?"

Racing back to her room, Katie picked up Timmy and found the Tylenol. His cries filled the room. "Can you hold him, Brad, please? Noah has been trying for weeks to get his parents here so I could meet them, and I'm not even dressed yet."

Brad took Timmy. "Give me the Tylenol and go get dressed, Katie. I've got this. I'd rather you were going out with CJ, but that's none of my business. Just go get dressed.

Timmy can stay with me, if that's okay with you. I've helped Julie watch him a couple of times, you know."

Setting down the Tylenol, Katie hesitated. "Are you sure? I promise I won't be late."

"Go. I've got this."

Katie turned and raced to her bedroom. Timmy's cries had quieted but not stopped. Pulling her dress from the closet, she stepped into it and tugged it over her bottom and tummy. She had been right. It was a tight fit. But acceptable. She stepped into her only pair of black pumps and grabbed a small purse off the closet shelf.

The doorbell rang. It was ten to six.

"Katie, it's Noah," Brad called.

"Are your parents here with you?" Katie asked as she came in the family room. She smoothed back a strand of hair that had escaped the braid. Adrenaline pumped fast and furiously through her system. Guilt at leaving her baby, even though she trusted Brad, caused her stomach to knot.

"No, we're meeting them at Jake's."

"And who is Jake again?"

"It's a restaurant. In Del Mar. We should get going." He patted Timmy on the back. "Thanks, Brad, for watching him. My folks will really appreciate getting to know Katie without, you know, without her having to—"

Katie interrupted. "I've got my phone, so I'll check in with you, and call me if he gets any more miserable." She rubbed Timmy's head and blew him a kiss.

"I will. Just have a good time."

~ ~ ~

Thirty minutes later, Noah turned the car into the parking lot at Jake's and pulled up to the valet stand. "Let's see if my folks are here yet. I think we beat them. That was my plan, at least."

The breeze from the ocean caught Katie's hair and fanned her neck when she got out of the car. Longing to take off her shoes and feel sand between her toes, she turned to Noah. "It's been way too long since we walked on the beach. We should go tomorrow."

Noah planted a light kiss on her lips and took her arm. "Men's Breakfast and cleanup day, but how about Sunday? We could pack a picnic and spend the day together after church."

"I would love that, but Timmy probably wouldn't last the whole day. Maybe for a little while if Julie and Brad have a beach umbrella."

"Let's play it by ear," he said as he opened the restaurant door.

Within minutes of being seated, Noah grinned. "Here they are," he said and stood.

Katie stood and peered around him. Mrs. Davidson was petite and pretty. She exuded energy and confidence as she made her way through the crowded restaurant in front of her husband. Impeccably dressed in a soft pastel silk dress and jacket, she had dark eyes, like Noah's. She smiled a greeting when she saw him and hugged him gently before turning her attention to Katie.

"So, this is Katie," she said with a smile and turned to her husband. "And Katie, this is my husband. Most people call him Pastor Sam."

Katie extended her hand, grateful when he gave her a genuine smile. But in his very proper suit and tie, she couldn't think of him as anything but Pastor Davidson.

"And where is this baby you've told us so much about, Noah?" he asked.

"He's with friends, the family that Katie lives with, actually," Noah said.

Katie added, "He just felt hot, like he's running a fever, and Brad offered to watch him for me."

"Oh dear, and who is Brad again?" Mrs. Davidson asked.

"He's the man who owns the house where Katie has a room," Noah said.

"He's a Navy SEAL," Katie added.

"Special forces, huh? Well, let's hope Timmy behaves himself then!" Pastor Davidson said.

They all laughed and Katie breathed a sigh of relief. Noah held out his mother's seat, then hers before sitting down. Katie studied the menu.

"What are you having?" she asked Noah.

"Lobster. What about you?"

"I think the poached pear salad and seared scallops look good. But just water to drink, please."

"Good choice." Noah gave their order to the waiter.

"So, Katie, tell us about yourself," Mrs. Davidson said. "Your southern accent is charming."

Katie blushed. "Thank you. Actually, years of singing in the school choir helped get rid of some of it. I was born and raised in the Charleston, South Carolina area."

"And what about your parents? Any siblings?"

"My parents still live there. I have two older brothers. Both married, but they live close by my folks. One owns a plumbing business and one's career Army. I came along twelve years after my younger brother. The girl my mom always wanted." Katie fielded Mrs. Davidson's questions, trying her best to make a good first impression. When there was a break in the men's conversation, Mrs. Davidson joined the discussion with them. Relieved to end the questioning, Katie took out her phone to check for any messages from Brad.

When she looked up, Mrs. Davidson's hand was on her husband's arm. "I think those elders were way out of line. What they've done to that church is outrageous. You are going to have to go in there and take control."

From her tone of voice, Katie could tell that something major had upset Mrs. Davidson. She hoped fervently that it wasn't the elders at Pastor Davidson's church. Hard as she tried, she couldn't quite follow the conversation. She was relieved when her food arrived and she had something to occupy her thoughts and hands.

With the meal finished and the plates cleared, Pastor Davidson sat back. "Well, Katie, I apologize for that little business meeting. There's always something happening in one church or another and since I'm the chairman of our denomination, I hear a lot. So, let's hear some more about you. You work at Cornerstone, and have been a believer for a while, I think Noah told us."

Katie smiled. "Yes, I'm on staff part-time doing graphic design work, and I became a believer when a friend invited me to her youth group. One night the director told us that this was *the* night."

Noah gave her shoulder a squeeze. "From what Katie's told me, that youth group didn't do more than games and costume parties, Dad." He shook his head. "No Bible study. No discipleship. But she's really getting . . ."

"What he's saying is I didn't even have a Bible for years." Katie wanted to defend her youth director, but what Noah said was mostly true. "And I didn't know much about how to study it. But I did have an experience with Jesus that night, and that's never left me."

"Well, that's great, Katie," Pastor Davidson said. "Experience is important but it can't replace knowing Scripture."

Mrs. Davidson added, "You know, it's never too late to become a solid Bible student. I'm sure Noah has helped you with that, hasn't he?"

"He's been wonderful. I've really learned a lot."

"Oh, yes, Noah is an outstanding teacher. Of course,

he's learned from the best." Mrs. Davidson nodded toward her husband and chuckled softly.

Katie smiled. There was a coolness in Mrs. Davidson's demeanor, slight but still there. Probably because they did know far more about the Bible than she did, Katie thought. And, they were looking out for their son. They knew she had a baby out of wedlock. Did they approve of Noah having a relationship with her?

"How about some coffee?" Mrs. Davidson asked. "Decaf, of course, at this time of night."

"Thank you so much, but I really should be getting home to Timmy."

"Of course, dear. If he has a fever, he will be wanting you," Mrs. Davidson said. "Noah, you should get Katie home. We'll have a little decaf and enjoy this lovely view before we head to our room. We can talk tomorrow. We'll be staying at Rancho Valencia, as usual."

Noah stood and pulled out Katie's chair. "It was lovely to meet you both," she said, stepping away from the table. "Thank you for a lovely evening. Good night," she said and turned with Noah. When he took her hand, she breathed a sigh of relief that the evening was over.

~ ~ ~

"Your parents are really nice," Katie said once they were in the car.

"Yeah, they have a lot on their plate right now, so it was good of them to come. They really liked you, Katie, I could tell. You and my mom seemed to be hitting it off."

Katie smiled. "You think so? She asked a lot of questions, but she was interested in what you guys were saying, too. She seems to be just as involved as your dad."

"They're a team. Always have been. A power couple." He chuckled. "Seriously. They're known for how to get things done and get them done well."

"You're proud of them, aren't you?"

"Well, why shouldn't I be?"

Katie laughed. "You should be. They raised you to be wonderful, and sweet, and smart and fun, and a terrific teacher!" She reached across the console and rubbed his shoulder. "And I am crazy about you."

Noah took his eyes off the road to glance at her. "Ah, Katie, I love you. You make me feel more alive than anyone ever has."

At the house, Noah helped her out of the car and took her in his arms. "Too much light on the front porch to say good night like I want," he said, kissing her neck.

Katie giggled. "Your beard is tickling me." He was getting a little more amorous than she thought was appropriate. His hand found her bottom. "Noah," she said sharply and stepped away from him.

"I'm sorry. You're just so beautiful, Katie."

She took his hand and led him to the porch. When she turned, she could see he had banked his desire. "I want to be beautiful for you, but we have to take it slow, okay? I've already made one big mistake. That's enough." She kissed him gently. "Thanks for a lovely evening. I'll see you Sunday, okay?"

"Okay, but if you want to come help with clean up at the church tomorrow, you're welcome to."

"Good night, Noah. Love you."

He kissed her again. "Love you, too. Night."

She followed Noah's car down the street with her eyes. Behind her, through the screen door, she heard the TV playing in the family room. No sound of crying. She opened the screen door and went in to the house. Brad's laugh reached her and she looked up. CJ sat on the sofa holding Timmy.

In six long strides, she was at the entrance to the room. "Why are you here?" she said to CJ, keeping her voice low so she wouldn't scare Timmy.

Brad got up and picked up his Dr. Pepper can, crossing t the kitchen. "I invited him, actually, last week when I knew Julie was going to be out. Didn't know until he called afte you left that he was coming. He was a big help with Timmy."

CJ smiled at Katie but didn't get up. "Yep, it's me again I've got to say, Wow, Katie. That dress on you is a killer Want to join us?" He patted the seat beside him.

"No way, but I want to see how my baby is doing." She made her way around the coffee table and perched on the edge of the sofa seat near him. She felt Timmy's forehead When Timmy saw her, his activity level shot up. "Did you have to give him some Tylenol?" His arms and legs were in motion, his coos and gurgles making her smile.

"Brad gave him some Tylenol before I got here, and he's been okay. If he needs more"—he checked his watch—"you have to wait until ten, maybe ten-thirty."

"Did you give him a bottle?" She could tell she would be ready to nurse him soon.

"Right after you left and a half hour ago," Brad said. "And we changed his diaper. That was CJ's job."

Katie's gaze swung to him. He shrugged. "Yeah, that was nasty this time. I emptied the trash can, too. It was full, and smelled worse than a whole team of SWCCs after burrito night."

Brad and CJ started laughing, a loud raucous sound. Katie got up. "You guys, honestly." Then she laughed. "When you've had enough of him, you can bring him in my room. I'm going to get out of these shoes." She walked the short distance to her bedroom, taking her shoes off as she went.

"Guess that's my cue to go." CJ stood. He shifted Timmy to the crook of his arm. "Thanks for having me over. It was nice of you to offer to watch Timmy, too."

"Glad to help. I'm going to turn in," Brad said, hitting

the power off on the remote. "Stay as long as you like. Catch you later." The men shook hands and bump hugged.

CJ made his way around the dining table to Katie's bedroom with Timmy. The door was open so he went in. Katie stretched to put her evening purse on the closet shelf. CJ swallowed, admiring the back view of her shapely form in the black dress. No way he could tamp down his attraction.

He cleared his throat. "Is Timmy okay to sleep in this?"

Katie turned. "Sure, that sleeper's fine. Just lay him down. If he starts to fuss, I'll feed him again. That usually puts him to sleep."

CJ crossed to the crib, snuggled and kissed Timmy a bunch of times before laying him down. Instead of leaving, he stood staring at his son.

Katie studied his face, the soft warmth in his eyes as he gazed at his son. Putting Timmy to bed was something she had done every night on her own for six weeks. This was CJ's first time. It wasn't fair to him, but what could she do about it?

When CJ looked up, he smiled and stepped back. "He's the most amazing little guy. I just can't get enough of him." He laughed. "He's got an amazing mom, too." He stepped closer and pierced her with his stare. "I'm sorry about today, Katie, at the zoo. I said all the wrong things, I know. But you have to know I didn't mean to scare you when we got separated. I wouldn't do anything to harm you or Timmy. You have to know that."

Katie nodded, too moved by his sincerity to speak.

He stepped closer and spoke quietly. "And I just want to set the record straight on something you said today." He lifted her chin gently with one finger and leaned in. "Your old boyfriend didn't find someone better than you. Different maybe, but not better." His gaze scorched her in its intensity. "And if you ask me, he was a fool to ever let you go." His eyes dropped to her lips, and for a moment Katie thought he was going to kiss her. But his hand fell away and he turned to the door.

Her heart in her throat, she finally found her voice. "CJ." When he turned, she wasn't sure she could say what she had wanted to say all day without breaking down. But she had to try. "You-You were the only one I saw . . . when we were together."

For a moment, he stood still. Then he nodded and went out the door.

Chapter 11

Lifting and shoving, Katie maneuvered the box with Timmy's swing onto Brad's dolly in the garage and wheeled it around the side of the house. Voices came from the backyard. She opened the gate and went through with the swing. In the far corner of the yard, Brad, CJ, and another man Katie didn't recognize were pulling parts out of the boxes containing Brad's new shed.

Pushing the dolly to the patio, she unloaded the swing. How had she forgotten that Brad was building the shed today? Why couldn't he have asked someone besides CJ to help? After last night's confession, she hadn't slept well, her mind refusing to shut off the memories of their time together in Las Vegas. How they had hiked and gone rock climbing in Red Rock Canyon, won a hundred bucks at blackjack, snuggled at the dinner table. And ultimately surrendered to passion. Katie blew out a long, shaky breath. God had forgiven her. She needed to forget. Bury the feelings. Move on. So, why couldn't she? As if reading her thoughts, CJ materialized beside her.

"Want some help with that?" he asked, squatting down beside her.

For several long seconds, she stared at him, caught between the past and the present.

CJ chuckled. "What? I didn't shave, so it can't be that I missed a spot."

How could he look so good, so full of energy when she felt emotionally exhausted? Katie bristled. This was all his fault. He had cast a spell on her. And was still trying to work his magic. She pictured pushing him over on his butt. Instead, she turned away. "I don't need your help." She pried open the box with a violent tug.

"Wow. Got it. Okay." He laughed as he stood. "But if you change your mind, let me know."

Forcing herself not to watch him walk away, she dumped out the box, not caring about the noise. Until she remembered she wanted Timmy to stay sleeping. She checked the baby monitor. He hadn't stirred.

When all the pieces were laid out, she glanced over the instructions and got to work. Within minutes, she had the mainframe assembled. But the wayward direction of her thoughts couldn't so easily be brought in line.

"Looks like you know your way around a wrench and a screwdriver," CJ said an hour later. He stripped off his shirt and slung it over his shoulder. "Man, it's hot. Nothing like Bahrain, but still hot." He opened a cooler and pulled out an icy bottled water. "Want one?"

"No thanks," Katie said, not looking up.

After several long gulps, CJ tossed his shirt on a nearby patio chair and came over to admire her work.

Katie deliberately averted her eyes and kept working. "Yeah, I know my way around a few tools. Thanks to my dad."

"Is your dad in construction, a mechanic, what?"

"He was a mechanic, but he doesn't work anymore. He was in a car accident when I was in tenth grade and had to go on disability. He's in a wheelchair."

"Wow. I'm sorry to hear that. Must be tough on your mom now that you're all the way across the country."

Katie's mouth tightened. "Yeah, she can't really get away much. My brothers help some, but"—she shrugged—"they have jobs and families."

"So, it would be tough for her to get out here, I guess."

"Yeah, too tough."

"Have you been sending her pictures of Timmy?"

Katie kept working. "Every week. And we FaceTime."

"By the way, I need to change my time with Timmy today. We'll be a while getting this shed up. Tomorrow after lunch okay?"

Inwardly, Katie fumed. CJ could have asked her last night, couldn't he? She had the day planned so he would watch Timmy while she worked on Noah's project. But how could she demand CJ help her with Timmy instead of helping Brad, after all Brad and Julie did for her?

"I have other plans tomorrow after church. With Noah. So, you can come next week." She sounded like a total grouch, even to her own ears. Why did he have to look so good?

CJ squatted down so close he almost touched her with his bare shoulder. "Nope, not happening that way."

She nodded toward Brad. "I think the other guys need you." She turned to him. "And it is happening that way. You get to see him on Saturday mornings, unless you give me some notice. And you didn't. So, you can't see him this week."

CJ stood. "We'll see about that, Katie."

~ ~ ~

With Timmy strapped in his sling on her chest, Katie stood at the door of the church the next morning with the welcome team. One of the church members, who had been particularly nasty about Katie being pregnant and still on staff, walked in the door with his wife. Katie sucked in a deep breath. Pasting a smile on her face, she nodded but didn't offer her hand.

"Well, young lady, I certainly think it would be more

appropriate for you to be behind the scenes instead of right out here in front flaunting your . . . your . . ." He pointed to Timmy, his face turning a shade of red that reflected his disgust.

"I think you mean her son."

Katie gasped. "CJ!"

He towered over the irate parishioner, his eyes flashing daggers at the man. "And I don't think you have any business judging anybody. Haven't you heard Jesus' teaching about taking the plank out of your own eye?"

The man's gaze swung to CJ, then back to Katie. "Pastor Dale will hear about this, you can be sure. And you'll be out of a job, mark my words." He marched off with his wife.

Caught between shame and fear, Katie gaped at CJ. "Just what are you doing here?" She took his arm. "Come with me." Not bothering to let the welcome team know she was leaving her post, she walked across the lobby to a corner near the coffee bar and turned on him.

"So, guests aren't welcome here?" he said before she could speak.

"Yes, of course they are. But not you." She shook her head. "I mean, you don't care about church. You're doing this to get back at me because I said you couldn't see Timmy until next week."

CJ sighed and smoothed his hand over Timmy's head in the sling. "Who says I don't care about church? Just because I don't go any more doesn't mean I don't care about it. As an institution, it does some good in the world. Not enough, but some. Of course, I could easily deck some of the people . . ."

Katie cut him off. "I don't believe you. You didn't come here for any other reason but to give me a hard time." She glanced around him, her face suffusing with color when some friends waved to her. She waved back before stepping closer to CJ. "I'm on staff here, CJ. People know me. They're going to put their own spin on why a guy like you is here talking to me, and what do you think that's going to do to Noah?"

CJ grimaced. "This is a public place. I came for church. I'd like to experience it with my son. And you, if you'll let me."

"Why don't I believe you?"

"Maybe you have trust issues?" CJ held out both hands. "C'mon, Katie. The music's starting. Take off that sling thing and let me hold Timmy."

As he said it, Katie glimpsed Pastor Dale going toward the sanctuary doors. She groaned as he detoured her way.

"Hey, Katie." He turned and extended his hand to CJ. "I'm Pastor Dale. I don't think we've met, have we?"

CJ took his hand. "No sir, Connor Jansen, CJ to most folks. I'm just visiting."

"Well, glad to see you found Katie. She's our artist in residence, aren't you, Katie?"

He looked at Katie. She couldn't meet his gaze. Guilt and shame overwhelmed her. Sighing, she confessed, "CJ isn't just visiting. He's Timmy's father, Pastor Dale." She looked away, fighting tears.

He nodded. "Thought that might be the case." He laid his hand on CJ's shoulder. "Well, CJ, we're glad to have you today, and I hope you'll come back. If you ever want to talk, my door's always open." He turned away. After greeting the usher at the sanctuary door, he disappeared inside.

"Do you want me to leave?" CJ asked, his voice low.

Katie bit on her lower lip. What would Jesus do? Did He know the turmoil and confusion raging inside her? Was CJ a Christian? It seemed like he knew a lot about the Bible. But did he believe in the God of the Bible? She'd never really asked him. With a loud sigh, she took his arm. "No. Let's get a seat and you can hold Timmy."

~ ~ ~

Noah finished loading the car for the beach and turned to Katie. "Do you have everything you need for Timmy? I've got lunch and some waters and sodas in my cooler."

"Yeah, I think we're good to go. Julie loaned me a beach umbrella and a baby tent. I brought an old quilt for us to sit on."

The ride to La Jolla Shores took twenty minutes. Not bothering with small talk, Noah brooded. What he had seen at church in the Parents' Room that morning was disconcerting. And Katie hadn't even mentioned it. Did she think he didn't care about her being seen sitting so close to CJ? The guy couldn't be a Christian, not after what he'd done with Katie in Vegas. Why had he come to Cornerstone today, except to rub his connection with Katie in Noah's face? He grimaced, annoyed. The beach was the last place he wanted to be. He didn't like sand. But he'd do it for Katie. He pulled in to a parking spot and unloaded the gear.

Once on the beach, Noah slipped off his sandals and sprawled on the quilt next to Timmy. Katie finished assembling the baby tent.

"There, that's perfect for Timmy," she said, putting the baby in the tent with a couple of toys. "He'll probably be asleep in no time." She stretched out her legs and leaned back on her hands beside Noah. "Julie has an amazing assortment of baby stuff. And why not? They always knew they wanted more children. She just told me last week that she and Brad are pregnant again. Deployment baby, you know? Isn't that great?"

Draping his arm around Katie's shoulder, he said, "Great."

Katie turned to look at him, puzzled. "You don't sound very excited about it."

Noah sighed. "I'm just distracted, that's all." He took her hand. "You know I'm crazy about you, Katie. And my parents loved you. I'm thinking we need to talk about the next step for us. I saw you come into church with CJ and sit with him this morning. What's with that?"

Katie leaned on Noah's shoulder. "I had no idea he was coming. He wanted to see Timmy after lunch and I told him no, that I had plans with you." She stroked his cheek. "Are you jealous?"

"Should I be? How can I not be? Every time I turn around, he's at your place."

Katie scooted away and sat crossed-legged looking at him. Guilt flooded her. Did he know they went to the zoo? "I'm sorry. He's Timmy's father. What am I supposed to do?"

"For starters, you could have less fun when you're with him."

At her dropped jaw, he continued, his frustration evident. "Oh, don't give me that! I saw you laughing with him during Pastor Dale's sermon this morning. He was all over you with his eyes."

"Oh that." Laughter spilled out of her. When she finally could talk, she said, "Timmy had a blowout. I mean, he just let it rip and the shock on CJ's face was priceless. Everyone around us heard it, too."

"Well, I guess that was funny. But Katie, I'm serious. I don't think you should have anything to do with him, beyond letting him see Timmy." His voice low, he pleaded, "I guess I just want him out of your life."

Katie shifted and draped herself over Noah's back. She rubbed his bald head and put her lips to his ear. "I'm sorry. Really. He's Timmy's dad, so I have to let him come over. But you don't have a thing to worry about." She stood and pulled off her T-shirt and shorts to reveal a modest blue one-piece bathing suit. "I know you don't like swimming in the ocean, so thanks for coming with me today. As soon as Timmy's asleep, I'll get in a quick swim. We don't have to stay long."

"You want to have lunch in the meantime?" Noah opened the cooler to pull out sandwiches and a couple of waters. "I hope turkey subs are okay."

Katie peeked into the tent. "Okay if we wait? Looks like Timmy's out already, so I should swim before we eat. I'll just be a minute." She jogged to the ocean.

Swimming parallel to shore, Katie felt herself finally relax. They had made it through their first squabble. She knew Noah didn't want to be jealous. It was an emotion that meant he wasn't in control, and that was a feeling he avoided at all costs. She could relate. She didn't like the feeling either. But CJ wasn't giving either of them a choice. He just kept showing up.

Rolling over on her back, Katie gazed at the sky as she stroked the water. Noah didn't like the beach, or sports, or pretty much any activity that caused him to sweat. Did she want to marry him? Give her body to him? What would their life together look like? She had dreamed of raising Timmy with him once upon a time. Until CJ barged back into her life with his demands and apologies. Now she didn't know what she wanted.

Lord, I need some help here, Katie prayed between strokes. Noah had come alongside her at a time when she felt lonely and abandoned, forsaken by CJ, and the object of speculation and pity by some people at church. She had resisted thinking of him as anything but a friend for several months, knowing he had a job and a reputation to build at Cornerstone, not wanting to cause any trouble for him. But when she started to show her pregnancy, he hadn't averted his eyes, like some. Instead, he had walked with her, studied the Bible with her and encouraged her. How could CJ match what Noah offered? Turning in the water, she swam hard for the shore. But in the space of time it took to reach the beach, she made up her mind to do what she could to slow things way down with both men. And pray. A lot.

~ ~ ~

Worn out, Katie loaded the dishwasher after dinner that evening. Timmy and Megan were already tucked in bed, and Brad and Julie were snuggling on the sofa watching a movie. She set the start timer on the dishwasher for nine o'clock so the noise wouldn't interfere with the movie and turned to go to her room. The doorbell rang.

"I'll get it," Katie said when Brad started to get up. Almost to the screen door, she didn't see anyone outside. But when she put her hand on the door knob, CJ turned and came to the door.

"What are you doing here?" Katie asked. Noah would not be pleased if he knew. She stepped out on the porch, hoping to deal quickly with whatever he wanted and get back inside. The streetlamps provided enough light for her to see that he was agitated. "Has something happened?"

"Is Timmy in bed? Can you talk for a minute?"

"Yes, he's been asleep for an hour or so. What's wrong?"

"I can't get that guy at church out of my head." He paced away from her, then back. "Pastor Dale says he's been in your face for months."

"You talked to Pastor Dale?" Katie moved to sit on the bench Julie had bought for the front porch earlier in the summer.

"Yeah, he says the guy's been after him to fire you because you got pregnant and had the nerve to keep Timmy." He ran a hand over his head. "Thank God for that."

Touched by his earnestness, Katie said, "We worked it out a long time ago. Pastor Dale lets me do my work at home. It's not perfect, but it's working for now."

CJ sat down beside her and braced his elbows on his knees. For several moments, he didn't speak. "I messed up your life pretty good, didn't I?" He glanced back at her before turning away.

Was that an apology? He would have to do better than that. "Why are you here, CJ? There's nothing you can do to change anything."

"I know that." He sat back, his gaze sweeping her face, his eyes tender. The warm night air enveloped her, a slight breeze caressing her skin. They weren't touching, and yet, he was touching every part of her.

"I guess I just want you to know I care about you. And what happens to you. I thought about you a whole lot while I was deployed. Even thought, hoped, maybe we'd take up where we left off when I got back. But I never counted on Timmy." He shook his head. "He's rocked my world. I know that sounds lame . . . compared to how things have changed for you." He stood and shoved his hands in his pockets, his back to her. "But there it is." He turned and pinned her with eyes that smoldered. "And some old geezer who doesn't care a thing about the sanctity of life isn't going to mess up yours, Katie. I promise you that."

He had no sooner said the words than a car pulled up in the Skidmore's driveway. It was all Katie could do not to groan. Noah got out of his car. He had made his dislike of CJ, and any time she spent with him, very clear at the beach.

"Looks like a party," CJ said under his breath.

Giving him a look that could kill, Katie went to meet Noah. She stopped halfway down the driveway. "Hey you. What's up? I didn't expect to see you again today." She felt like a schoolgirl caught by the principal for passing notes in class. Her stomach ached.

"Obviously," Noah said. He glanced at CJ. "I guess you don't care what I want, do you? When it comes to him."

Katie glanced at the porch. CJ hadn't moved. "That's not true. He just stopped by. What was I to say? Go away?"

"Yeah, something like that."

Suddenly impatient with Noah's petty jealousy, Katie grabbed him by the shoulders. "Well, that's just poor manners and you know it. Nothing's going on with CJ and me. Except Timmy."

CJ laughed. "Oh, I'm not sure that's exactly true."

Katie spun around to find CJ only a foot away. "Ooooo . . ." Her hands clenched into fists, ready to pummel him, and in a moment of lucidity she wondered why only CJ could bring out this urge in her to physically fight.

Over her head, he said to Noah, "She get feisty like this with you, man?" When Noah didn't respond, he smirked. "Didn't think so."

"You need to leave, CJ." Katie barely resisted clawing at him. But she didn't. She couldn't touch him. Her feelings for him were too intense. Too raw. In a flash of understanding, she saw it, this need for him that could consume her. "Now!" she shouted.

Hands up, CJ took a step back. But instead of leaving, he said, "I have something else I want to talk to you about, Katie. But, it'll wait." He moved past her and stopped alongside Noah. "I'm not going anywhere, man. Deal with it."

Chapter 12

Over coffee and orange scones at Panera Bread on Monday afternoon, with Timmy sleeping in his car seat next to her, Katie asked the question that had been gnawing at her since the beach trip. "Noah, yesterday you said we need to talk about the next step for us. What exactly did you mean? I thought we defined our relationship already. Didn't we?"

Noah took her hand. "That was before Timmy. Before CJ came back. I can't help thinking you're not so sure about what you want from me now. Am I right?"

Katie sighed. Of all the things she loved about Noah, this one attracted her most, his willingness to look head on at a situation and talk about it without getting emotional or defensive. At least until CJ came on the scene.

"You're so good to me, Noah. I-I wish I could understand what I'm feeling right now. I guess you could say I'm just overwhelmed and confused. I'm attracted to CJ. I mean, I was. That's how I got pregnant in the first place. But now, I'm just . . ." She groped for the right words and came up short. How could she explain the chemistry? The constant desire to give in to CJ's charm and charisma? To what end? He had said he cared about her last night on the porch. But what exactly did he mean?

Finally, she said, "I just know this, Noah. At every rough patch these last months, you've helped me to see the good and give the rest to the Lord. I've grown so much stronger in my faith. And I don't want to do anything that would displease the Lord. I'm tempted by CJ, but that's just how the devil works, right? I love you. That's the one thing I do know."

Noah smiled, a big toothy grin that made his whole face light up. "That's what I wanted to hear." He kissed her hand. "So, the next step is a weekend with my folks. Labor Day weekend. It'll give you a chance to see where I'm going to be working next. What do you think? Can you swing it with Timmy? I mean, my folks don't have any gear for babies, but he doesn't need much, right? We do have a couple of nice guest rooms."

Caught up in his excitement, Katie ignored Noah's omission of how she might fit into his next job plans. That would come eventually if the weekend went well, wouldn't it? But she couldn't ignore the little voice in her head, reminding her of the invitation from Mary Jansen to meet her family on that same weekend. She had made no promises to her, and yet, she didn't want to let her down. Suppressing a sigh, Katie withdrew her hand from Noah's and lifted it for a high five.

"Let's do it," she said. "And trust the Lord for what happens next."

~ ~ ~

The shooting range was crowded Monday evening. CJ didn't care. After Katie's denial to Noah the night before, he had some steam to blow off. Some thinking to do. Figure out what else he could do to convince Katie there was something going on between them that needed a chance. She still hadn't mentioned the ruby knot bracelet, and that irked him. Had she read his card? Maybe he'd ask her. Shoving the thought away, he looked around for Dustin. When he didn't see him at any of the apparel racks or at a table, he walked to the desk. "How's it going, Craig? Have you seen Dustin?"

"CJ. Heard you were back." Craig offered his fist and connected with CJ's. "Good to see you. Heard you had some excitement over there in the Gulf." When CJ shook his head, he chuckled and dropped the subject. "Haven't seen Dustin. Want me to put you on the list?"

"Yeah, I think he's bringing his girlfriend, so sign us up for three lanes."

"Need ammo tonight? What'd you bring?"

CJ held up his gun case. "Going with my favorite. The Glock. Yeah, put a couple of boxes on my tray. How long's the wait?"

"Count on an hour. Maybe hour fifteen."

CJ nodded and looked around at the crowd in the reception area. The downside of paying to shoot was the waiting. He was on his way to a display about Wounded Warriors when he heard Dustin call his name. He turned to see his teammate. As usual, Dustin practically sprinted instead of walked, while Ashley and another girl—a very attractive blonde with a gun case in each hand—sauntered behind.

"Did you get us on the list?" Dustin asked.

"Yeah. It's an hour wait. Who's the blonde with Ashley?"

"That's a friend of one of her new roommates. She's a Marine up at Pendleton."

"She got a name?" CJ hadn't planned on the evening turning social, but it looked like he would have to make some small talk until their lanes opened. Maybe he could discover why Katie was so down on Dustin.

"She goes by Midge or something like that. Not sure if that's her last or first name."

CJ shook his head. Typical Dustin. He was all about the action. Forget the details. He decided to let Ashley make the first move and come to him. It didn't take long.

"How's it going, CJ?" Ashley asked when she had made her way through the crowd, her blonde friend following. She high fived him and stepped back. "Are you and Katie together yet? Cause if not, you'll want to get to know Midge here." She pulled the blonde toward him. "Midge, this is CJ. CJ, Midge."

CJ nodded. "Hi," he mumbled, the memory of Katie chastising Noah for his poor manners flashing through his mind. There was no way he wanted anything to do with this girl, but since they had an hour to kill, he figured he didn't have to be a total jerk.

"What are you using tonight?" he asked, nodding at her gun cases.

She met his gaze with the most brilliant blue eyes CJ had ever seen. "I like to practice with my .357 Magnum, but I also just got a Browning 1911. So, I wanted to try it out." Her voice was low and husky. "How about you?"

A Marine? *Try eye candy.* CJ cleared his throat. "Uh, I use a Glock 19. It's enough fun for now. Although I've heard the Browning is a sweet deal."

"Oh, very sweet," she laughed, a low rumble that sounded like the purr of a predatory cat.

"So, tell me about it."

To pass the time, CJ listened to the best sales pitch he'd ever heard for a gun. Midge knew her weapons, all right, including the kind that women don't carry in a case.

"Dustin says you're up at Pendleton. Where's home?"

"West Virginia. Almost heaven." She laughed. "At least that's what some say. I'm not one of them. I like California."

"I don't actually know much about West Virginia except they've got great whitewater rafting. I spent some time kayaking on the Gauley River about ten years ago. I go closer to home now."

"Oh, you'll want to put more than the Gauley on your list." She launched into a litany of outdoor adventures in West Virginia. Twenty minutes later, CJ ran his hand through his hair and laughed. "I think you missed your calling, Midge. You sold me on the Browning, now I'm itching to go whitewater kayaking in West Virginia again. Among other sports. Got anything else you need to unload on me?" He walked to an apparel rack. "Which line of sport's gear do you like?"

By the time his name was called to pick up his tray of eye and ear protection, ammo, and target sheet, CJ had offered to share his lane with Midge.

~ ~ ~

Pastor Dale's office was comfortably furnished with a worn leather love seat, several upholstered chairs and a well-used coffee table. Rather than sit behind his desk, he was known for his warm hospitality when people came for counseling, consolation, or just to chat. His office manager, Dana, was already in his office with her cup of coffee and a homemade cookie when Katie arrived for her appointment on Tuesday morning.

At the door, Katie hesitated when Pastor Dale wasn't in his office. "Hey, Dana, am I here at the right time? Right day?"

Dana put down her coffee and cookie and crossed the room to Katie. "You are. But, just where is that darling baby of yours?" She gave Katie a quick hug.

"Julie offered to watch him and I accepted. I'll bring him by in a day or two to visit. I think Pastor Dale wanted to talk about work today so I didn't want to risk him fussing." She eyed the cookies but didn't take one as she made her way to the love seat.

"Yep, we've got the fall projects on our mind. Pastor Dale just texted. He'll be here any minute. He had an early appointment off-site with the new president of the Council. Brent Hellman. Were you at the business meeting last week?"

"No, I'm not officially a member yet, and my presence seems to rile certain people. You know, the ones who always attend the business meetings, so I decided to lay low."

"Gotcha. It actually went well. Just a little hassle about the color of the new chairs for the fellowship hall. Brent was the Council VP last couple of years so he was ready for his new title."

"He's here." Dana said, gesturing to the doorway.

Katie stood and turned.

"Hi, Katie." Pastor Dale gave her a quick hug. "Thanks for holding down the fort, Dana. I see my wife brought us cookies. Another new recipe, I'm sure."

He swiped a cookie and started munching as he took a seat.

"So, Katie, I asked Dana to sit in so she can help me remember all the projects we want your help with between now and the end of the year. I think you and Noah have already started work on the Men's Steak Dinner for the end of September, right?"

"Yes, it's about ready. The only thing that hasn't been decided is whether or not you want a banner for the street. Noah said it's your call on that."

"Has he got a high-profile speaker?"

Katie nodded several times. "I think you'd call his dad pretty high profile."

"Oh, that's right. My memory . . ." he said. "Then, yes, a banner at the street. Let's go with big, bold lettering and how to register online. We wouldn't want to run out of steaks with such an honored speaker in the house."

Katie quipped, "Yeah, the stakes are too high for that, huh?"

The groaning was immediate. And friendly. Pastor Dale began naming the projects: the Country Fair in October, the Thanksgiving Pie Social, the Preschool Christmas Dessert, Advent and Christmas Eve services. Every few minutes, Dana chimed in with "We'd also really like . . ."

When the string of design projects seemed to be coming to an end, Katie took a deep breath. "I'm really excited by all this work, and all the programs," she began, "but I have to be honest here. What you've laid out will take me more than the hours I'm currently working." She looked at her hastily scribbled notes. "I'd say probably half again above the time I'm already doing." Swallowing her nervousness, she added, "I would love that much work, but does Cornerstone have the budget for it?"

"So, you're saying it would take you thirty, instead of the twenty hours a week you work for us now?" Dana's expression said she was clearly skeptical. She'd done the weekly bulletin before Katie took over the job, and didn't really have an understanding—or appreciation—for the changes and upgrades Katie had made.

"Well, yes, that's just an estimate, but I think it actually favors the church. Even now, I sometimes put in more hours than I bill for. I love my work, and I want to do the best job I can. So—"

Pastor Dale interrupted, "You get raves from me, Katie, even though I confess I have no idea how long it takes to do any of the creative work you do. I talked with Brent this morning, knowing we were meeting, and we're hopeful that we can get by with twenty-four hours a week and still get these jobs done. Of course, if that's not going to work, then I'll have the staff make some cuts. Bite the bullet and prioritize. We're hoping these new campaigns will help get people opening their hearts to Christ. That's first and foremost our heart's desire. But, it would be helpful if they could cheerfully open their wallets a little wider for Cornerstone, too."

"Maybe I could take a little time to look these projects over," Katie said, "before I commit to doing all of them. See if what I think should be a priority matches what you and the staff think."

Pastor Dale and Dana nodded in agreement. "Just keep the weekly bulletins coming," Dana said. "I love not having to spend time on those. And I think people are actually reading them."

"Yes, those are a given," Pastor Dale said. "And just let me know in a day or two about the rest. We don't want to take advantage of you, especially since you've got your hands full with Timmy right now. By the way, speaking of Timmy, I talked with CJ on Sunday. Such a nice young man. He's very concerned about you, you know?" He gave her a pointed look. "Caught him last night at the gun range, too. That was a surprise. But I guess being in special forces, guns are a way of life."

Katie nodded, not really knowing that side of CJ's life. Whenever she asked about his work, he said a little, but mostly said he didn't like talking about it. "I didn't know you like guns."

"Oh, yes. I came to Cornerstone from Minnesota. Guns, hunting, fishing. That's a way of life there. My dad first took me out deer hunting when I was twelve. Maybe my interest in firearms will be a good connection point for me with CJ. Give me a chance to see where he is with the Lord."

Guilt washed over Katie. CJ's salvation had been the last thing on her mind. She had been too busy fighting the attraction. Had he been with a woman at the gun range? Did she dare ask? Deciding against it, she said, "Yes, he said he talked to you. He . . . a . . . he's . . . he's very good with Timmy," she finally managed.

"Well, that's good to know. As I said, he seems like a very caring young man."

Not knowing what else to say, Katie just nodded. Did Pastor Dale think she should ditch Noah for CJ? Ignoring the implications, she said her goodbyes and hurried out the door. If Pastor Dale wanted her answer about the work load in a couple of days, she needed to get home and get started.

~ ~ ~

At noon, Noah arrived with lunch. Katie opened the screen door. "Your timing is perfect. I was just making sandwiches. Timmy's still sleeping."

Noah held up a fast-food bag. "KFC. Much better than peanut butter."

"How do you stay so skinny, eating that junk?" She gave him a quick kiss. "Come on in. You need some vegetables, too. And water."

"Hmmm . . . a little bossy today, aren't you?" Noah laughed. He followed her to the kitchen.

"I'm only looking out for your health," she said, cutting the sandwiches in half. "I don't want you to have a heart attack when you're fifty." She slipped her arms around his waist and hugged him. "Let's eat in the backyard."

"I'll warn you, it's hot out. Another scorcher. But at least the table's in the shade." Noah slid open the back door. Katie put the sandwiches and vegetables on the picnic table and went back in to the kitchen for two tall glasses of water and a couple of napkins.

"So, are you excited about the weekend?" Noah asked. "My folks have invited some friends of ours from Sacramento to come down. You'll get to meet their daughter, too. Amanda. She's been in Honduras the last two years working with a guy and his wife who take homeless boys off the streets and give them a home."

"Just boys?" Katie bit into one of the chicken drumsticks.

"Yeah, just boys for now. They only take one or two new boys at a time, too. Otherwise, it's too hard for everyone to adjust. They homeschool the boys, feed them, counsel them, and try to find their parents. But basically, they just pour a lot of love into them, one boy at a time. In Amanda's last letter she wrote that the first boy they ever took in is a senior in high school this year, and making plans to go to college."

"That's wonderful. So, you know Amanda pretty well, it seems. Your face lights up when you talk about her."

Noah laughed. "Are you jealous?"

"Should I be?"

"No. She's been a friend for a long time, that's all. Her family went to our church before moving to Sacramento, and we've supported Amanda as our missionary in Honduras since she got out of college. I actually haven't seen her for years. She's back in the states to raise funds to go back, I think. You'll like her."

"I'm sure I will. Speaking of the weekend, what will we be doing? I mean, are shorts okay? Do I need a dress? Do your parents have a pool? Will we be swimming?"

"We have a pool so you're welcome to swim. I'll be in the lounge chair in the pool sipping an Arnold Palmer." He laughed. "That's my idea of fun. And cards. We play a lot of bridge."

"Sorry, I don't play bridge. How about bocce ball or tennis?"

"Amanda might play tennis. Not sure. You can bring your racket if you want, and I'll take you to the club not far from us. We don't play bocce ball."

"So, what do you do? I mean, Friday to Monday is a long time to sit around."

"We like to sit around, talk. You know, discuss trends in the church, politics, the latest books. And since we work hard, it's a great time to catch up on sleep. Take naps. Mom's friend Rosa makes all kinds of good eats, too. There's always a snack bar."

"Oh brother! Just what I need. I've almost lost the last five pounds I gained with Timmy. I could easily gain it back."

"Don't worry. I saw you at the beach, remember? You look perfect. But it might be best if you just bring your blue suit instead of a bikini. I can just imagine how great you'd look in one of those."

Katie blushed, pleased at Noah's interest in her, but disappointed, too. The blue suit was her only one-piece, leftover from her days on the swim team. Otherwise, she always wore bikinis. The thought of spending the weekend in the same suit every day was depressing. No chance of controlling her tan lines. "Okay. We'll save my bikinis for another time."

Noah crumbled up his lunch trash and stuffed it into the bag. "We'll probably go to a nice restaurant on Sunday evening, so do you have something fancy you can wear?"

"I don't, but maybe I can borrow something from Ashley or Julie." She had worn several of Ashley's outfits in Las Vegas. The thought reminded her of CJ. "I'll figure something out." She stood and began collecting their lunch remains.

"And bring your Bible." Noah laughed. "You don't want to get behind on your reading plan."

"What you mean is, I'll finally have time to catch up. I'm five days behind." She hated to confess her failings to Noah. She wanted to be perfect in his eyes. But she had to be honest, too. What kind of relationship would they have otherwise?

"You have to keep up with your reading, Katie. Being disciplined is important."

Feeling like an errant schoolgirl, Katie turned away and went into the house. "I'll catch up, I promise."

She walked with Noah to the door. "I want to make you proud of me. You know, be your star student."

He cupped her face and kissed her tenderly. "You are my star student. And much more." He kissed her again. "I'll see you Friday."

Chapter 13

Katie folded the skirt she had borrowed from Ashley and put it in her suitcase on top of the other things she had packed for the weekend at the Davidsons. She zipped the suitcase and turned to find her journal. Opening her desk drawer, she spotted the picture of CJ, Timmy, and her at the zoo staring up at her. She turned it over with a groan. Why couldn't she get CJ out of her head? His mother had been clearly disappointed when she called her this morning to say she couldn't come to her party, but she was understanding. She hoped, she said, that it might still work out on Monday afternoon for Katie to stop by on her way home, but she didn't push. Her sweet acceptance didn't help Katie's guilty conscience. Timmy was her only grandchild. This would be one of the few chances for her whole family to meet him.

The doorbell startled her from her thoughts. Pulling her bedroom door almost closed, she went to the front door. CJ stood on the porch.

"Ah . . . Hi. I didn't expect you today. I texted you I was going out of town. Didn't you get it?"

CJ pulled open the screen door and stepped in to the house. "I got it. And I get it. You're ditching me and my family for *him*, aren't you? A romantic weekend away. You know all about how to turn on the charm for a guy, don't you?"

Katie stepped back, caught off guard by the hostility emanating from CJ. Was he blaming *her* for what happened in Las Vegas? She hadn't seen him since Sunday night's fiasco, when Noah had caught him on her porch. Was he jealous?

CJ moved around her and turned, his eyes hard. "When it comes to *our* son, you don't get it, do you? You're his mother, but he has a father, too. Me. And grandparents, and an aunt, and plenty of others who want to be part of his life. But you can't even manage to let me have one day a week with him."

Katie bristled. "I'm not the one with the crazy schedule. I've tried my best to let you see Timmy. This weekend is different, that's all. I'm going to be away, but it's none of your concern where or with whom."

"Yeah right. It's none of my concern who you're hanging around, making plans with. Get real, Katie! You're making plans to take my son away from me. Do you think I was born yesterday? That I don't see what you're doing? You're so enamored with your boyfriend, you can't even give me or my family a few measly hours with him this weekend. There's a house full of people who are counting on meeting the newest member of the Jansen family. Did you think about that?"

"I called your mom and explained it won't be possible. She was very understanding."

CJ closed the short distance between them. "You think so? You think she understands? Think again. Sure, she puts on a good front. But she's crushed and heartbroken, believe me. Not to mention what your petty, selfish, self-interests are doing to my dad, who only wants to make my mom happy. And what about my sister, Lynn, our aunts and uncles? And me, Katie." He rubbed his neck. "Did you think at all about how you not showing up to meet my family would affect me? No. I'm just a thorn in your side here, aren't I? I'm the jerk who got you pregnant and deserted you. Yeah, I get it. And nothing I've done since then makes any difference to you, does it? All you care about is that I get out of your way so you can have your preacher man and your holier-than-thou life together."

He turned sharply and strode into the family room. With his back to her, he rubbed his hand around his neck as if he had a cramp. His other hand was clenched in a fist. For several seconds he remained that way before turning to pierce her with daggers shooting from his eyes. "I was sure mistaken about you."

She cowered at his anger, his every word lashing at her heart. What could she say? She was trapped by feelings for him she couldn't get under control. How many nights had she cried herself to sleep, wishing CJ would call when she found out she was pregnant? Wishing they could be a real family? She had fallen in love with him in Vegas. But can love without commitment and communication survive? In the wake of his rejection who could blame her for turning bitter and angry? For leaning on Noah? How could she forgive CJ for not calling her after their time together in Vegas? How could she let him back in her life unless they cleared the slate?

Timmy's cries broke the silence, and a sob escaped from her. Before she could move, CJ did. He walked boldly into her room and picked up Timmy. All she could do was follow and watch.

And then her own anger flared. Her voice shaking, she railed at him, "You have a lot of nerve, yelling at me. Walking in here and condemning me for hurting your parents. Or not thinking about you. You're the one who started this mess! You came on to me in Vegas. Not the other way around. And you may have thought about me later on during deployment, but you sure never did anything about it. You've never even said you're sorry. I'm the one who had to deal with being single and pregnant. Not you. No one looks at you and gives a rip that you made a baby. Your parents may be great, but they sure as heck messed up with you." She ignored the pain she saw on his face and pressed on, too overcome with anger to care how she was hurting him. "I don't owe you anything. Or them, either. I'm entitled to see or go with anyone I want, any place."

She reached for Timmy. CJ let him go without a fight.

He stepped back from her, shook his head, and rubbed his neck again. "Yeah, you're entitled, Katie." His shoulders slumped. "I'm not sure how I ever thought there could be anything between us. That was some kind of act you put on in Vegas. You had me fooled, all right. But now, seeing how you really are, I guess I should feel sorry for the bald guy." He drew a deep breath. "I hope you two will be very happy." He strode from the room, the door slamming behind him as he left the house.

In his wake, Katie crumbled in a heap on the sofa with Timmy. *Where are you, Lord?* What could she do? She hadn't gone looking for a relationship with Noah. It had just happened. And it had been a balm to her wounded heart. But all she could think of now was how hopeless it all seemed. She had four days ahead with Noah and his family. She barely knew them. Unlike Mary Jansen, who stopped by often to see her and Timmy, she'd been with the Davidsons only once. Noah said they enjoyed sitting around and talking. What did she have to say that anyone with their level of biblical knowledge would want to hear? She stood to pace the room, filled with guilt and uncertainty.

Chewing on her lower lip, Katie tried to think, to be objective about CJ's anger, his harsh words and disappointment. He hated her now, and the thought filled her with such grief she could hardly contain it. He had to face his whole family. Own up to his mistake. They all knew he had messed up. He still wanted them to meet Timmy. It was a depth of family unity Katie had never experienced. She didn't even know how her own mother and father really felt about her and the baby. They had never said much about it, other than they were glad she had been invited to live with the Skidmores.

A wave of homesickness crashed over her and she strode to her bedroom. Collapsing in the glider chair, tears poured down her cheeks onto Timmy. She had never felt so alone.

The baby began to fuss, and she turned him so he could nurse. "You love me, don't you, baby doll? At least we have each other, and I would never walk out on you like your daddy walked out on me." Katie closed her eyes, remembering how dismayed she had been to find CJ gone in the morning after she's slept with him. Agitated at the memory, she set the glider chair in motion and prayed to forget and forgive. CJ had come back in her life, and Timmy's too, come what may. "Oh, God, please give me your wisdom and guidance."

Twenty minutes later, with her emotions finally settled and a plan in mind, she picked up the phone and called Noah. He answered on the third ring.

"Hey you, almost ready?" His voice sounded young and excited.

"Almost, but I've just decided, Noah, I need to drive myself."

"What? Why? I got the car seat base in my car. There's no reason."

"I just have to. What if I need to go out for a while? Do something besides sit and talk? I just have to, that's all. We can go at the same time and I'll follow you up the freeway, but my mind is made up." She heard Noah sigh, a long, drawn-out breath. She prayed he wouldn't argue or press her for why she suddenly felt the need to drive herself. She couldn't tell him about CJ's visit or the Jansen's house full of company. No way would he understand her need to see the Jansen family.

Or tell CJ she was sorry.

~ ~ ~

The Davidson's Mediterranean-style home was in a gated community of large, estate homes. "What in the world is a little ole South Carolina girl like me doing here?" she mumbled under her breath as she followed Noah through the neighborhood to their driveway. Nestled on a half-acre of land, the home's facade was a warm honey stucco with a red tile roof. Palm trees and neatly manicured shrubs and perennials graced the perimeter and nestled up to the house in curved beds.

From the front seat of her car, Katie studied the impressive front doors, jumping when Noah tapped on her window.

"This is it. We're home." He opened her door and helped her out. "Mom's got your room ready. Why don't you get Timmy and head up to the door? I'll unload your stuff. Then you can look around while I take things upstairs. How's that sound?"

"Okay." She glanced at the closed front door and back at Noah. "Do they know we're here? Should I just go ring the doorbell?" Her laugh betrayed her nervousness.

Noah smiled and smoothed his hand down her hair in a comforting gesture. "I'll take you in the house . . ." He looked up. "There's Mom now. C'mon. Let's get out of this heat." He took her arm to turn her.

"Wait. We need to get Timmy." Katie opened the back door of the car and quickly unstrapped her son. This would be his first introduction to the Davidsons so she was glad he was awake. "Come to Momma, darling boy. And behave yourself, okay?"

In the shade of the entryway, Mrs. Davidson hugged Noah and turned to Katie. "So, this is Timmy. Welcome to our home. Both of you. What a darling boy." She patted Timmy's back and stroked his cheek.

Timmy fussed in Katie's arms. "Thank you. He, well,

he's developed separation anxiety, I'm afraid. The minute he realizes he isn't in my arms. I hope it's only temporary."

"Yes, that happens. Come in. Come in. Noah, you can bring your bags later. Come and say hello to your father. Do you need a cold drink, Katie?"

She ushered them inside. Katie did her best not to gawk at the grand staircase and large two-story foyer. Straight ahead a formal living room had been done in whites, blues, and greens. Mrs. Davidson led them past the living room, down a hallway to the kitchen. "I'll give you a little tour after you get settled in your room, Katie, if you'd like."

"That would be wonderful. I'd enjoy that, I'm sure. Maybe after I get Timmy down for a nap."

In the kitchen, Mrs. Davidson introduced Katie to her friend, Rosa, and pointed out a snack bar that had been set up. "Don't go hungry while you're here, please. Rosa has offered to help me with dinner tonight. She's a wonder in the kitchen, and one of my dearest friends. What can I get you to drink, Katie? Noah?"

"A glass of water would be nice," Katie said. "Thank you."

"Iced tea, Mom. But I can get it."

"Well, well, glad to see you made it." Pastor Davidson came into the kitchen, his arms outstretched in welcome. He patted Timmy on the back with one hand and Katie on the shoulder with the other before turning to shake Noah's hand. "Dinner's not until seven so you've found the snack bar, right?"

Katie almost laughed. The snack bar, evidently, was a big deal to the Davidsons. She made a point of going to see what was available. "Wow, this looks amazing." Glad to see vegetables had been included in among chocolates, dips, cheeses, crackers, and cupcakes, she helped herself to a stick of celery. Rosa brought Katie's water while Noah helped himself to iced tea.

"I'll just set your water here," Rosa said, placing Katie's water on the island. "I'll have your cookies in a little bit, Noah," she said, patting his face.

"I'm counting on it," Noah said. He finished his drink in record time and set down his glass. "I'm going to get our bags. I'll meet you in your room, Katie."

"I'll show you to your room," Mrs. Davidson said. "Once Timmy is asleep, we'll take that tour."

"That sounds lovely," Katie said then followed Mrs. Davidson up the stairs.

~ ~ ~

An hour later, Katie sat down on a white butter-soft leather sofa in the living room to wait for Noah. After bringing in her bags, he had suggested they grab a nap. It hadn't been her first choice, but she had ended up enjoying a power nap and some time to journal in the sunroom Mrs. Davidson had showed her on their tour.

Determined once again to block out the morning's fight with CJ, Katie studied the large abstract painting above the fireplace in the Davidson's living room. The artist's bold use of color and complicated patterns spoke to her own feelings of confusion about CJ. When he could have backed off from having anything to do with Timmy, he hadn't. Instead, he came faithfully to see him. His family apparently meant a lot to him. Hadn't he warned her not to hurt his parents? Now, she was disappointing, not just CJ, but his whole family.

Katie turned away from the fireplace to look around the room and take her mind off the Jansen family. Timmy was napping. She had an hour to kill before dinner. Their friends from Sacramento, the Wolfes, were due to arrive at six-thirty. Snacks and punctuality, it seemed, were very important in the Davidson's household. A grin tugged at Katie's lips and she picked up a framed picture of the family off the baby grand piano. Noah had learned his lessons well. He constantly snacked and was always at least ten minutes early for whatever was happening.

"There you are," Noah said, coming around the corner into the room. "Did you have a snack yet?"

Katie laughed. "Several. How about you?"

"No, I wanted to get unpacked, and grab that nap. It may be a late night playing cards. How was the house tour?" Without waiting for an answer, he grabbed her hand. "Let's go see what else Rosa and Mom have put out. Ready?"

Together they walked down the hallway past a formal dining room that could seat ten or twelve people easily. In the kitchen, Rosa was adding a batch of fresh cookies to the snack bar, their aroma making Katie's mouth water.

"Rosa, you're a doll," Noah said, giving her a pat on the shoulder. To Katie he added, "Rosa knows these are my favorite cookies—chocolate macadamia nut. Can't beat 'em." He took almost half the cookie in his mouth with one bite.

Katie picked up a stalk of celery and dipped it in a dish of hummus. It would have to hold her until dinner. She'd already had her share of other snacks, including a couple of dark chocolate-covered potato chips.

Noah finished his cookie and grabbed Katie for a quick chocolaty kiss that made her want her own cookie.

Instead she laughed. "You are going to spoil your dinner. And mine too, if we don't get out of this kitchen. Let's play hide and seek. Or pool in the game room."

Noah checked his watch. "The Wolfes will be here in ten or fifteen minutes. Not really enough time for a game. But we have all weekend. You want to meet them when they get here? Or go get ready and meet them at dinner?"

"What time is it again?" She really wanted to spend more time with Noah.

"A little after six. We'll have drinks by the pool at six-forty-five."

"I guess I should go get ready then. If I have to wake up Timmy, he's usually not too happy about it. What should I wear to dinner?" Katie had never thought much about her wardrobe until she met Noah. Now, she liked to consult him. Was she subconsciously fishing for complements?

"We do barbecue tonight so just some capris would be perfect. Wait till you taste Dad's carne asada and Rosa's guacamole."

"Mmm, yum. My mom didn't make much Mexican food when I was growing up. I've come to really like it, now that I'm a California girl."

Noah smiled and looped his arms around her. "Cutest California girl I ever met." He pulled her close and began kissing her neck before working his way to her lips.

Several minutes later, Rosa came in the kitchen. Katie stepped back, self-conscious at being caught making out with Noah. "Okay, then. I should get going and get dressed."

At the top of the stairway, she turned left to her room. Opening the door quietly, she crossed to Timmy's portable crib. He stirred but didn't wake. She pushed her hair away from her face and gathered it in a ponytail to cool the heat generated by Noah's kisses. From the window at the back of the room, she looked out on the pool and gardens. The Davidsons came out on the terrace with another couple. The Wolfes. But where was the daughter? Just then Amanda came in view. Slim, with long blonde hair that fell almost to her waist. A short sundress showed off her perfect tan and long legs.

Katie turned away. No wonder Noah's eyes lit up when he talked about Amanda. Unless she had bad teeth or terrible acne, she was enough to turn any guy's head. Katie turned to her suitcase to find her makeup bag. It wouldn't hurt to look her best.

Chapter 14

Sliding open the back door, Katie went out to join the others on the terrace. Noah immediately left the group and came to meet her. "What happened? Are you okay? We've been waiting for you."

"Sorry. Timmy woke up cranky. Didn't you hear him crying? I finally took him in to the shower with me so I could get ready. I hope he's not going to be a problem during dinner."

"He seems okay now. Come on, I want you to meet Amanda and her parents." He took her by the elbow and led her forward.

Mrs. Davidson left the group and joined them. "Katie, I heard Timmy crying. Is everything okay now?"

"Yes, I'm so sorry we're late." She turned with Mrs. Davidson to meet Amanda. The young woman extended her hand, even more attractive in person than from Katie's window.

"What a darling little boy," Amanda said. "Will he let me hold him?"

"He's been a little fussy, so maybe later, if that's okay?"

"Oh, sure. I think we're almost ready for supper anyway. Where I work in Honduras, the youngest boy is eight. I've often thought of how wonderful it would be to work with babies. Fewer problems to deal with." She smiled. "But I love what I do now, too."

"I'm looking forward to hearing more about your life in Honduras," Katie said. "Noah tells me you work with boys off the streets."

Katie felt Mrs. Davidson's arm around her waist. "There's plenty of time to talk, isn't there, Mandy?" She patted Amanda's arm. "But first, Katie, I'd like you to meet Bill and Lydia Wolfe, longtime friends of ours."

Katie had barely said hello when Mrs. Davidson stepped away and began to direct the group to seats at an oval table where bouquets of bright yellow sunflowers and purple larkspur, multi-colored tableware, and colored napkins set a festive tone for the evening.

Half expecting a couple of mariachi musicians to suddenly appear, Katie swallowed a giggle. She scanned the terrace, the pool, and the neat flowerbeds against the back wall of the yard, amazed to find herself in yet another beautiful home. Being a pastor and an author must pay way more than she imagined. No wonder Noah looked forward to his future with his father.

The setting sun filled the western sky with bursts of pink, lavender, and blue, woven together like an intricate pastel tapestry. Music from a set of whole tone wind chimes wafted on the breeze, and the fragrance of larkspur perfumed the air. She silently gave thanks to God and bowed her head for Pastor Davidson's prayer. Seated between Noah and Amanda, with Timmy on her lap, she felt surrounded by love.

~ ~ ~

Noah had been right about Rosa's guacamole and his dad's carne asada. Comfortably full after the delicious meal, Katie relaxed and tried to follow the conversation. Again, the talk centered on church politics. She turned to Amanda. "So, the youngest boy you work with is eight. How long has he been at the home?"

"His name is Tomás, and he came right after I started working there two years ago. He had just turned six."

"And he lived on the streets?"

"Yes, slept on the street and worked in the city dump with his brother José, who's a glue addict. The first few weeks at the house, I could hardly sleep because I was so upset we couldn't take José in, too. But Michael and his wife, Rita, helped me adjust. We can't help them all, but we do what we can."

Shaking her head, Katie said, "I can't even imagine how hard that kind of life must be for those boys." Timmy, who had been restless, started to cry. Katie pulled his pacifier out of her pocket. "I think he needs a diaper change. I'll be right back. Unless you're interested in this conversation, let's sit by the pool. Save me a seat, okay?" Katie stood.

"I'm all for that," Amanda said, glancing at the men, still seated, deep in conversation.

By the time Katie returned, Amanda had staked out a couple of chairs by the pool. She motioned for Katie to join her. Two drinks sat on the table.

"These are virgin piña coladas, the only kind I drink," Amanda said.

"Thank you. That's perfect for me." With a quick glance at Noah, Katie skirted the table and sat down.

"So, how did you and Noah meet?" Amanda asked, lifting her drink.

Katie's stomach dropped. Would Amanda's questions lead to hearing the whole story of how she got pregnant? "He's an intern at the church where I work. I hadn't studied the Bible much growing up, so I went to the classes he started, and pretty soon we were good friends. He's really helped me grow in my relationship with the Lord. He's coming back here to help his father in November."

Amanda nodded and sighed. "I think that's always been their plan for him. I just didn't know it would be so soon. I hope Noah's ready to work for his father. And mother." She looked away as if she'd said something she hadn't meant to say. But just as quickly, her gaze returned to Katie. "I don't mean to pry, and you don't have to answer if you don't want to, but you and Noah are a couple, right? Is it serious?"

A blush crept up Katie's cheeks. "We're getting there. I think." Face-to-face with someone who knew Noah, she didn't want to take any missteps. Had Amanda and Noah ever been together?

"I think you're already there. Noah can't keep his eyes off you." Amanda laughed. "I'm so glad he's found someone who makes him happy. A ready-made family for him. How old is Timmy again?"

"Two months." *Here it comes*, Katie thought, preparing for rejection. "I-I was expecting him, hmm, before I met Noah. Timmy's father . . ." She trailed off, embarrassed. "Well, he and I aren't together, let's just say."

Amanda reached for Katie's hand. "I'm so sorry, Katie, I didn't mean to pry or to upset you. I can see you've had a hard time, and I'm the last person who will ever judge you for whatever happened. I had a tough go of it myself a few years ago. Two sessions in rehab for drugs and alcohol before I finally got to a support group and got right with God. No matter how far we stray, He doesn't give up on us. I'm proof of that."

"Wow, I never would have guessed. You seem so perfect. So real."

"Thanks for saying that. I'm far from perfect, that's for sure. And I've learned that being *real* is huge. With God and everyone else. It wasn't always that way. Just ask Noah."

"So, you have some history? Were you a couple?"

"Yeah, in high school. For about a year. I was still crazy about him, but he wanted to date other people so we broke up. He said we were too young to get serious. And he had a point, but it didn't help my feelings at the time. After that, I gained weight, couldn't control my acne, and kept my nose in a book. I was a mess." Amanda shook her head. "But that was a long time ago. We moved to Sacramento right before my junior year, and I got to start over. Noah told me earlier that his mom always makes him read the annual Christmas brag sheet from my parents. When I went to Honduras, he started praying for me, and he's been one of my most faithful financial supporters. I hadn't seen him for years until this trip." She laughed. "I think his looks have improved since high school."

Katie laughed. "Less hair, I'm sure, but he's got that nerdy kind of cool look about him now, doesn't he? And I can't imagine that you looked as bad as you think. You're certainly gorgeous now."

"Thanks, Katie. I finally outgrew that awkward stage, I'm glad to say. I give all the glory to the Lord for healing me from the inside out. I know who I am in Christ now, and that makes all the difference."

Before Katie could speak, she heard the sliding doors to the house open.

"Here you two are, same place I left you. We're getting out the cards. Want to play?" Noah rubbed his hands together as he approached them. "I'm feeling lucky."

"I'm in," Amanda said.

Katie inwardly cringed. More sitting around. She would have liked for Noah to ask her to go on a walk. She looked at Timmy. He had been perfect most of the evening. "I'd like to say yes, but I'm not sure Timmy will hold out much longer. I think I should turn in. Can I take a rain check?"

"Bummer! Of course I'll give you a rain check," he said, "if Amanda will be my partner."

Amanda looked at Katie. "Is that okay with you?"

"Sure, sure. It's just cards. Have fun and I'll see you at breakfast." With a quick kiss for Noah, she made her way inside and up the back steps. Sit-ups and push-ups would have to do if she wanted any exercise.

~ ~ ~

Throwing back the covers, Katie got out of bed the next morning and put on her robe. The sun was barely up, but she wanted to get to her daily Bible reading before having to deal with Timmy. The book of Ecclesiastes hadn't been her favorite, but at least today's reading would finish the book. In the dim light coming through the window, she began reading in the One-Year Bible Noah had given her, the tenth chapter. She stopped at the fourth verse. *If your boss is angry with you, don't quit. A quiet spirit can overcome even great mistakes.* Katie closed her eyes and let the words sink in, sensing the Lord's presence. *Don't quit.* She drew a deep breath. CJ wasn't her boss. But the verse had a ring that resonated with her. His angry words on Friday had cut deep and stirred up the pain inside her again. *Don't quit.* The slogan CJ lived by as a SWCC.

Katie gnawed on her thumbnail. How could she get a quiet spirit with so much hurt and anger inside? Her feelings for CJ had been real in Las Vegas. And intense. She had tried to throw off the hurt of his rejection and forgive him, but instead, she kept going in circles. He hadn't ever explained why he left her in Vegas without saying goodbye. Or why he hadn't called after he got home. He had come back into her life because of Timmy, and Timmy only. But then, a few weeks ago he'd said he cared for her. What did he mean? Tears filled her eyes.

She swiped at her tears and finished reading the day's assignment. She bowed her head. "God, help me. I want to do the right thing, to walk in the way of the wise, but I don't know how. Help me understand where I've gone wrong so I can make things right. Help me forgive CJ, and help him forgive me. Please help him to know you, Jesus, as his Savior." She opened her eyes, then quickly closed them again, and added, "And can you please take away these crazy feelings I have for him? Amen."

Closing her Bible, Katie wrestled with how to start over with CJ, and bring the secret things in their past to light. But would he be willing?

~ ~ ~

Alone in her room again on Sunday afternoon, Katie changed Timmy out of his dress clothes into shorts and a T-shirt. Frustrated with Noah's lack of attention for her, she put Timmy on his play mat and paced the room. They had barely had any time alone. And Timmy had embarrassed Noah at church this morning. Having to walk out of the church service halfway through Pastor Davidson's message, with Timmy screaming at the top of his lungs, had not gone down well. Why had Noah insisting they sit in the front row? He seemed to have no clue about how demanding a baby could be, or how difficult it was to keep them to a schedule.

With Timmy occupied on his play mat, Katie crossed to the window. Below, in the pool, Amanda swam laps. Her presentation to the congregation that morning had been a homerun. At lunch, she had been glowing, ready to get back to the job of helping homeless kids get off the streets. Instead, she and Noah had spent an hour going over fundraising strategies. Katie had barely seen him before he was off to play golf.

Turning back to Timmy, she reminded herself to be thankful. Her little guy swatted at the giraffe hanging over his head, his delighted coos filling the room with sweet sounds. She knelt and captured his feet in her hands. "You'll be walking before I know it, won't you, little guy?" A knock on the door startled her. "Come in," she called.

Noah peeked his head into the room. "Is it okay if I come in?"

She got to her feet and went to him. "You're back. Sure, come in. I was just thinking about how little I've seen of you this weekend."

"Yeah, sorry about that. It's just been so long since I had a chance to talk shop with my dad. And Bill. He used to be the administrator at the church, and he's a wealth of knowledge about everything from insurance to facility maintenance. Stuff I'll be doing once I'm done at Cornerstone." He sat down on the edge of Katie's bed.

"I thought you were going to preach and teach."

"Well, I was, but Dad now thinks it's best if I start with the nuts and bolts. Get some experience in that area. Bill will be like a mentor, sort of."

"Does that mean you'll be going to Sacramento?" Katie's heart sank. There was no way she and Timmy would see much of him if he was so far away. Was this his way of breaking off their relationship?

"No, no. Well, maybe for a couple of days. I'm not sure. Dad will let me know. First, I've got to finish up at Cornerstone and get through my last semester of seminary."

Katie sat beside him. "You've got a lot on your plate, haven't you?" She leaned her head on his shoulder. "I know you'll do well at whatever the job is. I just want you to be happy, and to be able to do the things God gifted you to do. I thought you didn't really like administrative work."

"It's not forever. I'll get back to teaching. Eventually." Noah wrapped his arm around her and lifted her chin so he could kiss her. "With you by my side, I can do anything. Right now, though, I should find out what the dinner plans are. I know we're going out but I don't know where."

Not ready to leave the comfort of his arms, she protested, "Let's get to that in a while. Tell me about your golf game." She stroked his cheek. "Who won?"

While Timmy played on the floor, Noah described his afternoon. "I made par twice, landed in a sand trap once, and lost two balls in the water. Bill won, of course. But I was a close third." He laughed. "Of course, there were only the three of us playing, but I have an excuse. I haven't golfed since I came to Cornerstone. And I certainly don't get out as regularly as those two. Dad plays a couple of times a week, and so does Bill. They've both studied with pros, too."

"At least you got some exercise," Katie said.

Chagrined, Noah confessed, "We used a golf cart, Katie."

"But at least you swing the club, right? That's exercise."

Noah bumped her shoulder with his. "I see I've come up a notch, in your eyes. How about if we play a game of pool? That's exercise. And after you trounced me yesterday, I need another shot at it. But first, let me see where we're going tonight."

"You are persistent, aren't you? But don't leave yet. I want you to help me choose what to wear." Katie crossed to the closet and pulled out a long black dress with a floral motif. "I borrowed this from Julie." She put the dress back and pulled out a black-and-white striped skirt. "And this is Ashley's. I have a white top that goes with it. If I need to nurse Timmy, this is the best outfit. But hopefully, I can nurse him right before we go, and he'll be okay for the evening. No guarantees on that, just so you know."

As she put the skirt away, Noah's arms encircled her from behind. He pulled her close and kissed her neck. She melted against him.

"I like the black one, but the other's nice, too." He turned her around. "Have I told you lately how beautiful you are?" He smoothed her hair away from her shoulder and looked deep in her eyes. "Because you are, you know?"

A blush rushed to her cheeks. "This is what I've wanted all weekend. Time alone with you." She smoothed her hand over his head. "Our lives are so busy, and my time with you is precious. And not nearly enough." She kissed him, hoping to stay in his arms a while longer.

Instead, he pulled back. "I know, I know. For me, either. But, right now . . ." He grimaced. "Well, right now, I've got to put my job and schoolwork just a little bit ahead of you and Timmy. But it won't always be that way, I promise." He dropped his arms from around her and reached for the doorknob. "Let me see where we're going and what time we're leaving. I'll come back and let you know, so you'll have plenty of time to get ready."

Disappointed, Katie clenched her hands together. "Sure. Just let me know."

Noah pulled open the door and went out.

Chapter 15

Katie shoved her bag onto the floor of the back seat of her car and turned to Noah. Clearly not happy that she was leaving him to go to the Jansen's, at least he had come out of the house to say goodbye.

"Forgive me, okay?" With her arms draped over his shoulders, Katie pressed her forehead to his and tried again to soothe his anger. "I won't stay long at CJ's. Promise." With Timmy already in the car, and her guilt at a record high, she wanted to get on the road and get the visit over with the Jansen family.

Noah pulled back. "You know I don't like it. But what can I say? Call me. Just as soon as you get home."

"I will." She got in her car and fastened the seat belt. Noah started for the house, not bothering to look back or wave.

"Let's go see your Grandma, Timmy." Katie sniffed back tears until, in the back seat, Timmy began to babble. "You're right, darling. Grandma Mary and Grandpa Tim will be thrilled to see you. And that Daddy of yours? Well, he just better watch out. I'm going to do everything I can to make him . . ." Katie stopped, trying to shut off her thoughts. But in her head, they kept going. She wanted CJ to like her again. To think the best of her instead of the worst, as he did now. Glancing in the rearview mirror, she said, "What can I say, Timmy? Your daddy and I had a huge fight, and now I'm on my way for what? More of his accusations? His insults? I don't want to fight with him." In the back seat, Timmy talked back in baby talk, and she smiled. "Yes, darling boy, for your sake, I know, I'm going to have to find a way to make peace. I need the right words." She switched to prayer. "Help me, Lord. Please. Open CJ's heart to hear and forgive me."

An hour and fifteen minutes later, Katie exited onto Highway 56 and headed east toward the Jansen's. At the top of their driveway, she stopped. Cars blocked the paved area in front of their house. Checking her rearview mirror, Katie backed down the driveway and parked on the street.

"Looks like it's a full house up there," she said as she lifted Timmy out of his car seat. Slinging the diaper bag over her shoulder, she walked up the hill. When no one answered the doorbell, she opened the door and went inside.

People crowded the backyard. Mary's family. A game of water volleyball was in full swing in the pool, and even from a distance she recognized CJ as he jumped to hit the ball. She made her way through the house and stepped outside. For what seemed like forever, she scanned the crowd, looking for a familiar face. Finally spotting Tim beside a cornhole platform, she waved. He tossed the bean bag aside and trotted over to her.

"Katie! I'm so glad to see you. I thought you couldn't make it. Mary will be so thrilled." He hugged her and Timmy and kissed her cheek. "Can I take your bag and get you something to eat? We have plenty." He eased the diaper bag off her shoulder and tossed it on a nearby chair. With his arm around her, he led her toward the outdoor kitchen where she could see people helping themselves to hot dogs, smoked salmon, and hamburgers.

Katie glanced back over her shoulder. "What about your game? I don't mean to interrupt."

"They'll wait on me. We were almost finished anyway. I want to make sure Mary knows you're here."

He didn't mention CJ. Did he know about the fight she had had with his son? Not that it mattered. She had changed her plans so she wouldn't disappoint Mary.

"There she is," Tim said, pointing at Mary. "Let me get that bowl before she drops it."

Mary came out of the house with a large bowl of salad in her arms. She spotted Katie, gave a cry of delight, and hurried to her. Tim intercepted her and grabbed the salad.

"Oh, Katie, you made it. You're here. God is so good!" She wrapped Katie and Timmy in a hug, laughing and crying at the same time. "We just started lunch. Are you hungry? I can hold Timmy while you get something to eat." Just then, a woman who could only be Mary's sister, walked up.

"This must be Katie. And Timmy," she said, draping her arm around Mary.

"Yes, and Katie, this is my sister, Patty. From Seattle. And here comes Beth. She's from Portland."

Another woman joined them. Katie looked from one woman to the other, the family resemblance unmistakable. "You're not triplets, are you?" she asked.

"Close as triplets, but actually, we're numbers two, four, and five in the family. Ben is the oldest of the five of us, and Jerry came after me," Patty said. "Mary is the baby."

How she would ever keep them all straight was beyond Katie, especially when their husbands and brothers joined the group. But soon Tim took charge and shooed them toward the lunch line.

"Katie, let me hold Timmy while you get some lunch. I'll save you a spot at the table." He took Timmy and headed for a table near the house in the shade.

Mary fell in beside Katie. "Does CJ know you're here yet? He invited a couple of his SWCC friends to join us. They're in the pool. I think I heard they're on game three. Each team has won a game, so, of course, there's a playoff game. I hope I have enough food." She laughed easily. "Tim is saving you a seat and I'll join you in a minute. Thank you again, Katie, for making the effort to come. You have made my day!" She hugged her once more before turning to go in to the house.

Katie glanced at the pool, then couldn't look away as CJ high fived a woman in a bikini. The game must be over. CJ turned and made his way to the pool steps, his arm draped over the woman's shoulders. A fist of anguish and jealousy rammed Katie's gut and she turned away, reminding herself there was no longer anything romantic between them. Wasn't she with Noah? CJ could date anyone he wanted. The voice of reason pounded in her head. She forced herself to take slow, steady breaths. But jealousy wouldn't obey her commands. Who was the woman with CJ?

Her appetite gone, Katie forced herself to put some tossed salad and mixed fruit on her plate. She turned away from the buffet table and almost collided with CJ. Water still dripped from him, and his board shorts hung so low on his hips she thought they might slip off.

"So, you came after all. Thanks, I guess." He pivoted and strode to the table where his dad held Timmy. Katie looked down at her plate. Tears pooled in her eyes. What was she doing here? After yelling at her for not coming, why was he angry that she had? Just then, she heard a familiar voice calling her name. She looked up to see Ashley.

Dashing away her tears, Katie hurried to her friend. Ashley was dripping wet, but it didn't stop Katie from giving her a one-armed hug.

"CJ said you weren't coming," Ashley said. "He wasn't too happy about it either. But here you are! Where's Timmy?"

"He's with CJ's dad." She glanced at the table where she had been invited to join Mary and Tim. It was full, now that CJ had sat down beside his dad. Katie felt her stomach drop. She wouldn't be welcome if CJ was still mad at her. And it seemed he was. "Their table's full. Can I sit with you?"

"Sure. Come with me while I get some food, and tell me

all about your weekend in Orange County. With Noah, right? Did you need the skirt I loaned you?"

"Yes, I was with Noah and his parents, and no, I ended up not needing to wear your skirt, but thanks for loaning it anyway."

"I thought for sure you and CJ would get back together. I mean, you were hot for each other in Vegas."

Katie bit her bottom lip, a blush rushing to her cheeks. She only had to be near him, and she still got overheated. She just couldn't and wouldn't do anything about the feeling. Not now. Not ever. Especially not after what he said about her putting on an act in Las Vegas.

"I-I know. I was. We were, I guess. It just didn't work out, that's all. Too many problems."

Ashley helped herself to a hamburger and as many sides as her plate would hold. "Bummer. You seemed so perfect for each other. So . . . how was your time with Noah?"

Forcing her thoughts away from what might have been with CJ, she followed Ashley. "Good, it was good. Busy. Lots of time just talking with his family. Timmy was a trooper. Except at church yesterday, when he screamed his head off."

"During the sermon? Way to go, Timmy!" Ashley found a table for them, and soon the conversation was as easy as it had ever been for Katie with her best friend.

"I've missed you, Ashley. I can't believe how we came out here together, clear across the country, and now we hardly see each other."

"I know, and I've been meaning to ask you to forgive me. I'm sorry I messed up with the rent stuff when we lived together. It killed me that you had to move out. I've been going to a support group, you know. I got in way over my head with gambling. And I just couldn't seem to quit. But that's all in the past. Dustin's been helping me, too. He won't let me near a casino."

As if hearing his name, Dustin appeared at the table and sat down with his plate of food. "Hey, Katie. Nice to see you again."

"You too." Katie said, and meant it. If what Ashley said was true, she needed to let go of her anger at Dustin. He may have been the one who introduced Ashley to gambling, but he hadn't forced her to continue until she became addicted. Hadn't God worked things out for them both when he provided a home with the Skidmore family for her, and a support group for Ashley? Just like Amanda, it seemed another friend had found hope and healing.

CJ interrupted her thoughts. "Katie, this is my sister, Lynn." She turned to see a tall, willowy young woman in a one-piece bathing suit standing next to CJ, her smile lighting her brown eyes. Not the woman with CJ in the pool.

"I'm so happy to finally meet you, Katie," Lynn said. "CJ told me all about you, and I'm already head over heels in love with Timmy. He's the cutest baby I've ever seen."

What had CJ told her? She stood to talk to Lynn. CJ excused himself and left. She glanced at the table where she had last seen Timmy with his grandfather. She didn't see either of them. "You've had a chance to hold him?"

"Oh, yes, Mom's showing him off, making sure everyone has a chance to meet him. She took him for a diaper change when I came to meet you."

Remembering how well-stocked the changing table was in the Jansen's guest room, Katie nodded. "Your mom is the best. She's wonderful with Timmy."

"She's crazy about him. Dad, too. You know, we're just about to start the tri-game competition. Will you be my partner?" Lynn asked.

"Well, sure. I guess. But what's the tri-game competition?"

"It's a Jansen family tradition when we get together. We're a competitive group. So, we play three games—

Cornhole, Texas Horseshoes, and Scrabble, one right after the other in teams of two. Three teams play at a time, one at each game. At the five-minute buzzer, we move to the next game. There's a coach at each game who keeps score. The whole thing's over in about twenty minutes for each round. Top score of all the teams wins a three-day cruise to Ensenada, Mexico, compliments of the family cash kitty we collected last time we were all together."

"Wow! That's some prize! I think I get how it works with Cornhole and Texas Horseshoes, but how does it work with Scrabble? Do you dump the board each time?"

"No. That's the crazy part. You and your teammate pick up where the last team left off. We work with whatever they left us on the board."

"This is crazy," Katie said. "But I'm in. Don't blame me if we lose at Scrabble, though. I'm not that great with spelling."

Having overheard Lynn's explanation, Dustin said. "Hey, that sounds like fun, and I've never been on a cruise." He winked at Ashley. "Want to try?"

"Why not?"

"We're in, too. Where do we sign up?"

Lynn grabbed Katie's hand and pulled her toward the house. "Follow me," she called over her shoulder.

In the house, a group of people crowded around the table in the family room. CJ stood with the woman from the pool. She hadn't bothered changing or putting a towel around herself. CJ gave her name to Tim as his partner. Midge. Katie's stomach tightened and she looked away. It was none of her business who CJ chose for his partner. But when she thought of him going on a cruise with Midge, a lump lodged in her throat that she couldn't swallow.

Finished with his administrative work, Tim got up from his seat and held a basket over his head. "Someone from each team will draw a number from the basket. That's the order your team plays in. Three teams play at a time. Who wants to draw first?

Beth's boys stepped up. Tim lowered the basket so they could draw their position number. Katie and Lynn waited until there were only three teams left to draw, including CJ and Midge, Mary's sister Beth and her husband, Frank.

"You draw, Katie. Get us a good slot, okay?" Lynn said. Katie reached into the basket and drew the number two position. "Woo-hoo! We're in the first group of players."

CJ drew next, pulling out the number ten position in the last round of play. "We can scope out the competition," he said to Midge.

Tim held up the next basket.

"Now your turn," Katie said to Lynn.

Lynn reached in the basket to find the order in which they would play the games. She opened the slip of paper. "We play Cornhole first, Scrabble second, and Texas Horseshoes last." She looked at Katie and grinned. "Perfect! Let's do this!"

After a quick high five, they made their way to the Cornhole game. The family and those yet to play had staked out territory around each game. Katie scanned the faces, relieved to see Mary holding Timmy. She picked up her four bean bags.

"We have five minutes, Katie. We each toss all our bags, then go get them at the other platform and try again from there, okay? Let's do this."

The buzzer sounded, and Katie could feel her competitive nature kick in. Out of the four bean bags, only one had gone in the hole. She waited while Lynn took her turn. Then, running to collect the bags on the other side, she turned, aimed and let go. Beside her Lynn first bag landed and slid in the hole, then a second one. "Yes!" Katie said, and let a bean bag fly. It landed on the edge of the hole a second before falling in.

It was the most exercise Katie had had all weekend, but it didn't take long to get in the rhythm of the game. When the buzzer sounded to go to the Scrabble board, the referee announced that they had racked up fourteen points. The crowd cheered as Katie and Lynn raced inside and slid into their chairs.

Katie's Scrabble tray had only three letters left, all vowels. The referee pointed to the pile of letters at the side of the board. "You can draw four more." She quickly chose her letters, excited when one of them was an 'S'. She tried to concentrate on the words already on the board, but her stomach had developed butterflies. Board games had always been a challenge for her.

She looked up to see CJ standing behind Lynn, staring at her. A slow smile spread across his face before he turned and whispered something to Midge. Katie bristled but didn't look away.

"Katie, it's your turn. Do you have anything you can use?"

Katie's gaze snapped back to her tray. She grabbed the S, holding it while she tried to focus on the words before her. She had to concentrate. Forget that CJ was staring at her. Finally, she recognized the team before her had placed a word she could make plural with her S. She quickly put it down, along with a K, I, and D, to make the word 'SKID.' She counted the points for the two words. Twenty!

Katie made two more plays before the buzzer sounded. Relieved to be done, she ran after Lynn to the Texas Horseshoes game. As they had with Cornhole, they went from one side of the playing field to the other, throwing as quickly and accurately as they could. When the final buzzer sounded, Lynn had put four washers in the hole and Katie had added five.

"That one was tough. The washers kept sliding off the

box." Katie walked with Lynn back inside. "It was fun though. I burned off some energy for sure."

"Me too. You're a super sport, Katie. Cool under pressure."

"Thanks. I didn't feel so cool trying to play Scrabble." She laughed. "And thanks for asking me to be your partner. I guess I should see how Timmy's doing. I hope your mom isn't getting tired of holding him."

"Not Mom. She's loving it."

By the time Katie found Mary and nursed Timmy, the last round of players were a third of the way through the competition. She made her way to the Texas Horseshoes game in time to see CJ make a perfect shot. The buzzer sounded as Midge's coin slid off the platform. Even so, together they had made fifteen points for their team at the one game. As they moved through the crowd into the house for the Scrabble game, Katie hung back. This would be the final game of the competition, and as soon as the results were in, she needed to get home. She had seen more than enough of CJ Jansen and his new girlfriend.

Chapter 16

The game results were in. Katie and Lynn had tied with Dustin and Ashley for third place. Mary's two nephews—Beth's boys—had won second, and CJ and Midge had claimed first place. Through the crowd, Katie caught sight of CJ hugging Midge, and ground her teeth. All around her there were high fives and pats on the backs from the family. The SWCC guys razzed Dustin and CJ as Tim passed out ribbons. Mary handed Katie a gift card and gave her a hug before turning to give the cruise information to Midge.

In Katie's arms, Timmy's head rested against her breast. She pocketed the gift card and slung the baby's diaper bag over her shoulder. Hoping to slip away unnoticed, she went out the front door. Good manners had been drilled into her as a kid, but she just couldn't face Mary and Tim. Not feeling so vulnerable. She would send a thank-you note as soon as she got home.

Outside, she maneuvered between cars, making her way to the street.

"Katie. Wait!"

She turned to see CJ. Her stomach rioted. "Oh. Hi. I need to . . . Timmy's really worn out. We have to go . . . sorry." She turned, and took two steps before CJ stopped her, his hand on her shoulder.

"Not so fast." He parked himself in front of her, blocking her way.

She met his stare, her heart pounding. "What?"

"I'm going out to Virginia for a few weeks, so I won't be over for a couple Saturdays."

That was all he wanted to say? Katie exhaled sharply. No apology for saying such mean things to her on Friday? No gratitude after all the effort she made to come meet his family? Her face flushed with anger, and just as quickly she heard a still small voice in her heart whisper, *a quiet spirit can overcome even great mistakes.* Taking a deep breath, she asked, "Will you help me get Timmy in the car?"

CJ looked around as he reached for Timmy. "Where'd you park?"

"On the street. There wasn't room up here by the time I arrived."

They walked down the hill in silence. Katie prayed for the right words to say. For words that would restore their friendship. At the car, she unlocked the door, expecting CJ to buckle Timmy in and leave. Instead, he leaned against the car and stared at her.

"Did you have a good time with Noah?"

Her face grew hot at the look on CJ's face. It was as if the need to know was pulled from the deepest, darkest place in him. A place he didn't allow himself to go very often. It made her feel heady and heartbroken at the same time.

"I . . . Yes. His family, well, they're very different from yours. They sit and talk a lot." A smile escaped. "They don't play games like Cornhole or have crazy competitions with buzzers going off, and referees shouting, and cheering mobs screaming."

CJ cocked his head a second before a laugh escaped him. Katie's heart flip-flopped. Suddenly, they were back on good terms, as if their fight had never happened.

Running his hand over his head, he said, "What are you saying? You think my family's strange?" A sloppy grin lit up his face.

The CJ she knew and loved was back, and the feeling brought such joy to her heart she could hardly contain it. She started to laugh. "No question about it! But wonderful, too. I had a blast with your sister. And everyone. They're special people, CJ. You're very lucky. Really."

He took a deep breath. "So, you're glad you came?"

"Yes. I am." She looked down, nervously clutching her hands together and praying for courage to say what was in her heart. "And CJ, I'm so sorry I said those mean, hurtful things to you on Friday. Your parents didn't mess up raising you. I never should have said that. You're, well, you're . . . ." She looked away, a blush rushing to her cheeks. She had left Noah only a few hours ago with a promise to stay only a short time with the Jansens, and here she was about to make a fool of herself with CJ. How did he do it? Whenever she was with him, she lost all reason.

His fingers brushed her cheek and lifted her chin. "I'm sorry, too, Katie. Let's leave it at that for now, okay? When I get back, let's talk. I mean, really talk, okay?" At her nod, he dropped his hand, opened the car door, and strapped Timmy in his car seat.

"I'll catch you later," he said and walked back up the driveway.

~ ~ ~

Two weeks turned into three as the month of September sped by with CJ in Virginia and Katie working every chance she got to keep up with her design projects.

"At least he texted," Katie said under her breath as she rooted through her drawer for her belt. The gift from CJ caught her eye and she lifted it out of the drawer, once again shaking it gently. Their last conversation echoed in her mind. He wanted to talk. Katie's breath hitched and a familiar flutter tickled her stomach. She missed him.

Tossing CJ's gift back in her drawer, she pulled out her belt. The church's steak dinner event would start in a half hour. While Timmy played on his play mat, she looped the belt around the waist of her black dress pants. She was hunting in the closet for her black flats when her phone rang.

"Hi," CJ said. "We're finally back and I just finished putting my gear away. Any chance I can see you and Timmy tonight?"

Katie's heartbeat sped up. "I was just thinking about you. I'm so glad you're back. We've missed you."

"Yeah? I missed you, too."

Katie sighed. "Actually, this isn't a good night. I've got to be at the church all evening. It's the men's steak dinner and I have to help with prep and serving. The women wait on the men." She laughed. "Nothing new there, right?"

"What are you doing with Timmy?"

"He's coming with me. Between the sling and his car seat, he'll be one of the guys." She laughed, but it sounded hollow, even to her ears. Noah had wanted her to get a sitter. Her budget was tight since it was the end of the month, so she had declined. When he hadn't offer to pay, she told him she could work and handle Timmy, too.

"Well, why don't I watch him?" CJ said. "I was hoping to see you, too, but one of you is better than none, I guess."

"Oh, that would be perfect. Noah will be thrilled. He'd put a lot of time and energy into this event." *And wanted very much to impress his father with how well organized and attended it was.* "Are you sure, though? You're not too worn out? I should be back by nine-thirty or so."

"When do you want me?" His voice had lost its boyish excitement.

"How soon can you come?"

"I'm ready to leave now. I can be there in twenty."

"That's perfect," she said again. "Thanks, CJ. Thanks. This really helps me a lot. I'll see you soon."

On the floor on his tummy, Timmy rolled onto his back

and gave an excited laugh. Katie knelt to pick him up. "Your daddy's going to be so proud of you, young man."

Timmy smiled and cooed as if he understood exactly what she'd said and who was coming. Katie put him on his play mat again and resumed searching for her flats. But her heartbeat had picked up speed.

CJ was back in town.

~ ~ ~

Four hours later, Katie was worn out. And incredibly grateful that CJ was taking care of Timmy. She had been assigned to wait on three tables of hungry men, including the head table with Pastor Davidson and Noah. As she finished collecting the empty dessert plates, she bent and whispered in Noah's ear, "I am so proud of you. You and your dad were super!" Adding Noah's plate to the stack already in her hand, she took the dishes to the church kitchen.

At the dishwasher, Julie took the plates. "We're almost done here, Katie. Why don't you head home? See how CJ got along with Timmy."

"Thanks, Julie. This was fun, but yeah, I'm curious about how the boys did. And I'll be happy to get off my feet and have some time with CJ." Grabbing her purse out of a closet, she went out the back door of the church and got in her car. Her tummy had butterflies again.

At the house, Katie was surprised to see Ashley's car parked on the street. She opened the screen door and went in to the house. Timmy's crying sent her into an immediate panic. She rushed to the family room and pulled up short. CJ was sitting beside Midge, who was holding a very unhappy baby.

"What happened? Why's he crying?" A quick glance told her that Dustin and Ashley were also keeping CJ company. "This is the worst time to get Timmy all stirred up. He'll be a bear to get to sleep."

CJ stood and lifted Timmy out of Midge's arms. "Calm down, Katie. He just started crying. They just stopped by ten minutes ago. Timmy's been fine all evening."

"Yeah, Katie, we dropped by to see how CJ was doing." Ashley came to stand by Katie. "Love this penguin outfit on you, by the way." She laughed. "Bet all the guys wanted you waiting on their table."

Katie made a conscious effort to relax and laugh with Ashley. Deep down she knew she was overreacting, but seeing Midge sitting so close to CJ had sent her pulse racing. She had been counting on coming home to a baby in bed and some time alone with CJ. The realization of how much she had been wanting to be with him sent a blush to her cheeks.

"I'll take him, CJ. It's past time for both of us to be in bed." She took Timmy from CJ, but couldn't meet his gaze. "You four go wherever it is you were planning on going. It's still early for you guys." She took several steps toward her room before turning back. "Thanks for watching him. I'll see you tomorrow." Without waiting for a reply, she hurried to her room. Their voices faded. Laying Timmy on the changing table, Katie hung her head. CJ and Midge had been partners at his house on Labor Day. Now she was helping him babysit. The writing was on the wall. He had moved on. She had to, too. For Timmy's sake, they needed to be friends. She changed Timmy's diaper and sleeper, all the while feeling as if she had been kicked in the gut. When she heard her name, she jumped. CJ stood at the door to her room.

"I thought you left," she said, hope making her voice raspy. *Was he ditching Midge?*

"I wanted to make sure you and Timmy are okay before I leave." He took a step into the room. "And let you know I gave him two of those bottles you left, but he might be hungry again. Oh, and I changed him once." As he said it, the sound of the garage door being activated filled the room.

Brad and Julie were home. "Guess that's my cue. I'll see you tomorrow." He rubbed the back of his neck and turned to leave.

"CJ?" Katie couldn't think what to say. She only knew she wanted him to stay.

He waited.

Katie picked up Timmy and walked to CJ. "I thought maybe we could talk."

"Well, maybe tomorrow, okay? It's after ten, and I'm running on East Coast time, so . . ."

Her hopes sinking, Katie said, "Sure, sure. We can talk tomorrow. Get some rest, and thanks again for watching Timmy."

For a moment, he lingered. Then he nodded and left her alone.

His voice reached her from the family room, talking to Brad. Julie poked her head in to Katie's room a few moments later. "You doing okay? Looks like you and CJ had a little time to talk. How did it go?"

"Ashley and Dustin were here with him when I got here. And Midge. We didn't have a chance to talk at all. And now he's going out with her. They're together, I guess." She rubbed her left ear, which had begun to hurt.

Julie silently urged Katie to sit in the glider chair. She knelt in front of her. "You seem depressed about it. I mean, I thought you wanted nothing to do with CJ, and loved Noah. Am I missing something?"

Cuddling Timmy, Katie sniffed. "No. I do love Noah. But that's the problem. I love CJ, too. I can't seem to help it. They're both so different, though. You know Noah. He's steadfast. And safe. CJ . . ." She huffed out a sigh. "CJ isn't. Safe, I mean. When I'm with him, it's a constant wrestling match in my heart and head. There's chemistry between us. It's just there, you know? But he's not even a Christian. How can I think of being with him? I can't. I just can't. I've come too far in my walk with Jesus to even think about being unequally yoked. Not that anything like marriage is even on CJ's radar. I don't know what he's thinking beyond how he's going to get custody of Timmy."

"Is that what he wants? To take Timmy away from you?"

"Yes. No. I honestly don't know at this point. We haven't talked about it for weeks, so I don't know what he's thinking anymore. And it looks like finding some time to really talk about what's going on with us is never going to happen. Not with Midge in his life."

Julie stood. "You don't know that for sure, do you? Let me take Timmy while you get out of those clothes. You're as worn out as I am, so we need to get to bed." She took Timmy. "Did CJ give him a bottle?"

"Yes, two, he said." Katie undressed while Julie held Timmy. Putting on her robe, she reached for him. "But I need to nurse him. It will help both of us sleep better, I hope." She sat down in the rocker again and turned Timmy to nurse.

Julie patted her knee. "Things will look different in the morning. At least I hope. We're with you in prayer on this, Katie, and you know we want God's best for you. There's a lot to be said for you and CJ trying to make something work, since he's Timmy's father. But Noah loves you, and he's a man of God. Maybe that counts for more than chemistry. Keep asking and trusting God. He has a plan for you."

"I know he does. Thanks, Julie, for your prayers. And for everything. You're a special gift from God, and I don't know what I would do without you."

"I feel the same about you. Get some sleep. I'll see you in the morning."

She turned off the light and closed the door behind her, leaving Katie in the dark.

~ ~ ~

The next morning, Katie woke at eight-thirty with her ear throbbing.

"Julie, I have to get to Urgent Care," she said, coming into the kitchen. "My ear is an eight or nine on the pain scale. Do you think you can watch Timmy until CJ arrives? He should be here in fifteen or twenty minutes. I'm hoping to get in and out, get a prescription filled, and get home to see him."

"Sure, I can watch Timmy. Is he still asleep?"

"No, he's awake and in his crib. I've already fed and changed him, and I should be back within an hour. I hope."

Two and a half hours later, Katie arrived home, frustrated and feeling lousy. Brad came in from the garage for lunch as she filled a glass with water.

"I can't believe how long I had to wait. The room was totally full of people waiting to be seen. I heard the receptionist finally call in another doctor to help after I'd been there forever. Unbelievable! Then I had to wait another twenty-five minutes for the prescription to be filled. I can't believe I didn't get to see CJ."

"It goes like that sometimes. But I'm sorry you missed him. He left you a note, at least," Julie said, handing her the note. "He said he's going to visit his grandmother in Riverside for the rest of the day."

"I didn't even know he has a grandmother living that close," Katie murmured under her breath. How many more things did she have to learn about the father of her baby?

"She's not in the best of health, so the family's talking about moving her to assisted living," Julie said.

Katie nodded and swallowed two pills. Finishing the entire glass of water, she opened CJ's note and read it quickly. She looked at Julie. "He wants to see Timmy and me next Friday. Did he say anything to you about what he's got planned?"

"Just that he hoped it would work out."

"He told me he's going to be gone again in a couple weeks, this time to Kentucky," Brad said. "So, he was hoping for some extra time when he's in town."

Katie chewed on her lower lip, stuffing her disappointment. "What's in Kentucky?"

"MEATS. Stands for Maritime External Air Transportation System." Brad took a bite of his sandwich and finished chewing before explaining. "I don't know how much CJ has told you about what the SWCCs do, but they work with us a lot to get us in and out of the places we need to go. They specialize in heavy weapons and fast boats, and this thing in Kentucky is one of the most high-risk training exercises they do. You see, sometimes the boats need to be positioned for special missions with us. So, they fly the boats in by helicopter. Before the mission even starts, it's the SWCCs job to secure the boat to the helicopter with special rings. After the mission, they do the same thing. And both ways, they do it while the helicopter hovers. It's right over their heads. I mean, there's like two feet between them and the copter. That's the kind of thing you have to practice."

"Oh, my gosh, they don't stay in the boat while the helicopter's in flight, do they?"

"No, once the boat's dropped, we all use a short ladder to get in and out of the boats. But only the SWCCs drive the boats. That's their job."

Katie tried to picture it, and felt a chill go down her back. What if the helicopter became unstable as it hovered? Brad had experienced a helicopter going down when it came under heavy fire on his first deployment; Julie had told her about it during one of their talks. Fortunately, the SEALs had already been on the ground and away from the thrashing blades when it happened. But hearing about the close call had been enough to give Julie nightmares for weeks.

"Sounds really dangerous," Katie said.

"Yup. Comes with the job." He shrugged. "Take anything that most of us think of as fun, let the Navy get a hold of it, it's no longer fun. Like skydiving. CJ's signed up for that in a couple months, too."

Katie looked at the salad on her plate, her appetite waning. She had always wanted to go skydiving. But Brad's words reminded her that what he and others like him and CJ did was serious, life-threatening business. Determined to pray more for Brad and CJ, she forced herself to eat. "I'll text him this afternoon and tell him we can come."

~ ~ ~

On Friday morning, Noah dropped by the house. His weekday visits had thinned out, mainly due to his seminary studies, he had reassured her several times. Katie had her doubts, especially since Noah only stopped by if Timmy was napping. Seated beside him on the sofa, she pulled up the computer file for the new design she had created for Pastor Dale.

"What do you think?" she asked. "This sermon series follows the *Life Together* one, so I wanted the design to have the same feel." On the screen, Katie's design included people from every age group walking together through the words *Passing the Faith*. "Pastor Dale says he's starting the series in two weeks, so I've got to hustle to get the banner out today. The other promotional stuff can be handled in the office."

"The banner should have been on the street already," Noah said. "I thought you met with him weeks ago to get the schedule of events. Why didn't you have this ready?"

Katie bristled at his criticism. "I met with him. But he's had trouble deciding what to title this series. You should know better than anyone that he has a lot on his plate. What was I supposed to do? It's Friday. At least people will see it this weekend."

"My dad would never stand for that kind of procrastination. No wonder Cornerstone's not a mega-church."

Katie's jaw dropped. "And your dad has a staff of how many? A hundred? Pastor Dale has one associate pastor and three directors plus some part-time people. And since when is becoming a mega-church the goal?"

"Numbers are important, Katie."

"No, people are important." Katie closed her computer and got up. "Which is why I used them in this design. Not that you really looked at it."

Noah stood too, but she had moved out of his reach. "Katie, Katie, I'm sorry. Your design is wonderful. I'm just on edge because I only have a few more weeks to wrap things up at Cornerstone. I've tried my best to please Pastor Dale and do a good job, but it doesn't seem as if I've made much of an impact."

At the kitchen table, Katie put down her computer and sighed. "It's okay. I understand. By the time Pastor Dale starts the series, you'll be packing to go home."

"Speaking of packing, do you think you can help me? I want to be out of my apartment so I can get home for Thanksgiving."

"Okay, sure, I should be able to do that. And you have made an impact. Just look at how my faith has grown. And I know there are lots of others who feel the same way."

Noah looped his arms around her. "You're my star student, no doubt about that. How about we go to the movies tonight? I'll spring for a sitter for Timmy."

Katie slumped against him. "I can't. Timmy has a date with his grandparents tonight. It's been a while since they've seen him."

Dropping his arms from around her, Noah turned away. "Ever think about having them take care of Timmy?

At least part of the time? CJ's his father. He should have some responsibility besides showing up here every once in a while." He turned back. "You want to build your design business, don't you? If you didn't have to spend so much time with Timmy, you could."

Katie gaped at him, wounded by his words. "Wow. I didn't see *that* coming. Are you saying you want me to give up Timmy for design work? Let someone else raise my child? I love Mary and Tim, but they've never even hinted that they want any more responsibility for Timmy than being his grandparents. I'm sure they think he belongs with me. I'm making enough for Timmy and me to live on. He's not complaining. Why should you?"

"I'm thinking of you, Katie. Your future. Our future. I've been thinking we have one together, but maybe I'm deluding myself. Timmy's got a father. Why not make him own up?"

"I can't believe we're having this conversation." Katie paced a few steps away and back. Her mind raced, her thoughts colliding. Was Noah saying he didn't want her if Timmy had to be part of the deal? Could she ever consider giving up her son? Was that what was best for him, to be with CJ and his family? Tears filled her eyes. The Jansens could give Timmy the world. What did she have? A rented room, an old car. She didn't even own the bed she slept in or Timmy's either. And if Noah didn't want him . . . ?

Katie stopped in front of Noah. "Is that what you really want? For me to give up Timmy?"

He took her face gently in his hands and looked her in the eye. "Look. I know he means the world to you. I'm just saying it's complicated. Maybe it's time to find out what the Jansens want. How can we build a future together for us when we don't have a plan for Timmy?"

A fresh rush of tears spilled down her cheeks.

"Don't cry. I didn't mean to make you cry."

Katie sniffed and wiped at her cheeks. "You're right. I have to face reality." Dr. Chang's words came racing back: *The innocent suffer for the guilty.* "I'll find out tonight what CJ's thinking we should do."

"Atta girl," Noah said. "I know it's hard to know what's best. I'll be praying for you."

Chapter 17

"Would you and Timmy be willing to stay overnight?" Mary's voice on the other end of the phone line sounded upbeat and happy. Katie frowned, uncertain, as Mary continued. "Tim's birthday is in a few days, and it would really be special if he could celebrate it with you and Timmy."

"Well, I guess we could," Katie answered, thinking of how fond she'd become of Tim, with his prayers of blessing for Timmy every time they were together. This would be a chance for her to pray blessings over him. With more enthusiasm, she said, "I guess you've got everything both Timmy and I need, so yes, that would be lovely."

"Okay, CJ will pick you up at four."

A little before four, with her nerves in overdrive, Katie stuffed her blue swimsuit into her backpack on top of her pajamas, workout clothes, and toiletries. Maybe she could get up early and hike before breakfast. For sure, she planned on getting in some laps in the pool. Anything to stall the conversation she needed to have with CJ.

Timmy's clothes were packed, enough for three days at least. Not that they would stay that long, Katie assured herself. Could she pretend everything was fine for even an hour, let alone overnight? For Tim's sake, she would do her best to squelch her worries and put on a happy face. But what if CJ wanted custody of Timmy? He had threatened as much at the hospital, hadn't he? Was his relationship with Midge serious? Questions she couldn't answer wouldn't stop pounding in her head.

The doorbell rang and she jumped. Relieved when Julie answered it, she zipped her pack and left her room.

In the family room, CJ was kneeling beside Timmy's car seat talking to his son. He looked up when she came out of her room and came to take her bags. She couldn't meet his eyes.

His gaze narrowed. "You okay? It's just my house, not the executioner's chair," he joked, giving her face his full attention.

"I'm fine." She crossed to Timmy and picked up the car seat. "See you tomorrow, Julie."

Julie gave her a hug. "Trust God, honey," she whispered.

Katie nodded and walked to the door without looking back.

CJ drew alongside Julie. "Something I'm missing here?"

Julie shook her head. "Have a good weekend."

Katie stopped at CJ's truck and waited with Timmy. She had managed to pull herself together, and was anxious to get the weekend over with. "He'll probably fall asleep as soon as you start the truck. He's overdue for his nap." She left Timmy, went to the passenger side door and got in without waiting for CJ's help.

When he had secured Timmy's car seat in the base and stowed the bags, CJ climbed into the truck. "All set?" he asked.

Out of the corner of her eye, she caught him staring at her. "Yes." She turned to look out the window.

They rode in silence. In the back seat, Timmy issued a stream of darling baby sounds. Katie clasped her hands in her lap. *Stop it*, she admonished herself. *CJ hasn't mentioned custody for weeks. Nothing's been settled. He probably doesn't even want him.* But she knew in her heart it wasn't true. CJ was crazy about his little guy, as he called him.

"I'll let you off at the front door with Timmy, then be in with the bags," CJ said as he pulled up the drive. He shut off the engine and lifted Timmy out of his car seat. "Mom has really been looking forward to this," he said as he handed Timmy to her and opened the door to the house.

Instead of going back for the bags, CJ walked with her into the house. "I think Mom's probably in the family room," he said, leading the way at a brisk pace.

Katie had to trot to keep up with him. *Where's the fire?* He stopped short in the doorway of the room, and Katie almost crashed into him. Instead, she gave a long, low scream and covered her mouth. Her mother stood in the family room beside Mary. Bursting into tears, she rushed forward with Timmy. "I don't believe this," she cried, crushing against her mother and sobbing her heart out.

Finally getting her tears under control, Katie pulled away.

"So, this is my grandson," Peggy Ryan said, her face wet with tears, too. "He is even more darling in person." Taking him from Katie, she didn't blink when he started to cry. "He's got separation anxiety, doesn't he?" She stroked Timmy's cheek. "I'm not your momma, am I, sweet boy? But you and I are going to get to know each other. It's okay." She bounced him up and down.

"I can't believe this," Katie said, turning to hug Mary. "Thank you, both of you," she said, turning next to hug Tim. Where was CJ? Had he been in on the planning?

"Are the waterworks over yet?" CJ asked from the doorway, grinning ear to ear. He had the diaper bag and Katie's backpack in his hands. "Your mom's in Lynn's room, so I'll put these in the guest room, where you stayed before."

Katie followed him. "I don't know if this was your idea or your mom's, but thank you. This means the world to me." She looked away, tears filling her eyes again. She swiped them away. "The timing couldn't be more perfect."

He set down the bags and turned to her. "You're welcome. I'm just glad it all worked out. Your mom had to do a lot of rearranging and call in some favors to get the details worked out so that your dad had the care he needed for a few days, but she was in from the minute I called her."

"So, you put this together?"

"Well, I started it, at least. It dawned on me the day you put the swing together that you missed her, and she probably was feeling left out of things. FaceTime is great, but it's not like holding your grandson in person. Mom helped with the details after I called your mom and got her to say yes."

Without conscious thought, Katie launched herself at CJ, hugging him. When his arms wrapped around her and pulled her in close, she reveled in how good he felt.

Until she remembered Midge.

She pulled back and stepped away. CJ's arms dropped. "Thank you, CJ. I'm just so grateful." She turned to go.

"Katie?"

She turned back.

"Do you think, well, would you be willing to go for a walk later? After supper, maybe after we get Timmy in bed? We could walk down to the park."

"I'd like that." Katie smiled, feeling optimistic for the first time in hours. "I'll need the exercise after whatever your mom's got cooking. It smells delicious."

"Sunday pot roast, she calls it. It cooks while we go to church."

"I didn't think you went to church."

"I went with you, didn't I?" CJ's gaze dropped momentarily to the carpet. "But no, I haven't gone for a long time." He looked up and grinned, mischief lighting his eyes. "But I still come over here for the pot roast."

A longing swelled in her spirit, a desire so great for CJ to come back to God, she couldn't keep silent. "I wish you believed in Jesus, CJ. I wish that more than anything."

CJ shoved his hands into his pockets and smiled.

"You're not alone in that one. I hear you, and thanks for your concern."

There was so much more she wanted to say, but couldn't. She knew this man. They'd been intimate. But did she really know him at all? Would she ever? "I'd better see how things are going with Mom and Timmy."

CJ smiled. "Enjoy. You've got all weekend."

Resisting the urge to hug him again, Katie left the room.

~ ~ ~

"Your pot roast was delicious," Peggy said, as they got up from the table. "Some of the best I've had. I'd love to have your recipe."

"I'll write it out for you," Mary said. "Why don't you and Katie sit by the pool for a bit with Timmy. Enjoy that beautiful sunset. I'll make some decaf if you'd like. CJ can help me clear the table and do the dishes since Tim had to go check on one of his patients. Won't you, CJ?"

"Sure. I can do that." He slid open the back door for Katie and her mom. "What do you want in your coffee, Mrs. Ryan?"

"Oh, honey, call me Peggy. Everyone does. And I take it black."

"Same as Katie, I guess then. Strong and black."

Katie's head shot around and caught his smile. She smiled back. "You're welcome to join us, you know?" She nodded toward the kitchen. "After you help your mom, that is." A flirtatious smile curved her lips.

CJ winked and smiled back. "Thanks, I'll bring the coffee right out. I'll make sure we're not too long in here." He slid the door shut behind them.

Katie strolled to a chaise lounge near the pool, sat down and stretched out, her heart doing a funny flip-flop from the encounter with CJ. The sunset lit the sky in layers of spectacular color, and her anxiety melted away. Surely they could work something out about Timmy. CJ had held her close in the guest room, molding her body against his. What good would it do to deny how good it felt? How right. Katie sighed. Had she ruined her chance to have a relationship with CJ by falling in love with Noah? What did God want for her? For them?

"That family certainly knows how to have fun," Peggy said.

Katie smiled, startled from her thoughts. "Well, who wouldn't laugh at the stories you told about life in the South? I hadn't ever heard some of those about my great, great grandfather. Did he really wear a skunk hat and always smell like one?"

"Oh, yes, that one was true. The one about your grandmother? She denied that to her dying day."

Hearing her mother's soft Southern accent and watching her enjoy Timmy was like a balm to her soul. "I'm so grateful you came to visit, Mom. CJ and his parents really kept me in the dark about it. They. Are. Amazing. You like them, don't you?"

"I do, honey. Timmy couldn't have a better father and grandparents. I can see why you, well, you know, you gave in to him in Las Vegas."

Katie's face heated. They had never really talked about the circumstances that led to her becoming pregnant. She couldn't justify what she had done with CJ, but Katie felt better knowing she had fallen for someone her mother liked. The sound of the sliding door interrupted her thoughts.

CJ held a large tray in both hands. "Here you are, ladies. Two cups of strong, black decaffeinated coffee. And two of Mom's salted caramel brownies." He looked at Katie and winked. "With ice cream on the side. Do you want me to hold Timmy while you dig in?" He put the tray on the table next to Katie and reached for Timmy.

"This is perfect," Katie said, savoring the aroma of the coffee. Glancing at CJ, she murmured, "You remembered. Ice cream on the side."

Every sight, every sound faded away, leaving her alone with CJ. Back in Vegas. Fully alive in his arms. She tore her gaze away, embarrassed.

CJ cleared his throat and stepped back. "Can I get you anything else?"

"Just you and your sweet momma joining us would be wonderful," Peggy said. "We shouldn't be enjoying this gorgeous evening all on our own."

"I'll do what I can," he said and left with Timmy.

Katie sipped her coffee, enjoying the strong, bitter taste. She had been content all evening. But now she wanted to get Timmy bathed and in bed so she could be with CJ. Alone. Her pulse wouldn't settle and her stomach had a bad case of butterflies. She would have to be careful, she warned herself. She had given in to his charm before. Feeling as vulnerable as she did, she could easily fall for him and give in to him again. *And would that be so bad?* Refusing to answer, she set down her cup and reached for the brownies. "Here, Mom. Dig in." She handed a plate with a neat square brownie in the center to her mom, then took her own. "These look amazing, don't they? Mary is a fabulous cook and baker. I don't care about the calories. Not tonight." She took a big bite, closed her eyes and savored the perfect combination of chocolate, salt and caramel. "Oh, yeah, I'll walk this off later," she said as she set down the brownie and reached for the bowl of ice cream.

~ ~ ~

At tubby time, Peggy surprised Katie with a monogramed hooded bath towel for Timmy. "I wanted to get him a little something, and my friend Lulu said these are always welcome."

"I love it, Mom, thanks. He'll be using this for years. I've been meaning to ask, who's taking care of Dad?"

"Your brothers are taking turns. Once I found out which weekend I was coming here, they got together and worked out a schedule. Even Owen is helping."

A picture of her nephew flashed through her mind. Her brother Ray's son. At just fourteen years old, he already knew he wanted to be a youth pastor. He had even learned to play guitar so he could be in the praise band. "That's wonderful. Owen is special, isn't he? I think God's put a servant's heart in him, and he's going to use him down the road even more than he is now."

After his bath, Katie nursed Timmy while Peggy chatted. "This sure is a beautiful house. CJ is a dreamboat. I think Mary's hoping you two will get together. I see you looking at each other. There's something still cooking. Does Mary know you have feelings for Noah?"

It was as if a fire hose had doused her. Katie took in a deep breath. "I think so." She didn't want to talk about Noah when she was getting ready to talk with CJ. Her mom wouldn't leave it alone.

"Does she like him?"

"They haven't met. So, not sure, Mom. She doesn't ask me about Noah, or talk about CJ. She comes over to Julie's to see Timmy. While I work, she watches him. Or helps with the laundry. She always brings us goodies. Some of the time, Tim comes with her, too, and he always prays a blessing over Timmy before they leave."

"That is so kind of him."

"Mom, I'm going to put Timmy down now and go for a walk. I'll see you in the morning, okay?"

"Oh, sure, honey. I'm plenty tired. It's been a long day. But exciting, that's for sure." She kissed Timmy good night and hugged Katie before turning to the door. "I'll just say good night to Mary before I turn in. Enjoy your walk."

When she was gone, Katie spent an extra few minutes hugging and kissing Timmy, trying to calm her nerves. A knock on the door startled her. "Come in."

CJ walked into the room. "Thought I'd say good night to my son."

"I'm sure he would love that," she said, and handed Timmy to him so she could go change.

~ ~ ~

The walk to the park was brisk, just what she needed to calm her nerves. CJ led her through the neighborhood while he entertained her with some of his high school escapades. "I've got my own place in Mira Mesa now with two of the guys on my team, but I come home to see my old stomping grounds every couple of weeks. And enjoy Mom's cooking and their spa." They turned a corner. "It's just up this hill and we're there," CJ said. "You keeping up okay or am I going too fast?"

"No, this feels great. I might have to take up walking late at night like this more often. It's so peaceful. I still haven't picked out a jogging stroller for Timmy. Guess I should put that higher on my priority list. Maybe we'd both sleep better."

At the top of the hill, CJ steered her right. They walked down a slope to the parking lot next to a kiddie playground. The park spread out behind a small building housing restrooms. "See that ball field?" he asked, pointing across a wide expanse of grass. "The path we're standing on makes a circle around it. We could do a mile if we walk or jog the path three times. Are you game? The walk here was a good warm-up."

"Let's do it. I love to jog. It clears my head."

They set off together, and whether CJ was slowing his pace, she didn't know, but she kept up easily. Along the way, she noticed signs that said VITA COURSE 2000. Each sign had instructions for using a piece of exercise equipmen near it. At the end of their third lap, Katie leaned over with her hands on her knees, winded. "Guess I'm not as ready for jogging as I thought. That felt good, but I don't want to overdo it. Some of those exercise stations looked inviting, though."

"You just had a baby a few weeks ago. It's going to take a while to get everything back to normal, you know? Want to walk back to the bars and do pull-ups? Or, we could try the beam walk or vaulting bar."

"The beam first," Katie said. "That's easy enough." But within minutes of walking forward and backward on the bar, CJ challenged her to walk the length of it on her hands, and demonstrated how easily he could do it. Katie laughed at his antics, and gave it a try. When she started to fall, he caught her feet and steadier her.

"I'm impressed. I see you've got gymnastics in your arsenal of tricks."

Huffing, Katie said, "A long time ago. I haven't done handstands in forever. I think we should move on."

At the bars, he easily beat her, doing fifty pull-ups without breaking a sweat. But she got him at the vaulting beam when she put one leg on the bar and stretched so she was almost doing a split.

When she was feeling pleasantly tired, CJ suggested the swings on the kiddie playground. In minutes, they were competing to see who could go highest. When CJ jumped from his swing, Katie followed and found herself rolling on the ground among the wood shavings.

Laughing so hard she could hardly talk, she finally got to her feet, staggering but having fun.

"Looks like you've had something besides ice cream on the side," he said. "Let's get some water, then talk." He led the way to a water fountain on the side of the restroom building. "The bathrooms are locked at night, so if you have to go, there are some bushes over there. I'll stand guard."

"Where?" Katie asked after she finished taking a long drink of water. "I do need to go."

CJ pointed to a spot that was at least somewhat secluded. He bent to drink.

When she finished, she walked with CJ to a couple of picnic tables on the far side of the kiddie playground. Her nerves, steady and calm during the workout, kicked into gear. She had wanted this talk. But now she was scared. She sat down and put her feet against the nearby boulder. CJ sat beside her.

"I've got a suggestion for how we conduct this talk," he said. "Let's play a game of rock, paper, scissors. If I win, we do it my way."

"And if I win?"

"Go at it any way you like."

Chapter 18

"Looks like I win. Paper covers rock," CJ said.

"Best two out of three?" Katie countered.

"Not a chance." CJ lifted a small stick from the picnic table, turning it in his hands as he talked. "Okay, here's the idea. I learned this from my folks who learned it in some marriage course or something. We take turns asking a question, and the person who's holding the stick gets to answer without the other person interrupting. When they're done talking, they ask their question and pass the stick. Seem fair to you?"

"What if the person answering leaves out something the other person wants to know?" Katie asked.

"They have to wait until it's their turn again."

Katie shook her head. "I'm not sure that'll work. Who gets to go first?"

He smiled and tapped the stick in his hand. "You do. Fire away."

Of all the questions she wanted to ask, Katie mentally kicked herself when she said, "What's your relationship with Midge? Is it serious?"

"One question, Katie. But the answer is Midge is a friend. My turn."

"You barely answered it. This isn't going to work if you don't answer the question."

"Clarification. Midge is a friend, more Ashley and Dustin's friend than mine. I first met her when Ashley brought her to the shooting range. She likes guns. I've seen her three times, each time when she's tagged along with them. And no, our relationship doesn't even come close to serious. Is that good enough?"

Katie wanted in the worst way to challenge him; to question how he could deny anything was going on with them after the way he acted with Midge at the Labor Day picnic. But, she swallowed hard and forced herself to keep quiet. Any more questions would totally expose her jealousy. Under her breath, she bit out, "Okay."

"My turn to ask a question." CJ rubbed his hand around the back of his neck before saying, "I guess I want to go back a year, back to the time right after Vegas, when you found out you were pregnant. Can you let me in on your reasons for not telling me?"

His question caught her off guard. Taking the stick from CJ, she tried to sort her thoughts. She had expected a question about Noah since she had brought up Midge. Not this. Katie blinked and licked her lips. Her mouth was dry. She concentrated on keeping her breathing steady, but couldn't stop the pounding of her heart. Could she talk about what that time had been like without breaking down? The hurt hadn't gone away. Exposing her feelings would only make her feel more vulnerable. Jesus' words . . . *the truth will set you free,* fluttered in her spirit. Closing her eyes, she prayed, *Give me courage, Lord. Help me to get through this.*

Beside her, she could feel CJ waiting.

Licking her lips again, she fixed her gaze on the swing she had enjoyed a little while ago, remembering the feeling of flying when she jumped. CJ needed to hear the truth. Even if he mocked her for it.

She clenched the stick. "The first few days we were home, Ashley and I couldn't stop talking about you and Dustin." She glanced at him and smiled, self-conscious. "I'd never had such a fun time. Or felt so crazy about a guy. But then, a week went by. Dustin called Ashley but you didn't call me." She looked away. "I was hurt. Then angry." Her eyes filled with tears. "I felt used. I blamed you for coming on to me, then I blamed myself for giving in." Looking down, Katie confessed, "I'm a Christian. We aren't supposed to sleep with guys before marriage. But I did. With you."

She waited, willing the gut-wrenching feelings of shame to pass. To remember her sins were covered by the blood of Jesus. Blood. She closed her eyes, remembering. "When I missed my period, I was scared. Panicked. I couldn't believe it. I totally shut down in denial." She looked down. "I felt dirty. Ashamed. I didn't buy a pregnancy test till I missed what should have been my next period. By then I was two months along. I prayed desperately every day to miscarry. My body was going through changes I didn't want. I hated you." She stopped and swallowed hard. Then she glanced at CJ. "But I wanted you at the same time. To come make things right. To want me. Of course, you were only days away from being deployed. Ashley kept me posted, even though I didn't want to hear anything more about you. When she figured out I was pregnant, I made her swear she wouldn't tell Dustin. It wasn't until after you deployed that I finally couldn't keep it a secret any longer." She slid her hands over the stick, back and forth as she talked. "I told Pastor Dale the whole story, and he set me up with Julie as my Stephen Minister. She wanted me to tell you. I refused to even try to find out your last name."

Katie stopped, her pulse racing. She wanted to get it out and be done. Talking about it was more painful than she realized it would be. "It's all a blur now. And it doesn't matter. I've put it behind me."

Silence hung heavy for several ponderous moments until Katie jumped to her feet, throwing the stick away. "I've got to get out of here," she cried and started to walk quickly toward the park entrance. She had only gone a few steps when CJ grabbed her from behind.

"No," he said, lifting her off the ground, her legs still thrashing out in front of her. Instead of releasing her, he held her tightly against him. She lashed out at him, tears streaking down her face.

In one smooth move, he sank to the ground with her, turning her and pressing her against his chest as he sat cradling her on the grass. She pounded against him with her fists, to no avail. When she finally became still, he stroked her hair, shushing her with his voice. His heartbeat pounded beneath her ear as he held her close. His arms held her tight.

Katie lost track of time as CJ held and rocked her. When she finally felt calm, she shivered and pulled away. "I'm okay now." She wiped her wet cheeks with her hands. "We should probably get back."

He shook his head. His voice was gentle but firm. "Not yet." He smoothed her hair away from her face. "Look at me. Please."

Katie swiped again at her wet face, wishing for a tissue to blow her nose. Getting the words out had released her from their power over her. She finally looked at CJ. Even in the dim light, she could see his cheeks were wet.

When he spoke, his voice cracked. "If I could take back the decision I made that morning when I left you in bed in your hotel room, I would." He swallowed. "In a heartbeat."

She waited, glad he still held her.

"Being with you blew me away, Katie. I'd never had so much fun in so short a time with anyone. And I didn't want it to end. I cussed the timing all the way back to San Diego. Dustin talked about Ashley nonstop. He knew right away he was going to call her. I wanted to keep you to myself. I'd been . . . too busy being with you to get your number." He shifted his legs. "I didn't want to try to squeeze in a couple of dates in between all that was going on to get ready to deploy. In some crazy, convoluted way I thought I was doing you a favor." He swiped his hand through his hair. "In hindsight,

I see I was thinking mostly of myself. I'm so sorry, Katie. I know words don't change what you went through. But I mean them from the bottom of my heart."

Katie looked away, gathering her thoughts. His words had soothed and comforted her, but she wanted to know more. "I don't understand. How were you doing me a favor?"

CJ sighed and met her gaze. "My dad was in the Navy twenty years before he retired and went into private practice. He deployed a bunch of times. And every time, my mom cried. We all did. I know from experience how tough those times are on the people left stateside. The Middle East is a hotbox right now. I guess I thought if anything happened to me, it would be easier for you if we didn't have a relationship going." He rubbed his hand through his hair. "I promise you, I had every intention of calling you just as soon as I got back. If I got back. Dustin's announcement about Timmy beat me to it."

The minutes ticked by. Finally, scooping up her hair, Katie tilted her head to look at the stars. "Boy, did you get it wrong."

CJ dropped his head. "Yeah." When he looked up, he smiled and commandeered her chin. "Will you forgive me?"

Taking her time, Katie finally nodded. "Yes, I forgive you." Her body felt warm, touching up against his as they sat on the grass, their faces only inches apart. When CJ's gaze dropped to her lips, her breath caught.

"Kiss me, Katie. Please?"

His eyes met hers and she was lost. Palming his cheek, she stroked the path of his tears. Their lips met in a gentle kiss that rocked her to the core. Then it was over.

CJ leaned his forehead against hers. "Thank you," he whispered, his voice a husky growl.

The jangle of dog tags startled them and they pulled apart. A man with a large dog appeared on the path from the street into the park, jogging to keep up with the animal.

He glanced at CJ and Katie but kept going. When he was no longer in view, Katie leaned back on her hands and stretched out her legs. "Is it my turn to ask a question?"

"You want to keep going?" CJ laughed. "I'm not sure I can take much more."

"Me either." She bent her knees and pulled them up to her chest. "But there's more we need to talk about. That I need to talk about, at least."

"Yeah, me too. Let's go get another drink of water and head home. We can talk on the way. I won't walk so fast, and we can stop walking or talking any time you want." He helped her up and walked beside her to the water fountain.

When they had their fill of water, CJ pointed out a hill of boulders in the distance. "There's a shortcut among those rocks I usually take home after being at the park, but at night with the possibility of rattlers waiting on the trail, we'll have to forego it. Maybe I can show you tomorrow."

Katie stayed by his side, emotionally drained but exhilarated, too. A burden had been lifted, and reconciliation with CJ felt good. *What's next, Lord? Where do we go from here?* She prayed as they walked in companionable silence. CJ's next words were gentle, but they cast her back to earth all the same.

"Where are you and Noah on say, a scale of one to ten, ten being you're ready to marry the guy any day, and one being you realize that kiss we just shared changes everything?"

Put so succinctly, Katie was caught off guard. She stopped walking. Did their kiss change everything? It had for her, and yet she wasn't sure what it had meant to him. For so long she had harbored bitterness and anger toward him. Her feelings had changed when he came back into her life because of Timmy. But strong currents still swept her along on a course she couldn't control. Was their kiss anything more than putting a seal on forgiveness? "It-It's not quite so black and white," she finally managed, piercing him with a look that mirrored her confusion.

"Talk to me, Katie. Tell me why you say that? I'll try my best to just listen."

Slowly they started walking again.

"Okay, I'll try. But if I start to ramble, just stop me, okay?"

"Deal."

"Okay, first, Noah. When I met him, I was in the second trimester of my pregnancy. People at the church knew I was pregnant and unmarried, and that's not really cause for joy in the church, in case you didn't know that. Some, like that man you confronted when you came to church? He wanted me fired. Noah helped me through that, along with Pastor Dale and Julie. I came to depend on him. We studied the Bible. A lot. It was his job, but we went beyond that. When I made up my mind I was done with you, and would never try to find you to tell you about Timmy, my feelings for Noah were already bordering on love. When he made the first move toward becoming romantically involved, I guess you could say, I was ready. Are we at a ten now?" She paused. "I think Noah is."

"What about you?"

They turned the corner and started up the hill to the Jansen's home. It occurred to Katie that maybe she just needed a sounding board. Someone who could help her work through the pros and cons of marrying Noah, if and when he asked her. Help her discern the Lord's will. Did she dare ask CJ what he thought? Once the idea came, it wouldn't leave. "I know this sounds weird, but maybe you could help me with that."

CJ stopped and turned to her, his voice harsh. "What do you mean? Seems to me you're ready to marry him or you're not."

Unsettled by his tone of voice, she murmured, "Okay, I'm sorry. I told you this is weird. Noah hasn't even asked me. Yet. But I told you, things aren't exactly black or white for me."

He huffed out an impatient sigh. "Okay. How can I help?"

"Well, can I use you as a sounding board, sort of?"

He shook his head, his mouth drawn in a tight line. "I'm not sure I can be fair about this, you know?" He ran his hand around the back of his neck. "But okay. Talk to me."

They started walking again. For several minutes, Katie listed the pros and cons of her relationship with Noah, leaving Timmy out of her list. CJ listened patiently until she said, "And he hates exercise. And sports. Never played basketball, baseball, soccer. Not even roller skating. Well, golf. He plays golf."

"Wait a minute," CJ said, stopping again. "You're telling me you love a guy who will never play on a sports team with you? Never go hiking? Rock climbing? Biking? Does he even swim? Because you are part fish and you know it."

Katie laughed. She couldn't help it. "But he has a lot of other good qualities. I can exercise alone. No big deal. I do it now."

"I thought a husband was supposed to be a helpmate?"

"A helpmate, not a playmate," Katie countered.

"Let me get this straight. You're asking *me* to help *you* find enough reasons so you can feel good about marrying this guy? Do I have that right?"

"Well, when you put it that way . . ."

They had reached the bottom of the Jansen's driveway. He turned and pierced her with troubled eyes. "I can't do it, Katie. From what you just told me, all you've got in common with Noah is Jesus. Is that really going to be enough for you?" Without taking a breath, he said, "I'm getting in the spa. And I think you should join me. Especially after the workout we just had." He set off up the driveway.

Tears threatened. She had angered and upset him with her crazy thinking and runaway monologue. Why did she have to be so conflicted? She trotted after CJ, already halfway up the driveway. "Wouldn't a shower work just as well? What if Timmy wakes up and I don't hear him?"

"Mom's got a monitor set up. Bring it out with you." They were at the door. "It's your turn, you know?" At her puzzled look, he added, "To ask a question."

She went through the doorway ahead of him. Out the back window, the pool lights illuminated the water, making a silent appeal to her overheated body. "How can I say no to that?" Turning toward her room, she added, "See you in a minute."

Chapter 19

From the doorway, Katie saw that CJ had beat her to the spa. He lounged in the water, his arms stretched out on either side of him, his head tilted back. Relaxed. Waiting. She slid open the back door and went outside. Putting the baby's monitor a few feet away, she climbed in and sat across from him.

"Feels good, doesn't it?" He fisted his hand and shot a spray of water at her. It landed just short.

"You missed me."

"I wasn't trying to hit you or I would have."

"Oh yeah? I don't believe you."

This time the spray hit her chin and she laughed. "Luck, just plain luck."

"That was skill. This time I'm aiming for your right arm." He fired and missed. "You moved."

Shaking her head, Katie settled down so only her face was above the waterline. She closed her eyes. "Grow up," she challenged.

"Look who's talking." His foot found hers.

Rather than fight him, she played along until it began to feel too good. She sat up, putting her feet on the floor of the spa. "Okay, that's enough of that."

CJ smiled and Katie's pulse, already worked up, went into overdrive. It had been like this in Vegas. Fun, frivolous, hot. Crazy, burning hot.

"My turn to ask a question, right?"

"Can you make it an easy one?" His foot captured hers again.

She moved to another seat in the spa. "Sure. No. Probably not. I know you grew up going to church, but don't go now. Is that because of a bad experience, or do you have reasons for rejecting Christianity?

"That's two questions, Katie. But I'll let it slide. If you want details, you might try making the question open-ended.

"Are you saying you want me to reword the question, smarty pants? Or are you just procrastinating?"

That killer smile reached his eyes and burned a path to her heart.

"That's way more than one," CJ said.

Exasperated, Katie blurted, "Why don't you believe in God anymore?"

"Who says I don't believe in God?"

"I'm asking the question here, remember? So, you do believe in God?"

"Yes, I guess so. I haven't got any other explanation for all this." He gestured to the sky.

"You do?" Her hopes soared until she caught the smile lurking on his lips. "CJ, stop messing with me. It's been too crazy already tonight. Are you a Christian, or aren't you?"

"I'm not trying to mess with you. The jury's still out for me. As a worldview, Christianity has it hands down over any other religion. But I get hung up on the miracle thing. Men blind from birth seeing again? Water to wine? Jesus raised from the dead? Have you ever seen a miracle?"

"Yeah, our baby."

CJ smiled and cocked his head. "You got me there. Not the same, but still awesome. I look at that little guy and think, He's got my DNA, yours too. My ears and toes. Your eyes. Your personality."

"That's crazy. He's too young to be exhibiting much of a personality."

"Maybe you don't see it. But it's there. He's an extrovert, just like you."

Katie shook her head. "And you have now successfully changed the subject. Way to go."

"Can I ask one last question, and then I think we should get some sleep?"

Katie yawned. "An easy one, okay?"

"There are no easy ones with us, Katie. Haven't you figured that out yet?" He chuckled. "Here's the deal. You covered where you and Noah are on the scale of one to ten. What about the other end of the scale? That kiss we shared?"

Katie felt her breath catch. Color flooded her cheeks. What good would it do to deny their kiss hadn't released a flood of longing for him. "Are you asking me if I think our kiss changes anything between us?" At his nod, she continued. "Because, I think it does and it doesn't." He grimaced and shook his head.

"Come on, Katie, don't cop out on me."

"I'm not." She rushed on. "I mean, it does change things because all the secret hurts and misunderstandings are out in the open where we can deal with them now. Kissing you was a sign of peace between us. That's the best way I can describe it. But it doesn't change anything, CJ. I can't deny how I feel about you. Especially when you kiss me. I want more. You're lethal. But what do we really have— besides Timmy—if we don't have our faith in common? If it's not the foundation of our relationship? I can't compromise on that. I just can't."

"So, you're saying if I don't believe what you believe, there's no chance for us? Am I hearing that right?"

A verse of scripture rushed through her head. Try as she would to block it out, it still came. *No one who puts a hand to the plow and looks back is fit for service in the kingdom of God.* Her eyes filled with tears. "You're Timmy's father. There will always be room in my heart for you, CJ. But I have to follow what I think is God's plan for me. And Timmy."

As she said it, Timmy's cries came over the baby monitor. In one easy move, CJ was out of the spa. He grabbed a towel and headed for the house, his every move telegraphing his anger and frustration. Katie sent the water sloshing in her haste to follow him. "CJ, wait!" She picked up the monitor and her towel and rushed to catch him, heedless of the water she was getting on the living room floor. But when she got to her room, only Timmy was there.

Still dripping wet, she found her robe. Wrapping it snugly over her wet suit, she lifted Timmy out of the crib and sat down to nurse him. *Had CJ gone to his room?* It didn't take a rocket scientist to know he was angry. Hurt? Did she dare go to his room? As soon as she thought it, she dismissed the idea. She had only told him the truth. *What fellowship can light have with darkness?* But even as she remembered the scripture Noah had showed her in 2 Corinthians, tears poured down her cheeks. Why did loving CJ have to hurt so much?

~ ~ ~

Saturday, after breakfast, Mary drafted CJ to take Peggy and Katie to the nearby salon where she had arranged for them to have pedicures. "Don't worry about Timmy," she said to Katie, shifting the baby in her arms. "We'll play a little before I put him down for his nap." She stepped back as CJ opened both passenger side doors of the truck cab for the women. "Here's the bakery address, CJ," she said, handing him a business card, "where you can pick up a Bundt cake for tonight."

His expression grim, CJ took the card. He programmed the address in his phone as he walked around the hood of the truck.

Mary put Timmy down for his nap, then went to find Tim. "I saw CJ out here swimming last night after midnight,"

Mary said, leaning in to inspect Tim's progress cleaning the grill.

"He and Katie were out here in the spa earlier than that," Tim said. "I'd just come back from the hospital. You were already asleep."

"I guess I was. I didn't hear them. But when I got up to go to the bathroom, CJ was swimming as if he was racing someone. I think he and Katie had a tough conversation at the park last night. Her eyes were puffy this morning. And he . . ." She sighed.

"Did he tell you that, or is it just your mother's intuition?"

"He told me they had talked when he came in for breakfast. After I asked a few questions. He's having a hard time trying to figure out where he stands with Katie. I know he is."

Tim put down his scraper and opened his arms to hold her. As they embraced, he said, "I wish Katie could see how much he loves her. I've been asking the Lord to open her eyes and her heart. I'm afraid Noah Davidson has clouded her vision. Not that he isn't a fine young man. Just very different from our boy. Katie's always struck me as a go-getter, always ready for a challenge. The feisty kind. Just look at how she and Lynn went after the prize on Labor Day. From what I hear, Noah's the opposite. Maybe that's the appeal."

"I think it more likely Katie's relationship with Jesus. And CJ's lack of one."

"We gave him a good foundation, honey. All we can do is pray he'll return to it."

"I do. Day and night." Mary went back in the house, and Tim resumed cleaning the grill. But as she unloaded the dishwasher, she prayed once again for light to shine in CJ's darkness and illumine the way to Jesus.

~ ~ ~

With her mother napping on Saturday afternoon, Katie closed the door of her room and put Timmy on his play mat. Picking up her phone, she called Noah. He answered on the fourth ring, his breathing labored.

"Are you okay? You sound out of breath."

"I was taking the trash out, and had to sprint to get to the phone before it quit ringing. Are you home yet? I'd like to come over now that I've got my chores done."

"I'm not home. You won't believe this, but the Jansens flew my mom out to visit me and meet Timmy. Isn't that incredible? She's not leaving until tomorrow after dinner."

There was silence on the other end of the phone.

"Noah?" Katie asked.

His voice tight, he asked, "Are you bringing her to church? Do I get to meet her? Or is this an exclusive CJ and the Jansen's party?"

"Oh, Noah, don't be mad. Please. Of course I want you to meet her. I just don't want to be totally rude. Or offend Mary and Tim. I mean, they paid for everything for Mom. Mary even arranged for us to have pedicures this morning." She laughed, trying to interject some levity in the conversation. "You won't have any reason to complain about my scaly feet, at least for a couple of weeks."

Noah sighed. "Big deal."

His lack of enthusiasm for her news hurt. "Come on."

"Oh, okay. What color of polish?"

"Passion pink. It's totally cool. It's perfect with Julie's print dress. The one I wore to dinner with you and Amanda. But guess where I'm wearing it tonight?" Before he could answer, she exclaimed, "To a play at the Globe Theater."

"Great, just great. I suppose CJ's taking you, isn't he?"

"No, he's watching Timmy. Mary and Tim are taking us."

"Well, that's good at least."

"Come on, Noah, I thought you'd be happy for me. I haven't seen my mom in over a year. And how often do I get to go to the theater?"

"You're right. I'm being a jealous louse. I am happy for you, that you're getting to see your mom and go to the theater together. I'm just in a bad mood because I really wanted to see you tonight. I love you, Katie, remember? I can't help but be on edge when you're with CJ. I mean, you fell for him once. He and his folks seem to be pulling out all the stops to make you happy."

"I guess I hadn't thought of it that way. They're just incredibly generous, loving people. But maybe you're right. I'll be careful. I did find out from CJ that he doesn't consider himself a Christian. But he believes in God. That's a start, don't you think?"

"Most people believe in God, Katie. It doesn't mean much."

The conversation was becoming depressing, and Katie didn't know what to do about it. She was already feeling out of control emotionally after her conversation in the spa with CJ last night. He had barely looked at her after picking them up at the nail salon, and went to get his truck washed within minutes of finishing lunch. Now he was in the garage they used as a workout room, according to Tim.

Katie tickled Timmy with her big toe, admiring the bright pink polish. "It's time for me to put Timmy down for his nap, so I guess I'll see you tomorrow."

"So, you're coming to Cornerstone for church?"

"I don't know what the plan is, but I'll try to make that happen. I love you. Bye."

Katie hung up the phone and stretched out on the floor by Timmy. Noah hadn't asked about the baby. He didn't seem to care as much about him as she would have liked, and that bothered her. But, she brushed it off. Could she help it if Timmy looked just like CJ? "You're getting a workout just like your daddy is right now, aren't you, little man? He's mad at me, you know? And that makes me so sad. Do you have my personality? That's what your daddy thinks, you know?" She tickled his toes, reveling in his baby sounds and jerky hand motions. "Get that giraffe," she said, her voice high and breathy.

Timmy batted the giraffe that was swinging over his head. When he finally became frustrated, she pulled him into her arms to nurse. "It's dinnertime, little man, so drink up. You and your daddy have a date tonight, you lucky guy, and I want you to go to sleep for him when he says it's bedtime."

~ ~ ~

At the airport the next day, Katie had a hard time letting go of her mother. "The time went too quickly," she said, holding her tight. "I'm so glad you came."

"It was wonderful to meet all these folks you've been telling me about. And Noah, too. Such a nice young man. Reminds me of my Uncle Chucky Bob with that bald head and scruffy beard. He ran moonshine and preached on the side." They both burst out laughing.

CJ lifted Peggy's suitcase and tote bag out of the truck and placed them beside her.

"Thanks again, CJ. I had a wonderful time," Peggy said, giving him an extra-long hug.

"You're welcome. I'm glad it all worked out." He glanced at Katie. "Take your time saying goodbye. I'm in no hurry."

Katie gave her mom one final hug. "Have a good trip, Mom. I don't know when I'll see you next . . ." Tears choked her. "But we'll FaceTime, right?"

Peggy swiped at her tears. "We sure will. And Katie, don't worry so much, okay, honey? God has a plan and he's going to work things out. I know you're in love with two very different men right now. But keep praying. God will show you what to do."

"Thanks, Mom. I know you're right. I love you." She stepped back to let Peggy maneuver her suitcase. "Bye. I love you."

She turned when Peggy was almost in the terminal, and got in the truck. As CJ pulled away, she said, "Thanks again for everything you did to make this weekend happen. You and your parents are the most generous people I know." Swiping at her tears, she said, "I owe you, CJ, big time."

He was silent for several minutes as he merged into traffic. "I didn't do it so you would owe me, Katie. But you're welcome. You and your mom look a lot alike, you know? Act a little alike, too."

She wanted to dig deeper, to know why he had given her such a great gift. But she felt too vulnerable to ask. So instead she took the easy route. "We're close. Always have been. Mom had given up on having any more children, and along I came. The girl she always wanted."

"So, what was it like growing up? Did your brothers beat up on you?"

"No! Well, yeah, sometimes. But Mom didn't stand for it much, even when it was my fault they went after me. She wields a mean flyswatter." Katie laughed. "My brothers' names are Ray and Richard, but we call Richard, Ricky. He was twelve when I was born. Ray was fourteen. By the time I was six, Ray was in the Army and Ricky was an apprentice plumber. They didn't hang around home long. They both were married within a year of each other, but Ricky and his wife divorced after three years and three kids. He's having trouble again, this time with his second wife. Between them they have six kids. It's a handful."

"I'll say. I don't know anybody with that many kids under one roof."

Now that she had started talking about home, she couldn't seem to stop. Being with her mom had brought it all back. The fighting, the crying, the threats by her brother to walk out on his wife. "Mom tries to be the peacemaker. She watches the kids a lot while my brother works. My sister-in-law, Tammy, loves to shop. So, she calls Mom, drops off the kids, and spends hours at the mall. But it's especially confusing because half the time the kids . . ." Katie stopped mid-sentence, kicking herself for bringing up her brother's problems.

CJ finished the sentence for her. "They're with the other parent. Isn't that what you were going to say?"

The innocent suffer for the guilty. Dr. Chang's words echoed in her memory. Katie sighed. "Yes. Mom sometimes has to drop them off or pick them up, depending on who's where. At least everyone lives in the same school district, so that gives the older kids some stability." Almost under her breath, she added, "Ricky is the main problem. He has a temper and tends to blame everyone but himself when things go wrong."

"It takes two to make or break a marriage, Katie," CJ said. "A shopaholic can't be easy to live with. I mean, if she's a spender and he's a saver, that adds a lot of stress to a marriage." He turned the corner to home. "But I have a hard time imagining what it must be like for those kids to go back and forth like ping-pong balls. I never want to do that to Timmy. Never in a million years."

Guilt swamped Katie. Wasn't that what they would do to Timmy? If Noah asked her to marry him, and she said yes? Or was CJ saying he would fight to have full custody of their son? She hung her head. "Me either. But I—" She didn't have a chance to finish her sentence. She was hurled forward so fast the seat belt locked. "What the . . . ?" The truck came to an abrupt stop a few hundred feet from the Jansen's driveway, throwing her back against the seat.

"Sorry about that. A cat almost bought the last of its nine lives," CJ said, and resumed speed. "Are you okay?" He turned the truck into the driveway.

"Yeah. It just startled me, that's all. I'm glad the seat belt worked."

"We have a couple of stray cats in the neighborhood, my mom told me. They probably won't last long against the coyotes and rattlesnakes."

Katie stared out the window, a picture of a coyote catching a cat and going for the kill flashing through her mind. Was she like the cat, up against a predator who would show no mercy? What chance of keeping Timmy did she have if CJ wanted him all for himself?

Chapter 20

With Halloween only days away, Katie put the finishing touches on the design she had been working on for next month's Thanksgiving Pie Social at the church. She saved her work and closed her computer. Sliding off the kitchen barstool, she crossed to the refrigerator and pulled out a bag of baby carrots and some leftover tuna salad for lunch.

A text from CJ popped up on her phone as she forked tuna on a cracker. He wanted to stop by and see Timmy, if it was okay. Katie texted back that she was taking him shopping in an hour, but asked if he wanted to go with them. When the answer came back 'yes', she took a deep breath to calm her nerves. She hadn't seen much of him since her mom's visit. Between his time in Kentucky and his crazy hours, he had only been with Timmy one Saturday. The subject of custody hadn't come up again with either CJ or Noah. She didn't know whether to be worried or relieved.

She had just finished nursing Timmy when the doorbell rang. Dressed in jeans and a green Rogue T-shirt, she stepped back to let CJ through the door. "Would you mind burping him while I get the diaper bag ready?" She handed the burp cloth from her shoulder to him. "Are you off today?"

"No, we got off early because we worked late yesterday." He slung the burp cloth over his shoulder and took Timmy. Megan came running from the kitchen and wrapped her arms around CJ's legs.

"Hi, pumpkin," CJ said, squatting to give Megan a hug. "Are you ready for Halloween?"

"I'm going to be Princess Sofia," Megan said.

"Well, that sounds perfect for a beautiful girl like you." CJ stood as Katie came out of her bedroom with the diaper bag. "We're off to find a costume for Timmy. What do you think he should be?"

"How 'bout a monkey?" Megan suggested.

CJ nodded. "That's a great idea. I'll be on the lookout for a monkey suit. But, it might have to be something else. Is that okay?

"Okay. But I think it should be a monkey costume." Megan wrapped her arms around CJ's legs again before running off to her room.

"She gets more grown-up sounding every day," CJ said to Julie. "She's amazing."

Julie laughed. "You're telling me. She's four going on fourteen. Brad's pretty sure this next baby will have a fight for survival on his hands."

"So, you found out you're having a boy? Congratulations."

"Yes. Thanks. Brad's over the moon, of course. Me too."

Katie reached for Timmy. "We'd better get going if we're going to find that monkey. We'll be back in about an hour, Julie. I'll get going on the meatloaf just as soon as I get back."

~ ~ ~

At the Halloween store, Katie stopped at the entrance, appalled at the display of scary monsters, witches, and warlocks. "Do you believe this? I'm going to have nightmares. I can't imagine what this could do to a little kid."

"Yup. Seems like Halloween gets more popular every year. And bloodier. I better cover Timmy's eyes. Wouldn't want our four-month-old traumatized."

Katie rolled her eyes. "Very funny."

On the rack of baby costumes, Katie spotted a pirate suit. "He could look like Noah in this one," Katie said, holding it up for CJ to see.

"Not funny," CJ growled.

"Sorry." Katie pushed the costumes on the rack to the right and left, looking for something safe. "I knew I should have gone to Costco at the beginning of the month," she said under her breath. "Everything I like is either newborn size or for a toddler." Huffing out a loud sigh of frustration, she moved to the other side of the rack with CJ following.

"Dustin and Ashley are throwing a costume party on Friday," he said. "Want to come with me? We could be Papa, Mama, and Baby Bear."

Katie stopped rifling through the costumes and looked at him. "At Ashley's? And you want us to go as the Bear Family? You're crazy."

"Actually, it's at my place in Mira Mesa. I live with Dustin and a couple of other SWCCs. I have to be there to make sure my room doesn't get trashed."

Katie went back to looking at costumes without answering. Her mind was spinning. A costume party sounded like tons of fun, but did she dare give in to CJ? There was no way Noah would understand. He was carving out time from his schoolwork to talk on the phone occasionally. Their time together was precious. His job at Cornerstone would finish up the Sunday before Thanksgiving and he still hadn't given her any real sign that she was part of his future. Except to invite her to go with him to his best friend's wedding in San Francisco.

"What do you say?" CJ interrupted her thoughts. "A party's perfect for Timmy's first Halloween. He's too young to trick or treat, really."

"Well, yeah, he's too young to go out on his own, but I was going to show him off at the church office before it closes at three, then take him out with Julie and Megan to a few of the neighbors we know."

"You can still do that. I'll even come with you. The party

doesn't start until six or seven. C'mon, Katie, you know you want to." His eyes danced with mischief.

He was so close she could smell the fresh sunshine scent of his shirt. It tickled her nose and reminded her of the sheets on the bed in the Jansen's guest room. Shaking her head, she asked, "Does your mom still do your laundry?"

The change of topic threw him. "What makes you say that?"

"You smell like sunshine." Katie felt her cheeks heat and looked away.

CJ chuckled. "You like it, don't you? I do, too. That's why I have a clothesline in my backyard. I do my own laundry, have since fourth grade. You don't know my mom if you think she'd let me get away with that!"

Katie laughed. He was right. Mary wasn't the kind of mom to do her grown son's laundry.

"So, you'll go to the party with me, right?" CJ asked.

He knew her too well. And knew how to push all the right buttons. "You're incorrigible. You're not going to give up, are you?"

"Never quit. It's part of the SWCC creed. It's a party, Katie. Just a couple of hours. Ashley will be there, you'll be safe."

Mentioning Ashley reminded Katie of their renewed friendship. "Well, maybe. But only if we can find some costumes."

"Deal," CJ said. "Come with me." He started out of the store.

"Where are you going?" Katie said, hurrying after him. "We haven't found anything yet."

"Leave it to me. I've got a plan." In several long strides he was at his truck. Opening the back door, he pulled a bag from Party City off the floor and onto the seat. He shifted the baby to his left side. "This should work for Timmy," he said, lifting a brown, baby bear sleeper with a hood from the bag.

"Oh, that's darling," Katie said, turning the costume to see the little tail in the back. "The feet look like bear paws." She checked the tag. "You even got the size right. Impressive."

"And here's one for you." He pulled out a puffy cellophane bag with a neatly folded brown, one-piece costume inside.

"You bought one for me?" She squeezed the package. "Thanks, I think."

CJ dug into the bag again, his enthusiasm building. "Yeah, and here's some face paint. I figure being the artist you are, you can make us look like bears, easy."

Studying the picture on her bag, Katie laughed. "These are pajamas!"

"No," CJ said. "They just look like pajamas. But if you want to sleep in them, it's okay with me. Bears hibernate, you know?"

"Is that a joke?" Katie said, making a face at him. "Where's your costume?"

"It's at my place already. It looks just like yours except it's black instead of brown, and it's extra-extra-large. I'm going to stuff myself with a few pillows."

"Okay, I'm thinking you're just a little too over-the-top about this costume stuff. I mean, you're going to be Papa Bear. Not some cool, macho super hero. I think you're in for some serious teasing. And, I haven't said I'll come yet, have I?"

"Yeah, you did." At her questioning look, he said, "You said, and I quote, 'only if we can find some costumes.' And I did. You've got to give it to me for Timmy's at least. And I passed up a lot of other costumes that *you* would look over-the-top hot in." He winked at her.

A rush of heat she couldn't control raced up her chest to her cheeks. How could he charm her so easily? How did he know she loved parties? It wouldn't do to show too much excitement, would it? She studied his face as he tried to put Timmy's costume back in the bag, one-handed. Happy, excited. She reached in to help. Tension tightened the pit of her stomach. Noah would be upset if he found out she agreed to go to a party with CJ. So why would she do it? Why would she put her relationship with Noah in jeopardy? The answer came unbidden: CJ was fun in a way Noah would never be.

Katie sighed, blocking her errant thoughts and striving to think of how she could make things work. "Okay, I'll talk to Julie to see what time she wants to go out with Megan to trick or treat, and you can come along. If you still want to. We'll go back to your place to put on the costumes and do the makeup. Does that sound okay?" At CJ's nod, she went on. "I think Timmy and I can only stay a little while, so are you okay bringing us back when I say it's time to leave?"

"Whatever you want." CJ smiled, and it reached all the way to his eyes in a flash of daring. "I'm at your disposal. Anything you say."

Squinting at him, she said, "You're giving in too easily. Why don't I believe you?"

Leaning against the truck, his teeth worked his lower lip, doing his best to stop a grin. "You really want to know?"

Why couldn't she tear her gaze away from his lips? How did he know her so well? Know what she wanted better than she knew herself? The breeze caressed her skin, but couldn't cool the heat raging inside her. It had been like this in Las Vegas, the easy way he had looked at her, as if he couldn't get enough. They were in the middle of a public parking lot, with the sound of the freeway buzzing in her ears, and people coming and going to the Halloween store. The noise couldn't compete with the commotion raging in her heart. He had bought costumes—a family of costumes. Was he saying . . . ? *What?*

With a sigh, she tore her eyes away from him, jerked open the front door of the truck and hoisted herself in the seat. Anger covered deeper feelings of frustration. He hadn't said anything, really. Not in words at least. *Did he think she could read his mind?* Why did he have to be so attractive? So disarming? And why couldn't he just say what he really wanted from her. Felt for her? "I have to get home. Timmy needs his afternoon nap, and I'm in charge of supper tonight."

"Easy, Katie," he said, his hand on the seat belt, pulling it out for her to grasp. "Calm down. I'll get you home." Closing her door, he crawled into the back seat to secure Timmy in his car seat.

They rode home in silence. Katie fumed, torn between wanting him, wanting to go to the party, and wanting to stay true to Noah. Why couldn't she get it in her head that CJ was just toying with her? Hadn't Noah told her many times that what CJ wanted wouldn't last? That true love waits? CJ hadn't waited for love in Las Vegas. Of course, neither had she, a nasty, mocking voice reminded her. Did CJ even know what real love felt like? God's love? He said the jury was out on what he believed. What did that mean, anyway? Forcing herself to take slow, steady breaths, she stared out the window.

"I-I don't know about the party, CJ," she said when he pulled the truck in the driveway. "I-I'll have to think about it and let you know."

His temper flared. "For crying out loud, Katie. It's a party. No one's planning on making you worship the devil. Or do anything that would insult your Christian ethics." He turned to her. "I just want to be with you. Is that so wrong?"

Without giving her a chance to respond, CJ yanked on the door handle and got out. Controlling his movements in spite of his anger, he gently lifted Timmy out of the truck and set the car seat on the driveway.

Katie got out of the truck, CJ's remark reverberating through her mind. It filled her with hope, and it scared her, too. Could they be together, have a future? *Be a family?*

CJ's eyes smoldered with frustration. "Take the costumes. If you don't want to come, fine. At least you'll have something for Timmy to wear. I probably won't be able to make the neighborhood stuff anyway." He handed her the bag with both costumes and the makeup and turned away.

The truck engine turned over. She picked up Timmy and backed away. Heartsick. Confused. Frustrated. Following his truck with her gaze, she walked to the front door. The brake lights of CJ's truck glowed red at the corner. He turned at the same time another car came up the street. *Noah.* Katie's breath hitched. Had she been any slower getting home, Noah would have caught her with CJ. With a gasp, she raced in the house.

She was diapering Timmy when Noah knocked on her bedroom door. "Hey you," she said, pasting a smile on her face that didn't reach her heart. She had barely gotten Timmy's costume hung up in the closet and hers hidden behind her shoes before Noah knocked. Stuffing her guilt at being with CJ, she lifted Timmy off the changing table and hid her face in his neck, pretending to tickle him.

"Was that Jansen's truck I saw when I turned the corner? What was he doing here in the middle of a Tuesday afternoon?"

Katie swallowed hard, balancing Timmy on her hip while trying to think. She wanted to deny it, wanted to keep the time with CJ to herself until she could figure out what she was feeling, and what to do about it. But Noah was waiting. Out of the corner of her eye she could see his foot wriggling as he sat in the glider chair, a sure sign he was agitated. The longer she took to answer, the guiltier she would look.

"Oh, yeah, he, ah, he dropped off a Halloween costume for Timmy. Do you want to see it?"

"Not really." He sighed. At her crestfallen look, he softened his tone. "Well, okay. I never dressed up and went trick or treating when I was a kid."

Instead of getting the costume, Katie knelt at Noah's feet. "Well, I know it's the devil's holiday, but it's a fun time, too. CJ got Timmy a bear costume. It's adorable. He'll look so cute. And everyone at the office expects me to bring him to see them on Friday. Doesn't the preschool at Cornerstone have Halloween parties?"

"Yes, but I don't really think they're sending the right message. The Country Fair should have been sufficient. That's good, wholesome family fun. But enough about that. Let's talk about the weekend in San Francisco."

"Good idea, but let me put Timmy down for his nap and start on the meatloaf while we talk, okay?" She picked up her phone. "It's already four-thirty and we eat around six, so I have to get moving."

With one final barrage of kisses for the baby, she put him on his back in his crib, tickled him with the bear CJ had given him when he was born, and followed Noah to the kitchen. He sat at the table while she pulled out eggs, ketchup, mustard, and ground beef from the refrigerator. While she finished collecting the other ingredients she needed, she said, "Tell me again, who is the guy who's getting married, and what's his future wife's name?"

"It's Jeremy Dolton. And he's marrying his college sweetheart, Amy Winters."

"And you knew them at San Diego State, right?"

"Yes, Jeremy and I roomed together our freshman year, and every year after. We got an apartment, of course, after the first year. He met Amy at a Chess tournament, but Euchre is the game they're really good at."

"Euchre requires four players. Who was your partner?"

"Our other roommate. Sid Telchin. He's a Messianic Jew. You'll meet him at the wedding, too. There's a bride's brunch on Saturday morning. Did you know about that?"

"Yes, I got an invitation from someone, I can't remember

the name on it. And I already RSVP'd that I would come. But if you'd rather do something else with me, I'm all for that.

"No, that's perfect. I'm playing golf with Sid while you do that."

"Oh, some exercise. Good for you!" She winked. "What kind of clothes do I need to bring?"

"Well, knowing Amy and Jeremy, it's going to be very classy, from start to finish." He laughed. "Jeremy is marrying up. Amy's everyone's best friend. But, they both come from very well-to-do families of financial advisers, engineers, and artists. So, let's see. Friday evening is the rehearsal dinner, Saturday's the brunch, the wedding and reception. But first there's a gathering on Friday at the Dolton's. It will be casual, but I hope you'll wear something cute and sexy to show off those long legs of yours."

"Noah!" Picking up a hand full of the meatloaf she was mixing, she started walking around the counter, "How would you like a couple of meatloaf eye patches to cure you from gawking at my long legs?"

He pushed away from the table and came for her, laughing. "Oh, no you don't. Put that stuff down. And come here." He caught her in a hug, one hand making sure the wad of meatloaf didn't reach him. "You're going to have to be careful that you don't outshine the bride, you know? His lips touched hers in a light, sweet kiss. "You're so beautiful. You know that? Kiss me, Katie. I can't wait to have you all to myself."

Katie forgot about the meatloaf for a few minutes. "I just wish Timmy could come, too. I've never been away from my baby."

Noah released her and returned to his chair. "Well, I know. I know. But we need to get away. Alone. Timmy will be in good hands with Julie."

"You're right. Let me scrub the potatoes and get

everything baking, then we can talk more about San Francisco. How's that sound?"

"Good. I'm excited for you to meet some of my friends."

"Well . . ." Katie hesitated. "I just hope I can measure up. I think I might need some new clothes. What do you think?"

"Well, sure, that would be great. Maybe something from Nordstrom's."

Katie shook her head. "I've never even set foot in Nordstrom's. They're way out of my class. And pocketbook. Maybe I can try Nordstrom's Rack." Almost to herself, she said, "But anything I buy is going to have to work with my budget, and we're at the end of the month again."

"Sure, sure, I don't want you to wreck your budget. I guess I do care about making a good impression, though." He got up to meet her as she came around the kitchen counter. Pulling her close, he kissed her gently, then more aggressively. When he finished, he said, "And Katie. Maybe you could lose the ponytail."

Katie tugged on his beard, unexpectedly annoyed. "Sure. Just as soon as you lose the mop on your chin."

Chapter 21

"This is depressing," Katie said, closing her laptop. "C'mon, Timmy. We're going to the mall. But I am *not* going to Nordstrom's. Every dress I like there costs close to two hundred dollars." She picked up the baby. "I've got to find something gorgeous to wear to this wedding. On sale."

A sale sign lured her into stopping at the display window at Ann Taylor. But it was the green sheath dress on the mannequin that made her smile. It would be perfect for either the rehearsal dinner or the wedding, and later for Christmas. She wheeled Timmy in to the store.

In the dressing room, she put on the green dress and checked the price tag, groaning when she read $149. At this rate, she could afford one and a half dresses but no new shoes. Maneuvering around Timmy, she gazed in the mirror at herself, turning one way, then the other. She fluffed her hair and grinned at herself. The golden highlights in her brown hair glistened. Turning to see the back, she smoothed her hand over her bottom, sure that Noah would be impressed. But could she afford it?

Reluctantly, she put her jeans and T-shirt back on, at war with herself. She backed out of the dressing room pulling Timmy's stroller, and almost ran into Mary Jansen.

"Katie! How nice to see you!" She glanced at the dress over Katie's arm. "Did you find something you like?"

"Yes, but only if it's on sale. Noah and I are going to a wedding in a week and a half in San Francisco and I need three outfits. This one is perfect, but does some serious damage to my budget."

"Have you tried JCPenney or Kohl's? They have cute clothes but not usually as expensive."

"You're right. I should have stopped there first. What are you trying on?" Katie glanced at the blouse in Mary's hand.

"Tim and I are taking a little weekend trip to Napa Valley tomorrow, and I'm looking for something to wear on the plane." She held up a pale-blue blousy shirt with bell sleeves.

"Sounds like a fun trip, and that blouse will look perfect on you. Well, I guess we should go. It's nice seeing you." She started to give Mary a hug.

"Wait." Mary held up her hand. "Why don't you let me get this dress for you? Call it an early Christmas present. And some cute shoes to go with it?" She patted Katie's arm. "I so miss shopping with Lynn, and you would be doing me a huge favor by filling in for her. I can just imagine how darling you'll look in it."

Katie smiled and shook her head. "You've already done so much for me, Mary. My mom, the gifts for Timmy, I just can't take any more. It wouldn't be right. But thank you. Thank you so much for thinking of me." She tried to go past Mary, but she blocked the way.

"Nonsense," she said gently, cupping Katie's cheek. "You're letting your pride get in the way, Katie, and that's never a good thing. I came from a poor family, and being the baby, I always had to settle for hand-me-downs. Someone bought me a new outfit once, at a very important time, and it made all the difference. That's all I want to do for you. Please."

How could she resist the love shining in Mary's eyes? Before she could speak, Mary winked at her and remarked, "Besides, my next request is that you give CJ a chance to see you in it."

Katie laughed. Mary had never championed her son quite so blatantly. "You drive a hard bargain."

"Let's go find those shoes," Mary said, and took over pushing the stroller.

~ ~ ~

Two hours later, Timmy was asleep in his stroller and Katie was worn out. As she put the bags of clothes into the trunk of her car, she said a prayer of thanks for Mary and Tim. But it was Mary's challenge to wear the dress with CJ that wouldn't leave her alone. Did she know her son was angry with her? She had chewed on what to do for days, finally deciding there was no way she could go to the Halloween party with CJ and still face Noah. The decision had her tied in knots.

Surprised to see Noah's car in the driveway when she got home, she hurried to get Timmy and the shopping bags.

"There you are," he said, meeting her at the door. "I almost missed you. But I guess I can stay long enough for a fashion show." He planted a kiss on her lips and took the bags from her. "Pee . . . ew, what's that smell?"

"Timmy needs a diaper change, that's all." With his nap interrupted and his diaper loaded, he was crying loud, piercing sobs. "I'll just be a minute."

Julie and Brad were in the kitchen as she hurried past. "Hi, guys. Do you mind if I give Noah a fashion show? I got a couple of new things."

"Have at it," Brad answered at the same time Julie said, "Sounds fun. We're just marinating some pork chops for dinner and making a salad."

With Timmy changed and in his swing, Katie put on the green dress and new strappy shoes Mary had bought for her. She pulled the band from her ponytail and fluffed her hair with her fingers to give it that messy look.

Brad's wolf whistle split the air when she walked in the room. But it was Noah's face that made her smile. He clearly approved, and it felt so good she wanted to kiss him until he begged for mercy. Instead, she turned to Julie. She was smiling her approval and twisting her husband's ear in a friendly gesture of reprimand. Their love for each other made Katie's breath catch. She wanted what they had, that heart-pounding excitement coupled with love, respect, and an all-out commitment to each other and to making their marriage work.

"I think you nailed it," Noah said, coming to take her hand. "Very sharp." He looked down. "But I think you'll need a new pedicure before we go, okay? What else do you have?"

Knowing she had led with the showstopper, she didn't rush to put on the new top. But once she had it on with her black dress pants, she thought it looked perfect. She glanced at Timmy. He had fallen asleep in the swing, just as she hoped.

"I was thinking I could wear this to the brunch," she said, coming out of her bedroom. The top was light peach-pink with a jewel neckline, three-quarter length sleeves with flounce cuffs and a double flounce hem at the bottom.

"I love it," Julie said. "Very feminine and sexy. I have a necklace that would work beautifully with it. I'll get it."

"What do you think, Noah?" Katie asked.

"Very nice." He rubbed his ear. "I think I might have to skip the golf."

Brad laughed. "Good call."

Julie returned with a silver necklace. "Hold up your hair," she said as she fastened the necklace around Katie's neck.

"Oh, I love this," Katie said. Two rings were intertwined on a long silver chain. One ring was silver and the other a light pink. "What is this pink metal?" Katie asked.

"It's rubedo metal. Brad gave this to me when Megan was born." Under her breath, she whispered, "It's from Tiffany's."

"Oh, my gosh, there's no way I can wear this. It's too special."

"Sure you can. I insist. And so does Brad. Don't you, hotshot?"

"Whatever she says."

Katie lifted the two rings. It was the second time today that she had been overwhelmed by the love and generosity of others. "Thank you, Julie and Brad. It's perfect." She hugged Julie. "I think you should take it back now, and keep it until I start packing."

As Julie unfastened the necklace, Noah asked, "What about the gathering on Friday? And the rehearsal dinner. Did you find anything?"

"I thought I'd wear the black dress I already have for the rehearsal dinner. I think it would work, especially with my new shoes and some costume jewelry I found on sale."

Noah nodded. "Yeah, you look great in that dress. What about Friday afternoon?"

"I'll look for something next week. I ran out of steam today, and Timmy was starting to fuss. I should check on him and get my jeans back on. Do you want to meet me on the front porch, and we can talk a little out there?"

"Sure, that sounds good. Thanks for your hospitality and the input on the fashion show, you two. And thanks for watching Timmy next weekend. That's a blessing for both of us." He gave Julie a hug and shook hands with Brad before heading to the front door.

Katie settled Timmy in his crib and left her room to talk with Noah.

"Dinner in an hour," Brad said, as Katie passed him on her way to the front porch.

"Got it. I'll be back to set the table in plenty of time."

~ ~ ~

In the garage late Friday morning, Katie pulled the jogging stroller parts out of the box, determined to assemble it and go jogging when Timmy woke from his morning nap. She had almost finished when a text came in from CJ. He wouldn't be able to trick or treat with them; he had to work late. 'Pick you up at seven?' he had concluded his text. Katie's stomach clenched and she felt slightly sick. Picking up her phone, she stared at CJ's text. Regret swamped her. There was no way she could go to the party.

Katie sighed. CJ had bought them costumes, and been like a kid in a candy shop as he handed them out. Without caring that he would be teased mercilessly, he was going to put on a black Papa Bear body suit stuffed with pillows. Who would do that, except a man who loved his family?

Katie chewed on her bottom lip, one thought ricocheting off the next. He said he wanted to be with her. Did he mean for the evening? Or *with* her? No question he loved Timmy. He would do anything for his son. But what about her? He was attracted to her, sure. Liked to charm and tease her. But did he love her?

Another text came through as she got up off the garage floor, this time from Noah. 'Pizza at 7 tonight.'

Katie closed her eyes and groaned. She truly did feel sick. Could she use it as an excuse to stay home from either event? *Coward!* She'd known all week she couldn't go to the party. Why couldn't she text CJ and get it over with? She had to stamp out these feelings for him that churned inside her. Noah was her future. Why did her fleshly desires for CJ keep getting in the way? Grinding her teeth, she answered 'yes' to Noah. *Why God? Why does it have to be so hard?* With her head bowed, she pulled up CJ's text again and began to type.

'So sorry. We can't come after all. See you tomorrow.'

She could barely see the last words she typed as tears pooled in her eyes.

Sliding the phone in her pocket, she sniffed loudly and went back to the stroller to finish the job. But the churning in her gut wouldn't go away.

~ ~ ~

Sliding his sunglasses on his face, CJ picked his way around the debris left behind from the party and went outside. His head throbbed with a hangover, easily an eight on the pain chart, and for once, he cursed the bright San Diego sunshine as he got into his truck.

At the door to the Skidmore's home, he rang the doorbell, stepped back and turned away. He clenched his teeth and reminded himself to stay on task. He was here to see his son. He had nothing more to say to Katie. When she answered the door, he was relieved to see she was holding Timmy. Without so much as a glance at her, he reached for him. "Can you get his hat? I'm going to take him for a walk."

"Oh, sure. I-I'll be right back."

Her soft southern accent, usually so appealing to him, stoked his anger. He clenched his teeth and stared at the house across the street. The screen door opened behind him and he turned. Katie handed him the hat. "Thanks." He didn't wait, but took off down the driveway.

"I missed you last night, little bear. You and your mom." But he couldn't get the next sentence out before his eyes filled with tears.

~ ~ ~

Katie paced in her room, anxious for CJ to get back with Timmy. He said he was going for a walk, but where could he have gone that took almost two hours? His truck was still parked on the street, and he hadn't asked for a diaper bag. Had he been hit by a car? Tripped and fallen with Timmy? Chewing on her thumbnail, she found that the worst-case scenarios wouldn't go away. CJ was mad at her, and it didn't take a college degree to know why. What could she do about it? Nothing. He wasn't the type to punish her by making her anxious and worried, was he? She sat in the glider and hung her head in her hands. Where was he?

How would he take the news that she was going away with Noah next weekend? Without Timmy. Katie knew in her heart that they needed to talk soon about how they could arrange custody of Timmy. As much as she hated the idea of passing him back and forth, she needed to let CJ assume more of the responsibility for Timmy. Didn't she? Her breath caught at the thought. She planned to nurse him for a year. Would she get the chance? A sound at the front door had her jumping out of the glider and racing out of her room. CJ, still wearing his sunglasses, put his finger to his lips so she wouldn't speak and wake the baby. He passed her on his way to the bedroom and put Timmy in his crib. When he came out, he pulled the door almost shut.

"I'll see you next week," he said without looking at her as he walked past.

"CJ?" She whispered, following him when he didn't stop. "I won't be here next Saturday. I-I'm going to San Francisco for a wedding."

"I know. I'll talk to Julie about having Timmy at my folks' place some of the time."

"Oh . . . well . . ."

CJ turned abruptly, his voice low. "If that's okay with you."

With his eyes hidden behind sunglasses, she couldn't read him. Something about his tone of voice sent alarm bells off inside her. It was as if he had checked out, withdrawn all the warmth she was used to hearing in his voice. He stood waiting, his posture rigid and his body tense. Obviously, his mom had told him about the dress and why Katie needed it.

Did he think less of her for leaving Timmy? It was only an overnight. She hadn't been away from Timmy for over four months. Didn't she deserve a break? To have some fun?

"Of course it's okay," she said. "He's your son, too."

He pushed open the screen door without saying a word and walked out.

She ran out the door after him. "Just where do you think you're going? I don't like your attitude. I have every right to go away for a weekend. Every right. Julie's happy to take care of Timmy." She was talking to his back, and it infuriated her. She clenched her fists. "It's not as if I'm abandoning him."

He stopped. Turned. His every move precisely controlled. "It's fine, Katie. Have a nice time. I'll see you when you get back."

She was shaking she was so upset. CJ calmly got in his truck and drove away. Sinking to the sidewalk, she grabbed her head in her hands. "What is wrong with me?" she cried. But in her heart, she knew the answer.

Chapter 22

At the airport, Katie dragged her carry-on next to a seat at the gate and sat down beside Noah. Their flight wouldn't board for another thirty minutes, so she got out her phone to check for messages. A couple of men in military fatigues sat down nearby, reminding her of CJ. Guilt swamped her at leaving him and Julie to watch Timmy. What if the plane crashed and Timmy was left without a mother? Would CJ be relieved he didn't have to fight her for custody? Next to her, Noah played a game on his phone. His lack of attention irritated her. This trip was supposed to be a special weekend for them. Did he even care that she was nervous about flying?

"Did I mention that this is only my second plane ride?" Katie said.

"You're kidding?" Noah barely glanced up. "Where did you go the first time?" He continued his game.

"One of my college friends invited me to go to Houston for Spring Break my senior year. Her aunt and uncle had a boat and took us sailing. It was awesome."

"Hmm, I get seasick, so a cruise is more my style."

"Can you put your game away, please?"

"Oh, sure." Noah gave her a sheepish smile and shut off his game. He took her hand. "Besides, what's not to love about eating any time you want?"

"Is eating all you think about?" She squeezed his hand to make up for her sharp tone. "I think I would enjoy the land excursions more than time on the boat, but I don't know since I've never been on a cruise. I've always wanted to go to the Caribbean though, the Cayman Islands. How 'bout you? What's on your bucket list?"

"I don't have a bucket list. And I've seen plenty of beaches. I'd rather go to Italy. See the Vatican again."

"Well, yeah, a trip to Italy would be amazing. Maybe someday. But you should think about a bucket list. It's fun, and very revealing."

"Someday." He went back to his game.

Two hours later, with her nose against the window, the plane touched down at San Francisco International. After waiting for several minutes to deplane, Noah led the way to the rental cars. He signed forms while Katie stood with their bags. Shifting her purse on her shoulder, she studied the information about the hotel Noah had selected. When he took her hand, she breathed a sigh of relief.

An hour later, they pulled in to the underground garage at the Marriot in San Ramon, a suburb of San Francisco where Noah's friend Jeremy's parents lived. Noah pulled their bags out of the car trunk.

"I hope they have our rooms ready. I really need to use my pump."

Noah frowned. "Your pump? What do you mean?"

"I'm nursing Timmy. You know that. Since I'm not with him, I have to use a pump to express my milk."

"I thought you were all done with that. Didn't you say you were giving him cereal?"

She explained as they walked. "You have to introduce solids slowly. I'm giving him rice cereal, but only the tiniest amount in the breast milk I've bottled. I won't be able to save what I pump today and tomorrow, but I'm planning on nursing Timmy for a year, at least."

Noah held the door to the lobby open. "A year? I had no idea it would be that long. Do you have to?"

"No, I don't have to, but why wouldn't I? It's the healthiest thing for babies, and it's far less expensive."

In the lobby, Noah left her to go to the front desk.

Katie found the lobby restroom, quickly got out her breast pump, and breathed a sigh of relieve that she hadn't leaked all over her blouse. What would Noah say if she returned to the lobby with two big wet spots on her chest? Katie shook her head and sighed. The realities of motherhood. Noah didn't have much interest or understanding of what it took to take care of a baby. He also didn't seem to want much to do with Timmy, occasionally giving him a bottle, but never changing his diaper. During their time together, he focused on her.

Fifteen minutes later, Katie found Noah waiting in the lobby.

"Our rooms are ready. I got two that are connected." He winked at her. "I want to put on a fresh shirt, get a snack, and get out to the Dolton's house for the gathering." He glanced at Katie's jeans. "You want to change, right? We're in Rooms 307 and 309." He handed her a key card. "This is yours. We need to check out by eleven tomorrow, so we'll have to store the bags in the car while we wait for the wedding."

"Maybe we should extend it for a couple of hours, at least for one of the rooms. Isn't the Bride's Brunch tomorrow at ten? And you said you're playing golf. It's going to be awkward if we have to dress for the wedding in the lobby restroom."

"Well, that's going to be really expensive. We'll figure out something."

Noah inserted his card in the key slot and opened his door, then the one that connected their rooms.

"I hope you'll like my outfit for the gathering. It's really short, just for you." She blew him a kiss on her way in her bathroom with her suitcase. Stripping off her travel clothes, she put on the short, flared skirt outfit that she had seen on a mannequin in Nordstrom's Rack and brushed her hair until the curls bounced on her shoulders.

"Wow!" Noah said, turning from the window in his room with a smile. "I like the jacket especially. It tones down that wild print on the bottom."

Katie smoothed the collar of his button-down shirt. "You look very nice."

He glanced at his watch. "We're going to be late. But let's find a Starbucks on our way and get recharged."

"Sounds good to me."

At the Dolton's home, Katie tried her best to remember names. Eventually, while Noah helped himself to the food table, she turned to study the painting over the fireplace. A tall blond woman in red platform stiletto heels walked up beside her. "Hi, I don't think we've met. I'm Nicole, Jeremy's sister."

Katie turned. "I'm Katie Ryan. Noah's date. It's nice to meet you. You have a lovely home."

"Thank you. I live on my own downtown now, but I grew up here. Other than my old bedroom, this is my favorite room. So great for entertaining."

Katie nodded, amazed to find herself in another large estate home. Noah certainly ran with an affluent crowd. Could she ever fit in with this kind of lifestyle?

"Do you like the painting?" Nicole asked.

"Very much," Katie said. "It reminds me of one I saw in the Davidson's home. The artist's use of color is just so bold and daring. It makes me happy and hopeful."

"That describes my mom, all right. This is her work."

"You're kidding! She is incredibly talented."

"I agree. I didn't get that gene. Probably the one you saw at the Davidson's home is hers, too. Are you an artist?"

"A graphic designer, but I paint, too. Mostly portraits. I love abstracts, but I can't paint them. They always end up looking dull and boring. No depth, not at all like these your mom paints."

"Let me introduce you to her."

"I'd like that very much!" Katie followed her through the crowd.

An half hour later, Noah tapped Katie in the middle of a lively conversation with Trudy Dolton. "Hi, Trudy, I see you've met the love of my life." His words sent a warm glow through Katie. Noah leaned in to kiss Trudy on the cheek. "Time to go, Katie. You can continue your chat at dinner."

"That sounds perfect," Trudy said. "We have plenty more to say, don't we, Katie? I'll see you then."

~ ~ ~

Katie woke to loud snoring in the next room and pulled a pillow over her head. Aside from a thirty-minute conversation at the rehearsal dinner with the pastor who was performing the ceremony, Noah had been sweet and attentive. Would seeing his best friend get married tomorrow be the spark that galvanized him into action? Is that what she wanted? Had *she* climbed to a "ten" on the scale CJ had come up with after their talk at the park? Thinking of how CJ had listened as she laid out the pros and cons of marrying Noah brought a sadness to her heart she couldn't deny. If only CJ believed in Jesus. *If only, then what?* What would it change? Would she break up with Noah? With a sigh, Katie shoved the pillow away and sat on the side of the bed, too agitated to go back to sleep. What could she do but pray? Only God could change CJ's heart. But oh, how she wished He would hurry.

~ ~ ~

Dressed in her new pink top and black dress pants, Katie stood at the hotel banquet room door for the Bride's Brunch. She scanned the room, taking slow, deep breaths to calm her racing heart. The morning had not gone well with Noah. She had been late for breakfast, and not wanting to miss his tee time with Sid, he had left with a rushed goodbye and some last-minute instructions about extending their checkout time. Trying hard not to feel abandoned, Katie's gaze traveled from one stranger to the other, relieved when she spotted Nicole and Trudy. She worked her way through the crowd to them.

"You're at our table, Katie," Nicole said, after a sweet hug. She lifted two drinks from a tray of fruity cocktails and handed one to Katie. "These are non-alcoholic mimosas, in case you're wondering."

"That's perfect. Thanks for including me at your table since I don't think I know anyone else besides you and the bride."

Trudy gave her a hug. "Oh, we're only too happy to sit with you. As you can see, our Amy has a large family." She gestured to the crowd gathered around Amy. "I'm told they never miss weddings or funerals." Trudy laughed and turned to greet another woman. Katie settled in her seat at the table. She took a sip of her Mimosa.

The woman on her left leaned over. "I'm Amy's cousin, Alison. You're with Noah Davidson, aren't you?"

"Yes, I'm Katie Ryan. Do you know Noah?"

"We used to date on and off in college. His parents didn't care for me. They had other plans for him."

"Oh," Katie said. "Yes, he-he's graduating in another few weeks from seminary. And going to join his father in ministry."

"Well, yes, there's that," Alison said. "But I think they had someone already picked out for him to marry. You know, some vestal virgin of their choice. They're fanatics about, you know, waiting to have sex. The whole purity thing. Totally out of touch. I love your necklace, by the way. It's perfect with your blouse."

Katie swallowed hard, unsettled by Alison's comments. "Thanks. I borrowed it from my friend Julie. Her husband gave it to her when their daughter was born."

"Oh, that is so sweet. Julie sounds just like a sister, letting you borrow her things."

"In a way, she is my sister. We go to church together, and I live in her house. With my son." As soon as the words were out of her mouth, Katie wanted desperately to take them back.

Her shock was evident. "Oh, you have a son. With Noah? Really?"

"No, no, he's not Noah's son." Katie licked her lips. "His father's name is CJ. I, we, we're not together anymore."

"Oh, I'm sorry. How old is your son?"

Katie took a sip of her Mimosa. A blush reached her cheeks. How had the conversation gone so awry? Could she ignore Alison's question?

She persisted. "Is he with you?"

"No, he's just a baby. Four months old."

"Wow! And now you're with Noah. I'll bet his parents . . ." She swallowed whatever she was about to say. "Is Noah taking care of him? I have a hard time picturing that." She chuckled.

Katie looked around, wishing the floor would open up and swallow her. "No, he's with Julie. At home in San Diego."

"Oh, now I get the picture. Yeah, that makes more sense. Noah wanted a little time away without all the distractions another man's baby would bring to the party, didn't he?"

Katie's stomach dropped. "Well, I guess you could say that. As much as I love Timmy, he's . . ." How could she defend herself? "Do you have children?"

"Boy, do I. Two, and I don't care what anyone says, it changes things for a guy once a baby comes along. *They're* no longer the center of attention, and they don't like it one bit. My husband's the jealous kind. He still resents the time I put in with the kids. Says I spoil them."

"Well, they do take a lot of time. But I love being with Timmy." Katie wanted very much to change the subject. Was jealousy at the heart of Noah's lack of interest in Timmy? "Do you work outside the home?"

"No, and that's a problem, too. He wants me to get my career back. I tell him, the field has changed. Budget cuts axed a lot of programs. He blames the kids. It's a problem."

Katie sipped her Mimosa and nodded, wishing to be anywhere else. "What field did you used to work in?"

"Education. I was a teacher. Elementary art. I loved it, but with kids, I just couldn't do it."

Katie nearly cried out in relief. At last, a safe subject and a common interest. Doing her best to keep the focus on art and education, the rest of the time passed smoothly. So much so, that an hour later, the women exchanged contact information and promised to become Facebook friends. But Alison's comments about the Davidson's interest in Noah's love life weren't so easily forgotten. What did they really think about Noah's relationship with an unwed mother?

~ ~ ~

With her head resting on Noah's shoulder for the plane ride home, Katie let her mind wander. The wedding ceremony had been romantic from beginning to end, with a short message by the preacher. *Love keeps no records of wrongs . . . always protects, always hopes, always perseveres . . . never fails.* The cadence of the words from the Bible whispered through her mind, soothing her. She could trust God's love. His grace. Jesus had paid the price for her sins. And whether conceived in love or lust, Timmy was God's child. She would never let him forget it.

With a start, she woke up when the tires of the plane touched the runway.

"We're home," Noah said. "Too much dancing wore you out, didn't it? You were asleep within minutes of taking off."

"Well, I do love the dancing, almost as much as I love the wedding ceremony. I'm glad you have so many friends who were willing to take pity on me and fill in for you."

"Hey, I danced with you. Twice. And it was special."

Katie turned his face so she could look in his eyes. "You're special. And thank you for a lovely weekend. Now, get me home. I miss my baby."

"Come on, I thought I was your baby," Noah whined.

There is was again, that need to be the center of her attention. Katie shook her head. "No, Noah. One baby's enough for me."

~ ~ ~

Sunday after church, Katie unpacked while Timmy played on his play mat. Julie peeked her head through the open doorway. "Am I interrupting?"

"Hi, come in," Katie said. "I've got your necklace right here." She picked up a small drawstring bag off her desk and handed it to Julie. "It got a lot of attention with the pink blouse. Thanks again for letting me wear it."

"Anytime. How was the wedding?" Julie asked, sitting on Katie's bed.

"Beautiful, just perfect. Their soloist sang the Lord's Prayer and the ring bearer stopped in the middle of the aisle and had to be coaxed to keep going." She laughed. "He was adorable. How did Timmy do? He was sound asleep. In fact, everybody was when I got home. I didn't think we would be so late."

"He was a trooper both days. Brad and CJ went out to breakfast on Saturday, then CJ took Timmy to his folks' place so we could visit Brad's parents. It worked out beautifully. He brought him back about one o'clock and played with both kids for a while. It's good practice, I think, for Megan to play with Timmy. For this next baby." Julie rubbed her stomach where she was just beginning to show.

Katie pictured CJ on the floor with both children and smiled. "Don't you think it's so cute how Megan adores CJ? She's a sweetheart, Julie. Really. You and Brad are wonderful parents. And that's nice of Brad to go to breakfast with CJ. Did he tell you what they talked about?" Katie turned aside, embarrassed about voicing her curiosity.

"No, but Brad likes CJ a lot. You know these special forces guys. They have so much in common that they naturally bond. Brad and I pray every night for CJ to come to know Jesus. I think Brad is trying to get to know him as a friend, build their relationship, you know? He's invited him to his men's Bible study. But he doesn't tell me anything they talk about. He keeps it confidential, and that's the way it should be."

"You're right. I'm just curious, I guess, because CJ was so short with me last time I saw him. I think he's mad about me backing out on him for the Halloween party."

Julie stood. "You could be right. But probably more hurt than mad. Anger covers up a lot of other emotions. And it feels safer than admitting you feel hurt or helpless or scared."

"I never thought of it that way, but maybe . . . ."

Julie tossed the bag with her necklace up in the air and caught it. "Keep praying, Katie. God answers prayers, you know? Brad's gone out to grill the burgers. Will you be ready for lunch in ten minutes?"

"Sure, thanks. I'll be there." Katie picked up Timmy and blew on his tummy as Julie left the room. "I wish I knew what your daddy is really thinking, doll baby. Maybe then I could find some peace."

Chapter 23

CJ's text came on Friday. 'Helping my grandma move tomorrow. See you next week.' Disappointed and unsettled, Katie studied the text. Why hadn't he asked to see Timmy on another day, something he used to do when his Saturdays were tied up? Had his interest in his son changed? Rejecting the thought, she put Timmy down for his morning nap then grabbed her sweater and took her sketchbook to the backyard. She wanted to draw a picture of Timmy for Mary and Tim as a thank you gift.

The mid-November sunshine warmed her and the breeze fanned her skin. Settling in the chaise, she studied a picture of Timmy she had taken on her phone. She opened her sketchpad, turned past the drawings of Megan, and found a clean page. With light strokes, she drew the roundness of Timmy's head, the contour of his ears, and the placement of his eyes. In minutes, she could tell she had captured the essence of her baby.

Absorbed in filling in details, she started almost two hours later when she heard Timmy's cry over the monitor. She held the sketchbook at arm's length and smiled. The rendering was almost finished, Timmy's darling face staring back at her. Placing a piece of tracing paper over the drawing, she closed the sketchbook and went to get Timmy. Laundry was next on her list.

~ ~ ~

With Thanksgiving only six days away, Katie put the finishing touches on her drawing of Timmy. CJ would be coming for his visit in a few hours and she wanted to give it to him for Mary and Tim. *What mood would he be in today?* Other than one text, they hadn't had any communication since she yelled at him after his long walk with Timmy two weeks ago. Apologizing for her behavior was first on her list today.

The doorbell rang and she left Timmy in his crib to answer it. CJ's back was to her, his hand rubbing the back of his neck as she approached the screen door. He turned when he heard her open the door. She studied his face, thankful he wasn't wearing his sunglasses. The bags under his eyes alarmed her. Had he been up all night? She stepped back to let him in.

"Hi. It's been awhile. How's your grandma?" He didn't meet her eyes.

Katie's stomach lurched.

"Fine, she's settled in her new place." He moved past her to the family room. "Is Timmy still sleeping?"

"No, no, he's in his crib. I wanted to talk to you first. Tell you I'm sorry I flipped out on you, you know, the last time you were here."

CJ finally looked at her, his expression grim. "Apology accepted. I'd like to see Timmy, just for a while in the backyard today, and then I need to talk to you."

Katie's stomach leaped to her throat and her breath caught. "O-Okay. I have something for your folks I'd like to give you first. If you wouldn't mind taking it to them. I'll get it and then I'll get Timmy for you."

She disappeared in her room and returned with the drawing she'd had framed. She handed it to him without meeting his glance.

CJ studied it and swallowed hard. "It's . . . You're very talented." Turning away, he said, "I'll put it in the truck so I don't forget it."

Katie felt tears gather in her own eyes. Something was very wrong. What did he want to talk to her about? Couldn't they do it while he played with Timmy? She went to get the baby, her mind racing. It could only be the custody talk. She had been dreading it since the day CJ leaned over her bed at the hospital, demanding his rights.

When he returned, there was no longer any evidence of his feelings. He calmly took Timmy from her. "You probably have some work to do, so I won't keep you." He slid open the back door and went out.

Katie stared at the door. He had dismissed her, and it hurt. They hadn't been together to really talk since her mom's visit. And now, he wanted only Timmy. Alone. Katie turned and walked to the front door. The living room with its light gray walls, charcoal tweed sofas and tasteful botanical prints beckoned. She crossed to stand in front of the white brick fireplace. On one end of the mantle, Katie stared at a sculpture of an open Bible with a small sword resting on its open pages. Julie's weekly women's Bible study met in this room. The presence of the Lord was here. Tranquil, soothing. She shivered as a chill swept over her. Picking up the fireplace remote, she started a fire and stretched out on the floor to watch the flames dance and jump. *Help me, Lord. I'm afraid.* A scripture played through her mind. *Let the peace of Christ rule in your hearts . . . and be thankful.* Closing her eyes, Katie said the verse slowly in her mind several times, waiting in-between each time to let the Lord speak to her.

It took a while, but in time the richness of God's presence enfolded and comforted her. She rolled over on her stomach and buried her head in her arms.

A short time later, she heard the back door slide open. Katie got up in time to see CJ disappear through her bedroom door.

"Do you want to nurse him before he takes his nap?" CJ asked while changing Timmy's diaper. "I don't know his schedule."

"Or I could warm one of his bottles so you could feed him."

"I'd like that."

Katie left CJ and went in to the kitchen. She opened the freezer, pulled out a bottle of breast milk she had expressed and frozen, and put it in the microwave. "It will just be a minute."

Holding Timmy, CJ walked to the living room. "Did you start the fire? It's nice in here."

Katie joined him. "I didn't feel like working. This room is my go-to place when I need some peace."

CJ didn't comment, and Katie waited, praying. The microwave dinged. She left him to get Timmy's bottle.

"Here it is." She gave the bottle a shake and handed it to him. "Do you want to sit by the fire? I'll get you a burp cloth."

"And a blanket, since the room is still a little chilly."

When Katie returned, CJ was sitting in the easy chair nearest the fire, staring at Timmy. Wanting to be near him, she handed him the blanket and burp cloth and sat on the floor in front of the fire.

Neither of them spoke, and Katie once again repeated the scripture in her mind. CJ got up to burp the baby.

"Can we talk in here after you put him down?" Katie asked.

"Okay." CJ left the room.

Ten minutes passed. Anxious, Katie chewed on her thumbnail.

CJ's eyes were bloodshot and puffy when he returned. *Had he been crying?* He didn't sit in the chair by the fire, but instead, perched on the edge of the sofa and gave her his full attention. He clutched Timmy's blanket in his hands.

"I've been doing a lot of thinking lately," he began, and looked away for several long minutes, "and there's no easy way to say this. I-I think the time has come for . . ." He pierced her with tormented eyes. "For us to part ways."

His words slammed into her. "Wha-What do you mean?" Her eyes filled with tears.

CJ stood and took several steps away before turning back to her. The only sound came from the hissing of the fire and the pounding of her heart. Katie chewed on her lower lip, waiting. Terrified at the thought of losing him. CJ's next words didn't bring her any comfort.

"There's a story in the Bible, one you probably know or have read, about King Solomon and two women." He ran his hand around the back of his neck, a gesture so familiar to Katie, she wanted to jump up and massage his shoulders. Anything to ease the tension in him. And her own.

"Both women had babies, but in the night, one woman rolls over on her baby and kills him." He paused and swallowed. "She takes the dead child and exchanges him for the living baby. In the morning, both women, claiming the living child as theirs, ask Solomon to decide who should get the child." CJ looked away, visibly working to control his emotions. "Solomon says, 'Bring me a sword' and orders the child cut in half." He stopped, cleared his throat, then continued. "The true mother speaks up, giving up her rights to the other woman so the child can live."

Katie gasped and covered her mouth. "I-I've read that story, I think."

CJ sat down again and pierced her with eyes full of pain. Katie bit her lip to keep from crying out.

"It's not our story, Katie, but in a way, it is." His head dropped and his shoulders slumped.

"CJ—" Katie started to get up. He put his hand out to stop her.

"Wait until I finish. Please." He got up again. "Here's how it is for me. I only want the best for Timmy. And you. The best home life, the most stable environment, and the constant, unconditional love of two parents." He stopped. "And I get it. Noah's the guy you want, the one who believes what you believe." His voice faltered. He turned his head away. "It's time for me to bow out, Katie." His voice gaining strength, he said, "Timmy's our baby, but he belongs with you. You've nurtured and cared for him from the start. You've seen how demanding the life I've chosen is. The Navy owns me. For now, at least. I won't have Timmy divided in half. I can't . . . I won't do that to him. I give you all rights to him. And I'll put it in writing if you don't think you can trust me." He raced on. "I will still support him financially, same as I've been doing, and increase it as he gets older. And, sometime in the future, if he asks, I hope you will tell him that his father loved him and gave him up so he could have everything he needs and deserves. Love him for me. Please."

He turned and strode to the door.

"No," Katie cried, coming off the floor and stumbling as she tried to catch him. He outpaced her. On the porch, she screamed, "No! Come back. Don't do this!" But CJ didn't stop. She dropped to her knees and sobbed. "No, no," she cried over and over again.

~ ~ ~

Two hours later, when Brad and Julie came in the kitchen door with Megan, Katie was in the living room. One look at her face and Brad picked up Megan. "I'll play with Megan in her room. Looks like it's finally happened."

Julie sat beside Katie and put her arm around her. A fresh wave of tears spilled from Katie's eyes, down her cheeks and onto her T-shirt. A pile of used tissues told the tale. Instead of asking what happened, Julie waited.

Katie's breath hitched on a sob, "He doesn't want me," she finally choked out. "Or our baby." She told the rest of the story. "He thinks I want Noah."

Julie rubbed Katie's back. "Well, don't you?"

"Yes. No. I don't know. I just don't know. Don't you see? I want to do what God wants. But I love CJ. I can't help it." She broke down sobbing again.

How would Noah respond? Julie wondered. He loved Katie. But how much? Enough to be the father of another man's son? Julie had her doubts. He often ignored Timmy. Did he know what a treasure he had found in Katie? CJ did, of that she was sure. His every gift for her had given him away. The thought triggered Julie's memory.

"Katie, did you ever open the gift CJ gave you at the hospital?" Julie asked. "Maybe now would be a good time."

Timmy's cries broke the silence and Katie jerked and shivered. She swiped at her tears. "I've made such a mess of things, Julie. How can God ever forgive me?"

"Because that's who He is, the all-knowing, faithful One. There's nothing about what's happening that He doesn't care about. But I think it's time you owned up to what's in your heart. If you love CJ, you have to tell him. And end it with Noah. The rest is up to the Lord. Let's get Timmy. You'll always have him, and with or without CJ or Noah, you can raise him to love the Lord."

Julie walked with her to get Timmy. Picking up the baby, Katie cuddled him before sitting down to nurse him.

"I'm going to make you some tea," Julie said. "Here are your tissues. It's going to be okay, honey. Maybe not right now. But it will be."

~ ~ ~

Brad met Julie in the kitchen and wrapped his arms around her from behind. "Boy, am I glad we have each other."

Julie turned in his arms, "Me too." She looked up at him. "You knew this was coming, didn't you?"

"Yeah. After Halloween, there was a change in CJ. The fire had gone out. I knew he was wrestling with what to do. The weekend with Noah crushed his hope for something more with Katie. I think he made the right decision. For Timmy. I'm not giving up praying for them, though. I think he loves her, but just never felt confident enough about how she felt to say the words."

"God can use their mistakes. I know he can," Julie said. "But they each need some accountability for their actions. I hope we can help them see that in the future."

Gathering her in his arms, he held her tight.

~ ~ ~

Alone in her room, with Timmy asleep and the house quiet, Katie picked up the gift from CJ. He had caught her kissing Noah the day Timmy was born, and still refused to walk away. What kind of man did that? Refused to walk out on his son, even in the face of constant rejection? She turned the box and slid her finger under each piece of tape. The wrapping came away. For several long minutes, she stared at the box, her grief at CJ's decision to *part ways* as he put it, swamping her with anguish. She lifted the lid of the box. Her hand came to her mouth to cover her cry. Inside was a beautiful silver cuff bracelet with a central love knot and a ruby—Timmy's birthstone. She took it out of the box and slipped it on, loving the feel of it over her pulse. But, it was the card that brought fresh tears and bitter recriminations. He had written using block print letters: *'Knot' the end, but a new beginning . . . I hope. —CJ*

Katie pressed a tissue to her mouth to keep her cries from waking Timmy. Self-accusations came hard and fast. She had refused to call CJ before he deployed, and she had let her relationship with Noah go way beyond friendship, leaning on him more than she should have. Anger and hurt at CJ had owned her for months. Until their talk at the park. And their kiss. Why hadn't she seen it? He had wanted a new beginning from the start, and tried again at the park. Instead, she had focused on the state of his soul. Rather than being a witness of Jesus' love, she'd been a stumbling block. And driven CJ to make a choice he never should have had to make. Katie closed her eyes and let the tears fall.

~ ~ ~

Katie missed church the next day, and Noah texted, concerned. Using a stomach bug as her excuse, she stayed in her room all day, alternately hugging Timmy and crying. She clung to the verse she had been meditating on right before CJ shattered the peace she had been praying about. But giving thanks was beyond her understanding. How could she be thankful when her heart was shattered into a million pieces?

She texted CJ. 'Please, please, can I talk to you?' It bounced back. He had blocked her number. Erased her from his life? She drove past the Jansen's home, but couldn't find the courage to go up the driveway, and face Mary and Tim. CJ wouldn't have made his decision without consulting and informing them, devastating as it must have been. Would they still pray for her? Could they ever love her again? Had they blotted her out of their lives, too?

~ ~ ~

The next few days blurred in Katie's mind. Noah called to invite her to join his family for Thanksgiving, but she declined, without explanation. She would still help him pack for his move back home, she told him, then promptly hung up the phone.

On the day before Thanksgiving, she explained Timmy's routine to the young girl she had hired to babysit, and headed for Noah's apartment near the church. She had done the best she could to cover the puffy circles under her eyes, but with tears never far from the surface, it was a losing battle. She longed for peace, and she prayed for a second chance with CJ. But neither prayer received the answer she wanted.

Chapter 24

Dressed in scruffy jeans with a red bandanna tied around his head, Noah looked the sloppiest Katie had ever seen him. Already perspiring, he gave her a quick hug before stepping back to get her a box. "If you want, you can start on the kitchen," he said, doing a double take when he finally looked at her face.

"Boy, that flu really got you, didn't it? You look pale. Are you sure you're up to helping me?"

"Yes, I feel much better," she lied. Talking about CJ had to wait, if she was to be of any help to Noah. "What do you need done in the kitchen?"

"So, okay, how about if you empty the cabinets of all the food and then wipe them out. There's a sponge by the sink you can use."

Noah headed in to the bedroom, and Katie began opening cabinets. Every shelf except the highest ones had packaged food, mostly junk food. *How does he stay so thin?* She pulled out Pop-Tarts, crackers, sugar-laden cereal, ramen noodles, and packages of candy bars. The refrigerator and freezer were also full of processed food. Not only was nothing even remotely healthy, it looked like he could stay in the apartment at least another month. Squelching her judgmental attitude, she began packing the nonperishable items into the box. Three boxes later she was done, grabbed the kitchen sponge and went to work.

"What's next?" Katie asked, walking in the bedroom.

Noah called from the closet, "In here. Packing shoes."

Katie walked into the closet. "I could pack the clothes in your dresser drawers, or wash the sheets so you could take them home clean."

He walked out of the closet with her. "You don't mind doing the sheets?" When she shook her head, he tossed the pillows off the bed and stripped off the sheets.

Katie looked at the queen-sized sleigh bed. It was ornately carved and one of the most beautiful beds she had ever seen. *A bed made for lovers.* She sucked in a ragged breath and shut her eyes. She jumped when Noah spoke beside her.

"Katie? Are you okay?" With the sheets in his arms, he stared at her. "Is this job too personal?"

"No, no, I've just got some things on my mind, that's all." She looked around the disheveled room. "This packing stuff has you pretty tense, doesn't it?"

"Yeah, it's not my thing. I've always hired someone to do it. But this time, I was late trying to get it scheduled and no one was available."

"We'll get it done. The sitter I hired can stay with Timmy until four." Shaking off her thoughts of CJ, she went to work.

With the sheets in the washing machine, Katie found the vacuum cleaner without waiting for Noah to give her the next assignment. Shoving the sofa away from the wall, she went after the dust, gathering the junk mail that had fallen underneath. Next, she tackled the cushions, finding coins and crumbs underneath each one. She had moved on to the recliner when Noah came to the bedroom door with two large suitcases. Turning off the vacuum cleaner, she went to help.

"Should we get these in your car?" She looked at the boxes stacked by the door. "Do you have a cooler for the food in the refrigerator and freezer?"

"A small one. I'll put the rest in the church freezer for the food distribution night."

"I wonder if you're going to have room for everything. Maybe you should also give the unopened food to Cornerstone. It's not the kind of food they give out when people who need groceries stop by, but maybe they can use it for a kids' event."

"Yeah, that's a good idea."

Two hours later, encouraged by the amount of work they'd done, Katie looked around the living room. She had to quit stalling and talk to Noah about CJ's decision. And her own. Picking up her purse, she searched through it to find her tissues.

Noah came in from the balcony with a dead potted plant.

"I need a break, Noah, and I need to talk to you about something."

Noah closed the balcony door behind him. "Let me throw this dead thing away and get a Coke first, okay? Do you want one?"

"No, I'll stick with my water, thanks."

Noah popped the top on his soda and sat beside her on the sofa. He took a long swallow and put his arm around her shoulder. "You're a trooper, Katie. Thanks for helping me today. I wish you would reconsider and come for Thanksgiving though. Rosa makes the best oyster stuffing ever."

"I'm sure she does, but actually, there's more to the reason I can't come." She took a deep breath. "CJ and I talked Saturday, and he's giving me full custody of Timmy."

"What?" Noah pulled back and withdrew his arm from around her. "You're kidding!" He stood and paced.

"No, he's serious. And I've done a lot of thinking since then."

"Like, thinking what? Cause, I-I don't quite know what to say to this news. I mean, I-I, we, you know we've talked about getting married. But . . ." He shook his head. "Well, some things have changed for me. I think I, well, I thought we talked about CJ stepping up and accepting some responsibility for Timmy, for one thing."

"Well, yes, you did want me to talk to CJ, but the time was never right."

Noah pulled off his bandanna, his fist clenching it tight. "What's his reasoning for making you take all the responsibility for Timmy?"

"He doesn't see it that way. He's still going to support him. But he thinks I chose you over him, and he wants Timmy to have a stable home life, two parents who will love him unconditionally. Don't you agree that's best?"

Noah's whole body tensed. "Sure, that's best. It's God's way for a child to have a mom and a dad who are married." He pierced her with troubled eyes. "Oh, I get it. He thought the dad would be me, didn't he? That I'd step up and do his job for him."

Katie sucked in a deep breath. "And you're not interested, are you? That's the thing that's changed, isn't it? The love you have for me doesn't include Timmy."

Noah ran the bandana over his head where perspiration had gathered. He looked away. "Look, I'm sorry, Katie." He fidgeted with the headpiece. "You're right. The timing's all wrong. And . . . I'm not ready to be a full-time father. It's complicated. My mom . . . well, you know my parents counsel couples all the time, and they, well, they've encouraged me to break up with you. Because of Timmy. And other stuff." He wiped his eyes with the bandana.

Katie's stomach clenched. Alison, at the bridal brunch, had warned her, hadn't she? Noah's parents wanted an unspoiled virgin for their son. Not a single mom. Their interference hurt. A lot. But her pride wouldn't let her show it. "I understand. You don't have to say anymore. I mean, you want to honor your parents, being the experts that they are."

"Ah, Katie, don't get cynical." He paced away and back again. "They're just trying to look out for me. I mean, us. They have a point. I'm just starting my ministry. I graduate in a few weeks, and I'm trying to help my dad. Timmy's another man's child. You know I'm not good with babies. Or sharing."

Katie nodded, hurt and disgusted by his excuses. "I've noticed that. It's what I've been thinking about. You know, at one time, I thought you were the man God wanted me to marry." She shook her head. "I don't think that anymore. You've got a lot of good qualities, Noah, but generosity isn't one of them. CJ's got you beat, hands down, on that one."

Noah's head snapped up, but to his credit, he didn't try to defend himself.

She pushed her hair behind her ear and sighed. "I'm not trying to hurt you, Noah. You have helped me, immeasurably. But the truth is, since CJ came home I've been tied in knots." She twisted the ruby knot bracelet on her wrist, a smile tugging at her lips. "I've been trying to ignore how I feel about him. Stuffing my feelings because he's not a believer. I don't want to settle for someone who isn't. I don't know if we can ever have a future together but I'm going to try to set things right, and I'm not going to stop hoping and praying for him. He's Timmy's dad, so we'll always have that connection." She pushed up from the sofa and took a step toward Noah. "And the way I see it, you deserve someone who's heart is fully committed to you, Noah. That's just not me. Not anymore."

Noah's jaw tensed. "So, you're breaking up with me."

"And for the record, I don't really want a guy who would choose doing what his parents want instead of standing up for the woman he loves. But no hard feelings. You've been a good friend, especially when I needed one most, and for that I will always be grateful. But CJ's right about something he said one time about you and me. He said all we have in common is Jesus. And although that's the best foundation for a marriage, it's just the starting point. I want to be crazy in love and best friends with the man I marry."

A frown creased Noah's brow and his eyes filled with tears.

Katie walked to him. "I think you can handle the rest of the packing. I'm going to go home now, to that little boy I love with all my heart. If I have to raise him as a single mom, well, so be it. You've helped me see that I'm a new creation in Christ, and that's a priceless gift. I pray God will bless you in your ministry, Noah. But it won't be with me."

Picking up her purse, she crossed to the door and opened it. "Goodbye, Noah, and God bless you." She turned and went out into the sunshine.

~ ~ ~

Back at the house, Katie paid the babysitter and sat down to cuddle Timmy. A deep sigh welled up from her core. A terrible weight had been lifted, even if the outcome of her decision remained uncertain. A renewed appreciation for the tiny bundle who had brought her so much joy welled up inside her. What was it CJ had said? Timmy rocked his world? "Well, that make's two of us you've shook up, little man," Katie whispered. "From now on, you are my world. You're all the man I need. You and Jesus. But if your daddy wants to be part of our team, I would be the happiest woman on the planet." Katie sighed again and closed her eyes. "Oh, Lord, you know how I feel. You know everything. I love CJ so much. Please, please, do a miracle for Timmy and me."

A while later, Katie put Timmy in his crib, pulled two sheets of paper from her printer tray and found her favorite pen. What was next for her and Timmy? Did she dare follow through with a plan that had rippled through her mind on the way home. CJ loved his child so much He had given him away to save him. *But did he love her?*

Katie chewed on her lower lip. He'd never said the words, but had she ever really given him a chance? Hadn't she pushed him away, especially for his lack of faith? What good would it do to think about *what ifs*? With her pen poised, she wrote a quick note to Mary and Tim, vowing to always honor them as Timmy's grandparents. It took considerably longer, and several tries, but she finally found her voice and poured out her heart to CJ.

Then she began to pack. Tomorrow, she was leaving San Diego and heading home. Back to Charleston, South Carolina.

~ ~ ~

With the SWCC's evening training exercise in its final stages, CJ leaned against the side of the boat. They'd been pounding away at a fixed target on San Clemente Island for close to two hours, the noise from the guns ripping the night air. CJ huffed out a tired sigh. They had at least a couple of hours ahead, cleaning the guns and the brass on the boats, and making sure they were ready to go for tomorrow's drill. Three more days. Three more grueling days of training on the island. And then what? CJ glanced at the other RHIB boat sitting fifty feet away, a twin of the one he sat on. The heat from the .50-caliber machine guns the guys were using was so intense the weapons glowed in the dark. He glanced at the gun he'd been using. It glowed, too, then went dark. *Like my life.*

Much later, with their work all done and most of the guys relaxing, CJ left the barracks and walked along the shore, away from the noise of his teammates. He needed time alone. Time to think, and time to grieve. The hectic pace of the training and the comradery of the guys had been welcome distractions. For the most part. They didn't allow him time to think. Time to feel. Time to dwell on how he had lost the two people he loved most. Or, how barren his life would be without Katie and his son. But he knew better than to ignore the pain. Not that there was any chance he could. He sat down, drew his knees to his chest and buried his head in his arms.

A half hour later, he heard a sound and turned. Dustin had found him, the one guy who knew what he was going through. He swiped at his tears.

"You okay, man? You were kickin' it out there today."

His voice caught. "Yeah." He cleared his throat. "Yeah, I'm fine. It felt good to be in control of all that firepower tonight. I'm not in the mood for the chatter and rehash. That's all."

"Sure. Sure, I don't blame you. Couldn't believe you volunteered to swim out in the surf with live ammo whizzing overhead. You trying to get killed?"

CJ didn't answer.

After a while, Dustin said, "You know Ashley's been going to this group called Alpha. She's been talking a lot about Jesus. It's good stuff, nothing I ever heard growing up. I'm thinking about getting baptized."

A slow smile spread over CJ's face and he glanced at Dustin. "Is that right?"

"Yeah, being as Jesus died for my sins, you know?"

"You believe all that? Even the resurrection?"

"Well, yeah, I mean, no one ever found Jesus' body, the tomb was empty, and the disciples saw him. They even ate with him. But you know what really convinced me that he rose from the dead?"

CJ looked at Dustin. "None of the disciples ever recanted, did they? They died rather than deny Him."

"Yeah. And they turned the world upside down. How'd you know that?"

"I guess I've been thinking about it for a while. Since Timmy was born." He rubbed his hand down his face and looked away. ""*For God so loved the world, He gave his only son, that whoever believes in him shall not perish but have everlasting life.'* John 3:16, man. It's true. God gave his son. For me. I get it." Looking down, his voice dropped. "Just wish it wasn't too late to make a difference to Katie."

~ ~ ~

It had taken a week of driving six or more hours a day, nights spent in cheap hotels, and lots of songs on the radio, but Katie finally pulled in to the driveway behind her mother's car. The door of the mobile home opened and her mother came running out, her arms open wide. "Oh, honey, I'm so glad to see you. You're home and all the folks at the Nursing Center send their love, and want you to hurry back to work with them."

After a long hug, Katie pulled back. "It's good to be home, Mom. Thanks for saving my room for me. Let me text Julie and let her know I'm here. Then I'll get Timmy so he can meet his grandpa."

Chapter 25

CJ pulled open the door to the Quarter Deck on base a few days before Christmas. It had been a hard three weeks of training at San Clemente Island and he wanted to get the day done and get home. He hadn't even started his Christmas shopping. Didn't want to this year. But first he had to find Dustin to return the hundred bucks he'd borrowed on their Thanksgiving camping trip. CJ looked around the busy area, nodding when he spotted Brad. Keeping an eye out for Dustin, he met Brad halfway.

"Merry Christmas," CJ said, although in his heart he knew the reviews were mixed on the merry part for him. The ache for Timmy had been his constant companion. Katie, too, although he put her in a different compartment since she had chosen Noah over him. Losing her hurt like nothing he had ever known.

"Same to you. Where have you been? I've been looking for you just about every day."

"I owe you money, too?"

"You don't know, do you?"

"Know what?"

"About Katie."

CJ swallowed hard to keep the bile from rising in his throat at the thought of Katie with Noah, together, married. "That was quick." He turned away.

Brad grabbed his shoulder. "Yeah, it was. She was packed and ready to go when we got home from Thanksgiving dinner. Took her a week to get there, but she and Timmy got home just fine."

CJ stared at him. Why was Brad torturing him like this? He thought they were friends. "Well, I hope she's happy. That's why I gave Timmy up, you know? So she could have . . . he could be . . ." CJ backed away from Brad. "I gotta go."

Brad blocked him. "Didn't you hear what I said? She's home. In Charleston. She and Noah broke up."

If Brad had blasted him with a Taser, he wouldn't have been as stunned. He couldn't move.

Brad patted him on the shoulder. "Thought you should know. Seeing as how you love her. I still don't know how you let her go in the first place, man."

His heart threatened to jump out of his chest. He stared at Brad, searching for any sign he was messing with him. The guy was sincere. With crazy joy coursing through him, he rubbed his hand around the back of his neck. A laugh caught in his throat. "Look. I told her every which way that I love her. I thought she didn't want me. She kept shoving me away." His gut churned. He had to get to Katie. He stepped away, but Brad blocked him again.

"Yeah, you had some competition all right. And you did some incredibly nice things for her. Real generous. She should have known, I guess. Nice touch, that bracelet, by the way. But did you ever tell her, you know, with words that you love her? Women like to hear it said, you know? In words."

Hope flooded through him. His adrenaline pumped hard and fast. CJ tried to think, tried to understand what Brad wanted him to say. "Do you have her address?"

Brad put his face inches from CJ's, using his best drill sergeant voice. "Focus, man! Did you or did you not ever use words to tell Katie you love her? Answer me."

Heat raced to CJ's cheeks. Chatter around him stopped. Brad wasn't his boss, but it hadn't stopped him from acting like it. "No, sir, I did not. But I'm going to change that as soon as you supply her address." Then he laughed. "I've got to get a plane ticket to Charleston. Why am I standing here talking to you?"

Brad laughed with him and pounded him on the shoulder. "Good luck finding one at this time of year. Try the red-eye on Christmas Eve. There's a letter waiting for you at your folks' place. As soon as you get off, you might want to check in with them. Katie wrote one to them, too. I think she put her return address on it."

Forgetting that he wanted to pay Dustin back, CJ hurried to his locker cage. On the way, he pulled out his phone to call his mom. When her voice mail answered, he barely stopped himself from swearing, and instead said, "I'm back from training. I'll be home ASAP. Love you. Bye."

~ ~ ~

Finally, finished with his SWCC duties, CJ hopped in his truck. He had a good thirty-minute ride to his folks in heavy traffic. "Focus, man," he said to himself. *She didn't marry him. She didn't marry the guy.* His stomach in knots, he pulled up the drive to his parents' home, anxious to see if what Brad said was true. Had Katie left him a letter? He wanted to talk to her in the worst way, but knew it had to wait until he read what she had to say. Shutting off the truck engine, he jumped out and raced for the front door.

The dog barked a welcome. "Anybody home?" he called as he petted the dog. When no one answered, he groaned. It wasn't like his mom to not answer his voice mail, especially if she wasn't going to be home. He headed for the kitchen, hoping to find Katie's letter in an obvious spot.

On the island, he found a sheet of paper with a note. *Your dad and I are out walking. Be home soon.*

Under it, he found Katie's letter. He grabbed it and blew out a slow, steady breath. In his room on his bed, CJ barely stopped himself from ripping open her letter. The news that she hadn't married Noah filled him with hope, but still his hands shook and his heart galloped. He studied Katie's handwriting. Not script, but neat, professional block letters, the kind he'd seen on blueprints. Taking deep, calming breaths, he carefully worked open the envelope.

As he unfolded the letter, a picture fluttered to the floor. Without picking it up, he began to read.

Dear CJ,

By the time you get this, I will be back home in Charleston with Timmy. There was no future for me with Noah, and although I will always love him for the encouragement and hope he gave me during a tough time, Timmy and I don't plan to see him again. He is my brother in Christ, and like me, he's a work in progress.

I never meant to hurt you, CJ, although I know I did, many times, and I'm so sorry. Seeing your great, sacrificial love for our son has brought me to my knees. I don't deserve to be Timmy's mother, and yet, I love our son beyond words. I want you to know him, and him to know you. I don't know how to do that, on the other side of the country as we now are, but love always finds a way. I believe that with all my heart.

I never got a chance to say thank you for the beautiful bracelet. I love it! I wish I had opened it the day you gave it to me. Oh, how I wish that! Maybe then I wouldn't have made so many mistakes. I can only say I'm so sorry. Please forgive me, and know that I cherish this gift and wear it every day.

We've been through so much together since Timmy was born, some of it fun and some of it painful. But I wouldn't trade one minute I've spent with you for days with any other person. You are the man of my dreams, CJ. I love your big heart and your generous spirit, your kindness and strength. You've gone the extra mile for me again and again. You never quit. And no one has ever made me laugh and have fun the way you can, CJ. You have my heart and I don't want to deny my feelings for you any longer. I love you, always, no matter . . . .

    Katie

    P.S. I'm writing this wearing the cutest Mamma Bear PJs I've ever seen. I just had to take a selfie. XOXO

CJ tossed the letter on his bed and grabbed his head in his hands, leaning forward while tears of joy streamed down his face. He spotted the paper that had dropped out when he pulled the letter out of the envelope, and saw it was a picture. A great bellowing laugh came out of him when he saw Katie holding Timmy, both of them in the bear costumes he had bought. Katie had even made up their faces. Determined to get to her by Christmas, CJ pulled out his phone, reentered Katie's number in his contact list, and went looking for a plane ticket.

~ ~ ~

Christmas Day at the Nursing Center in North Charleston had been busy. Lots of visitors, happy smiles, and good cheer. But lots of lonely faces, too, when family didn't visit for one reason or another. Katie finished settling Mrs. Mason in her wheelchair by the window and knelt beside her. "I enjoyed meeting your granddaughter today," she said. "She's a real joy to be around." With a slight nod, Mrs. Mason's head dropped and her eyes closed. Katie pulled the lap blanket around the old woman and left the room.

She'd been lucky to get her old job back not long after moving home, but days like today filled her with sadness, too. There had been no word from CJ. No response to her letter. Katie sniffed and swiped at the tears on her cheeks. Why had she been so foolish? She passed the reception desk and took a piece of peppermint candy from the basket her mom had brought for the staff, and anyone else who had a sweet tooth. At her locker, she opened the candy and popped it in her mouth—an end-of-the-day ritual since coming back to work. Katie hung her head. Timmy's first Christmas Day and they hadn't spent a minute of it together.

"It's just a day," Katie murmured, then amended, "but the most wonderful day of all, the day God's love came to save us," But the sadness pressed in. Threatened to engulf her. She put on her jacket and slung her bag over her shoulder.

On her way out, she waved to Mr. Herrick in his wheelchair in the hallway. "Merry Christmas," she called. "I'm heading home to my baby. Sleep well tonight."

"Merry Christmas," Mr. Herrick said as he gave her a feeble wave. "Beautiful Katie."

Calling goodnight to Bev at the reception desk, Katie shoved open the door to the outside.

The crisp, cold air hit her in the face. She shivered and pulled her jacket collar up around her neck. She glanced up at the night sky. *Star light, star bright . . .* The children's rhyme sang through her head, it's ending request for her wish to be granted, filling her with such longing her breath caught. Where was CJ tonight? Was he with Midge? Katie rejected the thought. No, he'd said they were just friends, and she believed him. Swallowing hard, she adjusted her bag and started down the walk.

At the end of the portico, a large shape came from behind the last pillar. She jumped, startled. In an instant, her fear turned to jubilation. Her breath caught and she gasped. CJ held Timmy, each of them dressed in their bear costumes.

Katie couldn't hold back her cry of joy. She rushed to them, her heart pounding.

"Will you be our Momma Bear?" CJ asked, scooping her to him with his free arm.

Her arms wrapped around him and Timmy. She couldn't speak, her throat was constricted by so much happiness.

With his free hand, CJ stroked her hair and held her close. He kissed her hair, working his way down her wet cheek until his lips found hers in a long, slow kiss.

"Someone's been in the Christmas candy," he said, when the kiss ended, smiling against her lips. He smoothed her hair away from her face. "I like it." He tasted her again, finally pulling back to look her in the eye. "I'm not so good with words, Katie, but I love you, and I don't want to spend another day without you and this little guy in my life. Someway. Somehow."

She couldn't keep her hands off him, pushing the hood off his head to touch his hair and face. "I love you too, CJ, and I don't want to be with anyone but you. Always. No matter."

CJ laughed. "How did you know we say that in our family?"

"Your parents said it all the time to Timmy when they came over to the house. And to me. They told me it's a reminder of the vows they took on their wedding day."

CJ looked up as a woman came out of the nursing home door. "Let's move to that gazebo over there so we don't give that woman a heart attack. With his arm still around her, he led them out of the light.

"I would have been here sooner, but I had a three-week training session that just finished up two days ago." He sat beside her in the gazebo but didn't take his arm away.

"I wondered if you got my letter and if you still cared."

"You think I wouldn't go crazy with a letter like that? I got it, and I've read it so many times, it's starting to tear." He smoothed her hair. "It's the holidays. I couldn't get a plane ticket, babe, except by going through Boston first."

Katie's stomach fluttered at being called his 'babe.' She stroked his cheek. "You're kidding? Boston?"

"Yeah, I was in Boston at six this morning. But it doesn't

matter. I'm here, and I'm not going anywhere. Unless you come with me."

Leaning into him, Katie smoothed her hand over Timmy's head. "Wherever you want. We're ready." She twisted the ruby knot bracelet on her wrist, holding her arm up for him to see. "Knot, K-n-o-t, the end, but a new beginning, right?"

CJ grinned. "Basic boat guy stuff, those knots. I'm glad you like it. I wondered why you never mentioned it, and didn't wear it."

"Oh, CJ, can you ever forgive me? I was so wrong."

He stroked her hair without answering. "I have something else to tell you too, Katie. Something good." He cupped her chin and stroked her cheek. "I know you've been concerned that I'm not a believer. But that's all changed." He pulled her close so he could nuzzle her hair. "I've never felt so alone as I did after I told you I was giving you Timmy." He looked deep into her eyes. "Even Mom and Dad said it was the right thing to do, but we were all miserable. I didn't have anywhere to turn, so I just started talking to Jesus." He grinned. "And it finally dawned on me, why was I talking to someone I didn't believe in?"

Katie's eyes filled with tears, her throat too clogged with emotion to speak.

"So, if Jesus can forgive me, I can forgive you. And I do."

Tears pooled in Katie's eyes. "Thank you. That means the world to me."

"Dustin and I've done some talking, too. Thanks to Ashley's influence, he's even getting baptized, and I promised I'd be there to see it."

"Oh, I can't breathe!" Katie laughed. "This is amazing. Ashley's a believer now, too? I had a hunch something big had happened in her life."

CJ nodded. "You might want to talk to her. I think Dustin's in love."

She covered her mouth. "I don't know what to say. This is too beautiful!"

"Oh, it gets better. Brad's on our case. He's invited, no actually, he's ordered both of us to come to his men's Bible study group, and we said yes. I'm going to seek God with all my heart, and I think it says in the Bible, if you seek me, you'll find me. Am I right?"

"You are so right. Oh, CJ, you couldn't give me a better present in all the world. I love you so much!" She threw her arms around his head and hugged her cheek to his.

His lips found hers in a tender kiss. "I love you, too. With all my heart. You light up a room, Katie, just by being in it. You're fun and funny. The most kindhearted woman I've ever known. I love how I can be myself with you. Even after all the mistakes I've made, you humble me with your love. And I know I gave you a hard time, but I totally respect how you stuck to your faith. Your values and beliefs." Extricating himself from her arms, CJ slipped off the seat and got on his knees in front of Katie.

Her heart pounded so hard she was sure it would jump out of her chest. The two men she loved most knelt before her.

"Will you marry me, Katie? I want to be with you. Always. No matter."

"Yes, a thousand times, yes." She cupped his cheeks in her hands and reigned kisses over his face and eyes before opening her mouth over his in a long, slow kiss.

CJ's free hand found its way in to her hair and he deepened the kiss.

Loud voices came from the door of the nursing home, startling them. CJ pulled back and shifted Timmy. "We should probably continue this at home."

Suddenly self-conscious about her family's status, Katie sighed. "I guess since Timmy's with you, you've seen my home, haven't you? My dad's accident, well, it's been pretty tough making ends meet since then."

CJ smiled. "You come from good people, Katie. They love you, it's obvious. And want the best for you. Your mom seems to like me, so that's a plus, don't you think?" He laughed. "And your dad gave me his blessing to ask you to marry me, but he made it very clear that Timmy would have to come visit often."

"And you agreed?"

"Are you kidding? I'd have promised to fly him out here every week, if that's what it took." He got off his knees and snuggled beside her again. "By the way," he said, "I hope it's okay that Mom and Dad and Lynn and some of our friends are flying in tomorrow. Can you see any reason why we can't get married the day after that?" Even in the dark gazebo, his smile lit his entire face.

"No reason at all," she said, then sealed her words with another peppermint kiss.

Jane Josephs

Jane Josephs moved to San Diego, California, in 1999 when her husband Steve accepted a job in the biotech industry. Ready for a career change, Jane began writing. But four years later, Steve was laid off from his job, and they decided to move to West Virginia, where Jane grew up. God had other plans! A week before they were to leave, Steve was offered a new job. Soon after, Jane found work, too, in their home church, and began writing devotions for the church's newsletter. But the desire to write contemporary inspirational romances resurfaced.

In 2017, Jane was a finalist in The Stiletto Contest sponsored by Contemporary Romance Writers for her Inspirational Contemporary Romance, *The Ruby Knot.* She's been furiously writing ever since!

The mother of two adult children, and "Mimi" to five grandchildren and three grand-dogs, Jane still works full time. When she's not trying to beat her husband at Scrabble, Jane enjoys reading, traveling, painting with acrylics, hanging out with family and friends, and "soaking" in prayer and Bible study.

Jane is a member of the San Diego chapter of Romance Writers of America and the San Diego Christian Writers Guild.

Stop by and visit Jane at www.janejosephs.com.

CPSIA information can be obtained
at www.ICGtesting.com
Printed in the USA
FSHW011420290319
56667FS